A Reckoning for the Earl

Barrington's Brigade
Book 5

Ruth A. Casie

© Copyright 2026 by Ruth A. Casie
Text by Ruth A. Casie
Cover by Dar Albert

Dragonblade Publishing, Inc. is an imprint of Kathryn Le Veque Novels, Inc.
P.O. Box 23
Moreno Valley, CA 92556
ceo@dragonbladepublishing.com

Produced in the United States of America

First Edition January 2026
Trade Paperback Edition

Reproduction of any kind except where it pertains to short quotes in relation to advertising or promotion is strictly prohibited.

All Rights Reserved.

The characters and events portrayed in this book are fictitious. Any similarity to real persons, living or dead, is purely coincidental and not intended by the author.

AI Statement: No AI or ghostwriting was used in the creation of this story, or any story, published by Dragonblade Publishing. All text, structure, content, ideas, and concept are 100% human generated solely by the author whose name appears on the cover. It is prohibited to use this material, or any copyrighted material, for AI engine training.

ARE YOU SIGNED UP FOR DRAGONBLADE'S BLOG?

You'll get the latest news and information on exclusive giveaways, exclusive excerpts, coming releases, sales, free books, cover reveals and more.

Check out our complete list of authors, too!

No spam, no junk. That's a promise!

Sign Up Here

www.dragonbladepublishing.com

Dearest Reader;

Thank you for your support of a small press. At Dragonblade Publishing, we strive to bring you the highest quality Historical Romance from some of the best authors in the business. Without your support, there is no 'us', so we sincerely hope you adore these stories and find some new favorite authors along the way.

Happy Reading!

CEO, Dragonblade Publishing

Additional Dragonblade books by Author Ruth A. Casie

Barrington's Brigade Series
A Marriage for the Marquess (Book 1)
A Dilemma for the Duke (Book 2)
A Redemption for the Baron (Book 3)
A Vow for the Viscount (Book 4)
A Reckoning for the Earl (Book 5)

The Ladies of Sommer-by-the-Sea Series
The Lady and Her Quill (Book 1)
The Lady and the Spy (Book 2)
The Lady and Her Duke (Book 3)
The Duke's Lost Love (Novella)

Pirates of Britannia Series
Donald
Hugh
Graham
The Pirate's Jewel
The Pirate's Redemption

The Lyon's Den Series
The Lyon's Gambit
The Lyon's Alliance

Chapter One

L ADY GEORGINA RAVENSTOCK promised herself that this would be her last visit.

One year and one day ago, she buried her husband, and still the silence lingered. Not grief, precisely, but the burden of things unfinished, unsaid, unmourned.

She waited as her coachman climbed back onto the box after opening the iron gate. The autumn breeze sent leaves scurrying down the path, whipping them in circles against the stones. The coach's wheels had scarcely come to a halt before she stepped down, already certain of her path.

The last time she stood here, she had scattered earth upon her husband's grave and vowed it would be the final farewell. Now, after a deep breath, she made her way down the path, passing the final resting places of familiar names. Her late husband, Rowland, Baron Ravenstock, had been ten years her senior, a serious man, consumed by the responsibilities of his title and the coal mine that sustained it.

He had spent much of his time in Sommer-by-the-Sea, working alongside his men underground, while she remained in their London townhouse, managing the rest of their world. It was not distance born of disregard but of duty, carved out by expectation and necessity. A year ago, an urgent summons called her back to Sommer-by-the-Sea. There had been a terrible collapse in the mine, one that had taken Rowland's life.

Now, she approached his grave and stood solemnly, gazing at

the fine inscription. Try as she may, his features were fading from her memory. Rowland had always been a man of quiet strength, marked more by soot-stained hands than by society's polish. She smiled, remembering the dust smudged at the corner of his brow, more than the fine lines around his face.

She had done all that was expected. The silks, the silence, the seclusion. But expectation made poor company. And with the mourning veil still clinging to her like a shadow, she was no longer certain who she was meant to be.

Georgina drew a deep breath, then slowly exhaled. "Sleep well, my lord," she whispered, her gloved hand brushing the top of the headstone.

Tomorrow, she had an appointment with her solicitor and planned to settle all the accounts. This would be her final goodbye. Beyond that, she did not yet know where her path would lead, only that her path would be of her own choosing.

She lifted her chin, her gaze settling on the great oak at the edge of the cemetery. The wind stirred its amber leaves, revealing the figure of another mourner beneath its branches. She stilled. Although at this distance, his features were hidden, the gentleman was tall with a familiar bearing. There was no mistaking the broad set of his shoulders, or the way he stood with a soldier's stillness, braced against the wind, weathering the next military charge. For the briefest moment, their eyes might have met, or perhaps it was only her imagination.

Once, long ago, she had told a lanky, good-humored boy that one day he would fill those shoulders and trouble hearts without meaning to. She wondered if she had been correct.

She drew her shawl closer around her shoulders and turned away, casting her thoughts back to the matter at hand. She had returned for Rowland. To mark the year gone by and to close this chapter properly.

She turned and made her way back along the path toward the gates. The breeze shifted once more. She glanced up, and there was the shadow from beneath the branches. Closer now, he was unmistakably Alexander Weld.

Time had carved new lines at the corners of his eyes. There was a gravity to him now of a man who had seen too much and carried it quietly. But it was him, unmistakably him.

His gaze caught hers, sharp with recognition, and held. No words passed between them, but a flicker of something, surprise, perhaps, or memory, sparked in his eyes.

Her heart did not quicken. Absolutely not. It merely... remembered. A warmth, a shape, the ease of being seen without explanation. Nothing more. Of course, it was him. Broadshouldered stubbornness wrapped in a greatcoat. Only Alexander Weld could turn grief into a posture.

He always stood that way, unmovable when everyone else bent to please. She had once admired that certainty, even envied it.

And yet... something tugged at the edges of her composure. Surprise, perhaps, or an echo of the ease they'd once shared. There had been comfort in his presence, laughter once so effortless it had stitched itself into her memory. She had expected familiarity.

She had not expected a flicker of warmth. Not after all these years. Not after Rowland.

With a practiced nod, she acknowledged him and continued on her way, leaving the autumn wind to scatter the leaves in her wake.

THE SEA MIST clung to Alexander Weld's greatcoat like a widow's breath. He did not shake it off. He stood at the crest of Hawkesbury Hill. Earlier, he had followed the black-plumed hearse down the winding path toward the family vault. Below, the waves clawed at the cliffs with restless hunger, as though they too mourned his father's passing, their fury pounding against unyielding stone.

Five years ago, he'd walked away from this land, a broken man with blood on his boots and grief carved deep into his chest. He had left behind the mine, the manor, the title, and every expectation that came with them. Now, it all came rushing back.

"Welcome home, my lord," murmured Mr. Bexley, the estate steward, stepping beside him. "The tenants will gather in the hall to speak to you. There's much to be settled."

Weld didn't reply immediately. His eyes traced the jagged skyline of Sommer-by-the-Sea, its crooked chimneys, coal smoke, and glints of steel and soot. It was a town advancing into industry, growing hungrier by the day.

For a moment, his thoughts drifted from industry and death to the woman at the cemetery. Lady Georgina Ravenstock. Even from a distance, she had seemed unchanged, poised and composed, yet there was a tightness to her expression, as if the wind carried not a chill but rather a burden. Her gaze had met his across the graveyard, steady and unflinching. A faint memory drifted to the surface. Summer sunlight on the water, and her quiet laugh came to mind. He pushed it aside. There was no room for memory now.

"I received a report this morning," Bexley added. "Another accident in the lower shaft. One dead, two injured. Same cause as before. Equipment failure, but no explanation."

Of course. The mine wouldn't wait. Death did not pause for mourning.

Weld turned, his expression unreadable. "Send a message to Sommer Chase. To Lord Barrington himself."

Bexley blinked. "Barrington? The same man from—?"

"Yes." Weld reached into his inner coat pocket and drew out a gold medallion etched with double Bs, Barrington's Brigade. A calling card. A reckoning. "Bring him this. He'll know what to do."

Bexley paled slightly but nodded. "At once."

Rowland's father had given his life to the mine, as had generations before him. And now, it demanded more still. Weld turned back to the cliffs. His military life waited for him in London, his father lay in the earth, and the mine, his mine, was killing men in his name. He let out a breath. Enough.

The wind howled across the hills, and the new Earl Hawkesbury did not flinch.

⟫⟪

THE WIND CHASED Georgina up the front steps, tugging at her skirts like a child reluctant to let her go. She let herself inside, closing the door against its grasp.

"There you are," Eliza Langford, Georgina's close friend, said as Georgina removed her gloves. "I feared the cemetery might have swallowed you whole. We nearly lost two vicars that way. One to melancholia, the other to scandal. But that's another story."

Georgina managed a faint smile as she unpinned her hat. "It did try, but I managed to escape its clutches.

"What news, or should I say gossip, do you have to share?" Georgina asked as Mrs. Hemsley, the Ravenstock housekeeper, set down the tea tray.

The parlor at Ravenstock Manor bore the marks of years spent in quiet respectability. The upholstery had faded to soft hues of moss and cream, the once-vibrant curtains now gentled by the sun. A scattering of porcelain figurines perched along the mantel, relics of an earlier age, their glossy surfaces dulled. A stack of correspondence waited on a small table near the hearth, neatly bound with twine, the tidy habits of a woman determined to keep her affairs in order.

The fire crackled low, its warmth just enough to ward off the autumn chill, and the scent of beeswax polish lingered in the air. Mrs. Hemsley had, as always, prepared the room to welcome a guest, but it was Georgina's quiet presence that filled the space, lending it a sense of dignity the furnishings alone could not provide.

"The town grows restless," Eliza added more soberly. "There's talk of shortages. The bread from Thwaite's had nearly doubled in cost since Michaelmas. With several of the mines idle and wages unpaid, the women queued at dawn for half-loaves and onions. They've been trading eggs when coin ran thin. And for those who are fortunate enough to be working, there's been no improvement in wages."

"No improvement, and no end to accidents, I imagine." Georgina tucked her gloves into her hat, passed them to Mrs. Hemsley, settled into a seat across from Eliza, and began pouring tea.

"Lord Hawkesbury is the latest victim. His funeral was this morning." Eliza smoothed out her skirt.

Georgina froze as she was about to hand Eliza her tea. "Lord Hawkesbury? I thought I had seen Alexander Weld."

Eliza removed the tea from Georgina's grip. "Where did you see him? You only arrived yesterday."

"I had no idea." Georgina's voice was barely a whisper. She and Alex had known each other in Sommer-by-the-Sea as well as in London. He had gone off to war the year before she married Rowland.

"Where did you see him, Georgina?" Eliza leaned in to catch her friend's attention.

Georgina glanced at her and took a breath. "He was at the cemetery."

"The cemetery?" Eliza teased. "How perfectly dramatic. If only we had a storm to complete the picture.

"There is some exciting news." Eliza changed the subject. "Honoria Bainbridge is making a decision on her wedding gown. She is on the verge of pulling her hair out over the guest list. She received a message from Barrington's brother, Lord Edward, instructing her, not asking, mind you, that she include Michael Dane, the Viscount Albury." Eliza folded her arms. "She had no idea why the Chief Liaison to the East India Company needed an invitation."

"Has Lord Barrington come about, or did Honoria finally give him an ultimatum? It must be almost fifteen years since they became an item. I should give her kudos for remaining independent."

"Apparently, half the village wishes to attend, and the other half insists they've been scandalously overlooked, even though no invitations have been sent. And that's not even mentioning those from London. I still think it's wonderful. Those two make a wonderful pair. Everyone should be as fortunate."

Georgina didn't say a word.

"Oh, forgive me." Eliza placed her hand gently on Georgina's arm. "How unfeeling of me."

Georgina patted Eliza's hand. "There is no need for an apology. "My marriage was one of practicality and friendship. Rowland was a wonderful man in many ways. He gave his life to his miners."

She stood and crossed to the window, gazing out over the rooftops of Sommer-by-the-Sea. A breeze stirred the gold-edged leaves beyond the glass. "Even the air feels different," she murmured. "Autumn always brings change."

"It always does," Eliza replied, joining her side.

⥤⥤⥤⥢⥢⥢

OUTSIDE, THE WIND shifted again, stirring the autumn leaves and carrying whispers from the coast, soft as memory, and just as impossible to hold.

At Hawkesbury Hall, a fire crackled low in the hearth, holding back the chill as Weld turned toward the sound of approaching footsteps.

"You wasted no time," He remarked as Barrington entered the study.

"Neither did your steward," Barrington replied, returning the medallion to Weld's palm. "When a man sends this, it demands prompt attention. I was coming to see you today. Honoria is threatening I must sample more wedding cakes, and I thought Hawkesbury Hall would be a good place—"

"To hide." Weld chuckled and gestured for Barrington to have a seat by the fire while he went to the sideboard.

The study at Hawkesbury Manor smelled faintly of coal dust and old paper, as though the very bones of the house remembered the industry that sustained it. Heavy oak shelves lined the walls, their contents thick with ledgers and mining records, the spines cracked from handling.

Dust motes drifted lazily in the shafts of sunlight that pierced the tall windows. A scattering of maps and papers on the desk lay beneath an iron paperweight shaped like a miner's lantern, a tribute, or perhaps a warning.

The fire in the grate had been coaxed back to life, casting flickering light across the worn carpet and drawing long shadows up the paneled walls. It was not a room of comfort, but of command. And in Weld's presence, it was as if the house itself had roused from its long slumber.

"Brandy?" Weld offered, though his hand was already on the decanter.

Barrington nodded. Weld poured two glasses and handed one to him. The amber liquid caught the light, but neither man seemed to notice. Weld sat in the chair next to him.

"I've returned and found that my father has kept a great deal from me over the last few years. Accidents aren't uncommon, but the number my father endured…" Weld paused, swirling the branding in his glass. "It's suspect." He didn't look at Barrington right away. He wasn't ready to hear his agreement, not yet. He took a slow sip, then turned to face him.

"After nearly every accident, there was an outlay of money, supposedly for repairs. But." Weld shook his head. "I'm not so certain they were completed."

Barrington's gaze sharpened. "That's not carelessness. I've seen work undone, on purpose." He leaned forward slightly, his brandy forgotten. "Targeted disruptions. Financial siphons hidden behind false repairs. That's the Order's pattern."

The words struck. Weld paused mid-motion, surprise flickering across his features before he looked away, thinking, recalculating. "I thought they stuck to trade routes and political channels."

"They did. But we've choked off many of those." Barrington's voice was grim. "And now, in desperation, they'll take what they can. Coal…"

"…is a gold mine waiting to be bled dry." Weld finished.

"Then we move carefully." Barrington drained the last of his brandy. "Care is a luxury we cannot afford. Last year, Ravenstock. This year, my father. Who will be next?"

Weld's gaze settled on the map, its lines too neat to reflect the chaos beneath. He set down his glass, the fire catching in its depths, and rose. Side by side, they began.

Chapter Two

L ADY GEORGINA HAD not expected to feel anything upon her return to Sommer-by-the-Sea, least of all a pang. But there it was, sharp and unwelcome, as the carriage rolled past the familiar bend where lavender grew stubbornly wild against the stone.

It had been nearly four years since she'd truly traveled these roads. Her last real arrival was marked by a newly inked marriage certificate and guarded optimism. Since then, there had been fleeting visits, little more than duty and decorum. Now, widowed, unanchored, and oddly restless, she returned not to her husband's home but to a solicitor's office to settle Rowland's affairs.

The door latch was cool beneath her gloved hand, the luster of its brass dulled by sea air. She remembered touching it once before, years ago, when she'd stood beside her new husband, the future laid out like a map before them. Now, she traced that same handle, but the course had worn thin at the edges.

The nameplate on the door read *Hughes, Swift & Lacey*. She stood at the threshold. The office smelled of parchment and pipe smoke, as it always had, but now the air felt heavier somehow, as if burdened by unfinished affairs. She wondered if her husband had sat at this very desk, thumbing over the same ledgers.

She smoothed her gloves, stepped inside, and nearly came to a stop.

Alexander Weld stood beside the window, tall and severe in black, his profile as sharp as the last memory she had of him boarding a ship, eyes unreadable, jaw set against grief.

"My lord," she said carefully.

Weld turned, and for a moment, neither spoke.

She hadn't seen him in years, but the shape of him, still and steady in the morning light, was disarmingly familiar. He had always carried himself like a man preparing to be disappointed by the world, and yet, she remembered the boy who once believed it could be better.

Weld's shoulders stiffened, perhaps bracing for a tide of memory or something worse. "Lady Georgina," he said finally. "I didn't expect—" His gaze swept briefly over her, as if confirming she was not a ghost of the past but standing before him in truth.

"Nor I," she replied, offering a tight smile. "I am sorry to hear of your father's passing," she added, her voice measured but sincere. "I had not known."

His gaze flicked away, briefly. "It was sudden." He offered nothing more.

"Your husband's holdings are handled here. As are mine." His voice was rougher than she remembered. Deeper. Like coal dragged through velvet.

The solicitor entered before awkwardness could thicken.

"Ah, Lady Ravenstock, Lord Hawkesbury. How fortunate. You both have matters to settle regarding adjoining estates. Perhaps we might speak together?"

Georgina blinked. "Together?"

Weld gave her a wry glance. "It seems fate has a sense of humor, or a cruel imagination"

"The matter concerns the jointly held parcel at Ashdown Hill," Mr. Hughes said, thumbing through a thin stack of documents.

"Jointly held?" Georgina looked from Hughes to Alexander in surprise.

Mr. Hughes frowned as he shuffled the remaining papers. "Curious. There should be a transfer of trust documents here as well. Lord Ravenstock had requested it be drawn up separately from his will." He lifted his head and glanced at Georgina. "A precaution, he called it."

Weld's brow darkened. "And it is missing?"

"So it seems," Hughes admitted, troubled as he searched through the papers again. "Your father's copy resolves the joint use of the mine, but the question of Lady Ravenstock's legal stewardship of her late husband's holdings remains... incomplete."

Georgina tilted her head, keeping her tone neutral. "Then I expect we must search the estate records more thoroughly."

"Yes, it includes grazing land, timber rights, and the Ashdown Hill Mine. However, I must confess that there is no final agreement on record."

"Are you certain, Mr. Hughes?" Georgina was still in shock.

"It is uncommon, but not unheard of, for such parcels to benefit both estates, provided the parties remain amenable."

Weld's brow furrowed. "There should be a document." He reached inside his coat, and withdrew a folded parchment. "My father kept meticulous records," he added, passing it across the desk.

Mr. Hughes unfolded it, his eyes brightening. "Remarkable. This appears to settle matters precisely."

Georgina leaned closer, her gaze flicking from the solicitor to Weld. "I recall my husband mentioning this, but I hadn't realized the agreement was so well-preserved." She met Weld's eyes, a note of quiet appreciation in her voice. "Your father's diligence serves us both, my lord."

Weld offered a faint, wry smile. "For once, I find myself grateful for his obsession with detail."

An hour later, papers signed and tempers mostly intact, they stepped out into the sunlight.

"Would you allow me to buy you a cup of tea?" Weld asked, not quite looking at her. "For old times' sake."

She hesitated. Then: "Yes... Why not?"

As they walked, Georgina noted the way townsfolk greeted

Alex with quiet deference, their nods and brief glances, a silent acknowledgement of his new position. Had they always regarded him so, or was it the mantle of responsibility that now draped across his shoulders?

Once, they laughed over sweet rolls and squabbled over poetry in the Ravenstock library. Now he bore a title, a weight, a hush of respect wherever he walked. She studied him with quiet interest, wondering what years of command and loss had shaped him to be.

They continued toward the tea shop near the harbor, and the damp haze that had shrouded the morning began to lift.

The lane to the harbor sloped gently, worn smooth by years of salt air and boot heels. Georgina walked at an unhurried pace.

She stole a glance at Alex, not overt, but enough to note the changes time had carved. The rigid lines of his youth had eased, though his mouth still seemed a fraction too serious for a spring morning.

"You haven't changed as much as I expected," she said lightly, her eyes ahead.

"Nor you," he replied. "Though when I saw your name listed among the estate matters, I half-feared you might have turned into a mercenary, descending upon my holdings with a pack of solicitors."

Her brow arched, amused despite herself. "What a flattering impression."

"A foolish one," he conceded. "You were always too clever for such dramatics."

A breeze teased the hem of her pelisse as they rounded the corner near the harbor green. The scent of brine and wild thyme drifted in the air, and the familiar cry of gulls overhead tugged at a half-buried memory.

"You were abroad, then, when you heard of your father's passing?" she asked, her tone softened by curiosity rather than sympathy.

"I was," Weld answered. He hesitated before adding, "On the

Peninsula. News travels slowly, as you know."

She inclined her head. She did know. Too well. "You served with distinction, they say."

He gave a small shrug, as if brushing off both praise and memory. "I returned with enough scars to impress the uninformed, if that counts as distinction."

The wryness in his voice coaxed a genuine smile from her, small but real. "You were never one to boast, my lord."

"No," he said, glancing at her properly for the first time. His gaze lingered, thoughtful. "But I am grateful to be here, in spite of it all."

They reached the small tea shop overlooking the harbor, its windows clouded with the salt-fog that clung to the glass and softened the view beyond. The bell above the door gave a polite chime as they entered, and the familiar scent of bergamot and warm bread wrapped around them.

Tatiana Rostov looked up from arranging a tray near the counter, surprise brightening her features. "Lady Ravenstock! Lord Hawkesbury!" She set down the teapot and wiped her hands on her apron. "It has been too long."

Alex offered a nod of greeting. "Miss Rostov. I'd begun to think no one else dared rival your scones."

Tatiana laughed. "I do my best to uphold my family's reputation, my lord. Your usual table?"

He deferred to Georgina with a courteous tilt of his head. "If Lady Ravenstock approves."

They followed Tatiana to a corner near the window, where the hum of conversation and the low thrum of the sea blended in companionable rhythm. She returned a moment later with a fresh pot of tea and two delicate plates.

"Welcome home, my lord," Tatiana said warmly before leaving them to their privacy.

"It hasn't changed," Georgina observed, stirring her tea. "The village still keeps its secrets behind a polite façade."

"Some of them," Alex replied. "Others have learned new

tricks. There's talk of expanding the shipyards, and a new railway line from the north."

She smiled faintly. "Progress, then. Rowland would have liked that. He was forever sketching plans to bring more men to work."

"And you?" he asked, watching her over the rim of his cup. "Do you like the sound of progress?"

"I like the sound of fairness," she said. "If progress brings that, I'll applaud it. If not, I reserve judgment."

His mouth curved in a ghost of amusement. "You've not changed."

"I should hope I have. I was twenty when we last argued about fairness."

He gave a soft laugh. "You called me a moral philosopher without a cause."

"And you called me a dreamer with too much sense."

They shared a glance, brief but companionable, before she turned back to the window. The moment settled between them, comfortable in its simplicity.

Outside, gulls wheeled above the masts. Inside, the quiet clatter of cups and low conversation lent the room an intimacy that had nothing to do with sentiment, only the ease of two people remembering how to speak without pretense.

"Tell me," she said after a moment, "what brings you back here besides your father's affairs?"

He hesitated, setting his cup aside. "Obligation, mostly. The mine needs attention. There have been incidents."

She nodded, her expression thoughtful. "So I've heard. Rowland believed there were structural faults in the lower shafts. He was drafting proposals for reinforcement before the accident."

Weld's gaze sharpened slightly. "Did he leave those notes?"

"In his papers, I expect. I'll have them sent to you if you wish."

"Thank you."

The conversation slowed, not from discomfort but from

recognition of all that remained unspoken.

When they finally rose to leave, Georgina glanced once more toward the harbor, where sunlight glimmered over the tidepools.

"Strange," she murmured, reaching for her gloves. "The sea always looks the same, yet it never is."

"Like people," Alex said quietly.

She met his eyes—steady, unstartled—and smiled. "Perhaps."

Outside, the afternoon light had turned golden, softening the edges of the town. They stepped into it side by side, the distance between them measured not in years, but in the quiet possibility of knowing each other anew.

Chapter Three

THE NEXT MORNING brought sunlight with a chill. Fitting, Georgina thought, for the task ahead. She stood in the front room of Ravenstock Manor, her sleeves rolled and her expression tight as she surveyed the contents of the past. The portraits had been wrapped in muslin last year, after Rowland's funeral. Crates, with Rowland's personal effects, were labeled in her late husband's hand and had been destined for London, but there was no need to send them now.

She walked past the large side table and found a battered globe and a dented tea set. Both had suffered at Rowland's hand when, as a young boy, he and his father had played roughly in the room. They were amusing stories, difficult to imagine their playfulness, knowing how stiff and unbending Rowland's father had been. To Georgina, the items were less like keepsakes and more like echoes pretending to matter.

A soft knock at the door broke the stillness.

"Lady Georgina?" came a voice, warm and familiar. "I heard you might be parting with a few treasures. I thought I might offer a proper farewell to them, if you'll have me."

Georgina opened the door to find Mrs. Bainbridge standing crisply on the threshold, eyes sharp with curiosity and the floral scent following her like a herald.

Honoria crossed the threshold and, without hesitation, drew Georgina into a brief but genuine embrace. The scent of lilac clung to her, warm and familiar, and for a moment, the empty house breathed easier, as if releasing something it had held too long. It struck her how easily companionship could dispel a silence she had mistaken for peace.

"Honoria, how good it is to see you," Georgina released her and drew her further into the room.

Honoria's glance swept the chamber. "You have far better taste than your husband did. I knew Lord Ravenstock briefly. He was dreadful at cards. Worse than Barrington, and that is hard to do."

Georgina laughed before she meant to. "Would you like some tea?"

"Not right now. Mrs. Hemsley told my Ellen you wished to purge. I hope you were purging so she has less to dust. Yes, that is what she said," Honoria replied, her expression entirely innocent. "Am I accurate?"

Georgina couldn't help it. She laughed aloud, raising a hand to her mouth as she caught her breath. "You are correct."

"Good. I wouldn't want to miss an opportunity to help Mrs. Hemsley." Mrs. Bainbridge made a poor attempt at keeping a straight face, but finally broke down, her face blooming into a wide smile.

Georgina found herself returning the grin, surprised at how easily Honoria could lift the gloom.

"This way to my treasures." Georgina looped her arm in Honoria's as they walked to the side table. Honoria paused over a set of porcelain figurines, their painted faces faded, and a hairline crack running through the tallest shepherd's staff. "Sentimental or sellable?" she asked, lifting a brow.

"Neither," Georgina replied, flicking a finger against the cracked glaze. "My husband's mother fancied them, but I never could abide their facial expressions."

They came to a set of pewter candlesticks, squat and tarnished. "Well," Mrs. Bainbridge declared, hefting one as if to test its worth, "these could stop a thief at least, if not light a drawing room."

Her gaze swept the room again and caught on a battered globe tucked beneath a writing desk. She carefully drew it out, spinning it lightly beneath her palm as dust scattered into the air.

"My girls are forever convinced the world ends at Dover," she remarked, half to herself, half to Georgina. "This might expand their horizons, at least by an inch." With an approving nod, she set the globe aside as a claim, her attention turning to the wooden box with its intricate carvings and iron lock that sat on the desk.

"I have a student with a mind for puzzles," she added, lifting the box with care. "She will relish the challenge."

Georgina offered no objection. Let the box find use elsewhere, she thought. Better in curious hands than gathering dust in a forgotten corner.

"I understand congratulations are in order," Georgina said, leading her guest toward the library where Mrs. Helmsley had just laid out tea.

"It was rather exciting," Honoria replied, settling into a chair. "But I must tell you, I have no idea how you managed to plan your wedding."

"I had little say in it," Georgina admitted with a wry smile. "My mother and mother-in-law took it all upon themselves. I only had to be there." She poured the tea and looked up. Honoria's sober expression made her think she had said too much. She gathered her thoughts. "And when do you and Barrington plan to marry?"

"The week before the Hartleigh masquerade," Honoria said with a sigh. "And, before you ask, I have neither the gown nor the cake decided. What I do have is the date and the venue, the inn at Rosalynde Bay, where Barrington and I met."

"I am happy to help in any way I can."

"I'm glad for your offer," Honoria replied warmly. "I could use both inspiration and courage. In the meantime, I shall invite you to tea. There's quite a bit going on in Sommer-by-the-Sea that you ought to know about."

Mrs. Bainbridge set down her teacup, her gaze thoughtful. "And what of you, Georgina? Once this house is cleared, what will you do?"

Georgina hesitated, her fingers curling loosely around her saucer. "I had thought to return to London," she admitted. "Fortunately, the property is not entailed. The plan was to sell the manor, settle the affairs of the estate, and... begin anew. But things have changed."

There was a silence before Mrs. Bainbridge's lips curved into a knowing smile. "Well, that is a tidy turn of fate. Isn't it? "There's more Ravenstock in you than any of the men who came before," Mrs. Bainbridge said with a smile. "And I mean that as a compliment."

Georgina managed a soft laugh, though it carried a thread of unease beneath it. "I only hope I carry it well enough to see it through."

Mrs. Bainbridge's eyes sharpened, a gleam of approval there. "You will. Of that, I have no doubt."

Mrs. Bainbridge's gaze lingered over her tea, thoughtful. "Ravenstock holdings and the mine," she mused. "That is no small inheritance, Georgina."

"No," Georgina agreed quietly. She traced the rim of her cup with one finger, watching the faint reflection ripple across the liquid surface. "It is rather more than I intended to claim."

"You sound as though you've been burdened with an unwanted parcel from an aged relation," Honoria replied, her smile dry but not unkind.

"It feels nearly the same," Georgina admitted. "I had thought my ties to this place ended with Rowland. I never imagined the family would see fit to bind me so tightly to its affairs."

"Or so wisely," Mrs. Bainbridge countered. "The Hawkesburys might not have appreciated their good fortune at the time, but you are well suited to stewarding these lands." She paused, her eyes narrowing thoughtfully. "A woman of sense and strength, with her wits about her and no need to answer to a husband's vanity."

"Until I choose to marry again," Georgina said, her tone light but edged.

"Until then," Honoria allowed, lifting her cup. "But perhaps not even then, if you are clever."

Georgina offered a faint smile in reply. Her thoughts were less certain. The burden of responsibility had not yet settled, although she could feel its shape, like a cloak draped across her shoulders.

"Then perhaps it is time to surprise them," she said quietly.

Honoria raised her cup in salute. "That is precisely what I hoped to hear."

As they set their cups aside, Mrs. Bainbridge's gaze drifted toward the window, where the pale light of morning touched the edges of the old drapery. "And what of the household? Do you intend to keep the staff?"

Georgina followed her glance, considering. "Mrs. Hemsley has been with this house longer than I've been alive. I could not dismiss her even if I wished it. The others... we shall see. Some have family nearby and may prefer to find new positions rather than wait for my plans to settle."

"A fair approach," Honoria approved. "Better to let them choose their course than to bind them to uncertainty."

Georgina allowed herself a moment of reflection. "The house echoes more than it used to," she murmured. "I wonder if it always did, and I simply failed to hear it."

"It will echo less with purpose in its halls," Mrs. Bainbridge said, her tone matter-of-fact. "Houses are much like people in that regard."

Mrs. Bainbridge's gaze sharpened as she set down her empty cup. "You should know, Georgina, there are those in Sommer-by-the-Sea who expect you to sell. Quietly, of course. They whisper it over their accounts and at the market stalls."

Georgina's brows lifted, not in indignation but surprise. "I had not considered that anyone beyond myself cared what became of Ravenstock."

"Oh, they care," Honoria assured her. "Some because they fear change. Others because they hope for it. And more than a few because they wonder what manner of woman inherits a house and a mine and chooses to stay."

Georgina absorbed this with a quiet breath. "Then let them wonder."

"Good," Mrs. Bainbridge said, a spark of satisfaction in her tone. "Let them wonder, Georgina. Let them see what you choose to become next."

Georgina's gaze drifted to the window again. "Perhaps it's time I stop standing at the edge of my own life."

She watched Honoria lift her cup, her laughter still warm in the air, and for the first time in days, something like steadiness returned.

Honoria set down her cup and leaned back slightly, studying Georgina over the rim of her glasses. "And what of your neighbor, Lord Hawkesbury? It seems to me his return is not a mere coincidence. He's taken quite an interest in the mine, has he not?"

Georgina lifted her brow, affecting mild surprise. "Honoria, you make it sound as if you've appointed yourself mistress of Sommer-by-the-Sea's intelligence."

"A headmistress must keep informed of the important players in her town," Honoria replied crisply, a gleam of amusement in her eyes. "And since you are now co-owner of that mine, Georgina, I suspect Lord Hawkesbury's attentions may serve you well."

Georgina's fingers tightened subtly around her saucer. "So he has," she allowed.

"A fortunate arrangement," Honoria continued, "to have a neighbor with experience in both land and enterprise. You will need every sharp mind you can gather."

Georgina did not answer at once. The image of Alex Weld surfaced in her thoughts. The burden he carried on his shoulders, the measured calculation in his gaze. She had once assumed he was simply a steady hand at his father's side. Now she saw the steel beneath.

"He is capable," she said, keeping her tone even. "Practical."

Yes, there was something different in him. Not just purpose, but a quiet authority, as though command had become instinct rather than inheritance.

"And, I dare say," Honoria added smoothly, "loyal to the land and its people. He knows the veins of the mine as well as the veins on the back of his hand. Perhaps better."

Georgina met Honoria's gaze directly, her expression calm though her pulse quickened beneath it. "We shall see."

And yet, she had seen something already. Not the boy she once knew, nor the man shaped by war and duty. But the space between the two, a man who still surprised her.

Honoria's smile was sly but approving. "Indeed, we shall."

A quiet resolve began to form, threading through her doubts like a seam stitched tight. She was no longer simply closing a chapter. She was pausing to consider what the next might hold.

As their conversation ebbed into a comfortable quiet, Georgina let her gaze drift around the familiar room. It looked different today, not because of the absence of certain objects, but because of the presence of something she had not expected to find again, possibility.

She had intended to dismantle the pieces of her past and scatter them like autumn leaves, carried off by the next season's wind. Yet here she sat, not sifting through remnants, but considering foundations. Solid ground, as Honoria might say. If only it felt that way beneath her feet.

Her thoughts flicked to Mrs. Hemsley and the other staff. They had kept the house running long after its purpose had faltered. Perhaps it was not the walls that defined Ravenstock, but the people within them. And perhaps, she thought, that could include herself once more.

Mrs. Bainbridge rose, gathering the puzzle box beneath her

arm with the globe already claimed. She paused at the door, glancing at the room and the bundled memories left behind.

"When my pupil solves this box," she said, tapping it lightly with her gloved fingers, "I shall insist you join me to see what clever trickery lies inside."

Georgina allowed a smile to touch her lips. "Only if you promise not to let her outwit you first."

Honoria's answering laugh was genuine. "I make no promises, Georgina. Only that you will not face these challenges alone."

With that, she stepped into the sunlight, leaving behind the quiet assurance that, even in uncertainty, Georgina's course was hers to chart.

Alone again, Georgina stood for a long moment by the door, her hand resting on the frame. Through the rippled glass panes, sunlight caught the lingering mist, turning it to silver. Possibility, she thought once more, a fragile thing, yet glimmering all the same.

She lingered a moment longer in the stillness, her gaze drifting to the bundled memories stacked against the far wall. Her future might be uncertain, but at least she knew where it would begin.

A gentle rap at the doorframe drew her attention.

Mrs. Hemsley appeared, a folded note in her hand. "This arrived for you, miss. Brought by one of Lord Hawkesbury's men."

Georgina took the missive, her fingers brushing the rough paper. Breaking the seal, she read the concise lines:

Lady Georgina,

As we agreed, I shall call for you at half past nine tomorrow morning to visit the Ashdown Hill Mine.

—A. Weld

Her pulse quickened, but she folded the note with care, slipping it beneath the edge of a nearby ledger. No need to fret over it now. Tomorrow would come soon enough.

She stared a moment longer at the folded edge, wondering if it was anticipation for the task ahead, or something less easily named. Either way, she was done watching from a distance.

"Thank you, Mrs. Hemsley," she said, her voice steady.

"Shall I have a morning tray brought to the library, miss?" The housekeeper inquired, as if sensing her thoughts.

Georgina allowed herself a small smile. "Yes, please."

Chapter Four

THE MORNING LIGHT slanted through the library windows, casting long stripes across the worn spines of books that had not been touched in years. Dust swirled in the beams like restless thoughts, unsettled but not unwelcome.

Georgina drew her shawl tighter over her shoulders and reached for the folio Rowland had kept tucked between two ledgers on the lower shelf. The folio crackled faintly as she opened it, releasing a breath of cold, dry air along with its contents. The scent of old paper struck her. Ink, dust, and something sharper. She looked again at the folio. She found it surprising that she remembered his handwriting so well. Neat. Contained. Like the man himself. Like the lies he'd left behind.

Inside, she found diagrams and dense notations, some penned by Rowland, others copied from the respected engineer John Buddle's lectures and reports concerning ventilation shafts, coal seams, and timber supports. The terms were as foreign to her as any military dispatch, yet as she traced the careful sketches and annotations, they slowly began to take shape in her mind.

The diagrams told a different story than the tidy reports she had seen. Repairs had been delayed, inspections deferred. The mine had not merely failed Rowland. It had been failing for years.

Her gaze caught on a loose sheet, thinner than the rest, tucked between the pages and marked in Rowland's familiar script. He had underlined a passage concerning the dangers of slowed air currents and the accumulation of gas in older seams.

There was no commentary, no notes in the margin to explain why it had caught his attention, only the firm pressure of the ink, as if urgency alone had driven him to mark it.

Her breath caught, a prickle rising along her skin. A private warning from the past, too late to spare him, but not too late for her.

She pressed her palm to the cool edge of the table, steadying herself. The house still smelled faintly of old paper and cold hearthstones, but something new curled in her chest beneath the lingering chill. Determination.

Carefully, she gathered the loose papers back into the folio and set it aside for later study. She thought it best to understand the danger before stepping into it.

"Lord Hawkesbury's carriage just turned into the drive."

Mrs. Hemsley's quiet announcement had scarcely faded before Georgina rose from her chair, brushing the crumbs of her solitary breakfast from her skirts. She had chosen her attire with care, sturdy boots beneath her gown, a practical woolen pelisse, and a bonnet tied neatly beneath her chin. Sensible, but not so severe as to invite comment.

By the time she stepped into the front hall, Lord Hawkesbury stood just beyond the open door, his figure cut sharp against the soft gray of the morning mist. He did not fidget, nor glance about impatiently, but stood with the same quiet authority she remembered from their youth, tempered now by years and the burdens he carried.

"Lady Georgina," he greeted, offering a slight incline of his head, not quite a bow, but more than mere courtesy.

"Lord Hawkesbury," she returned, her tone even. She did not extend her hand, nor did he seem to expect it.

Mrs. Hemsley handed Georgina her gloves, which she drew on with careful precision, noting the way Alex's gaze lingered, as if assessing not her appearance, but her readiness.

Without further ceremony, he gestured to his carriage. "Shall we?"

They descended the front steps together, the crisp air stirring the ribbons at her bonnet. The carriage stood with its door open, dark wheels damp from the morning dew. Alex handed her up and settled opposite her a moment later as the vehicle jolted into motion.

For a stretch of road, neither spoke. Georgina traced the patterns of fog along the hedgerows, feeling the excitement of anticipation coil quietly beneath her ribs.

"The foreman has made his assurances," Alex began breaking the silence, his gaze steady on her, "but I trust my own senses more than any report. We'll inspect the main shaft, the timber supports, and the ventilation passages."

His words were methodical, plans of a commander, not a partner. Georgina suspected he sought order, while she sought truth. Two sides of the same purpose, perhaps, but not yet the same intent.

"And the firedamp?" she asked, her voice calm. The word still felt unfamiliar on her tongue, but she knew it meant danger, gas, invisible, and deadly.

His brow lifted, just slightly, a flicker of surprise passing over his features. "You've been studying Rowland's notes, then."

"I have," Georgina replied, smoothing her gloves against her skirt. "It seemed prudent to understand what dangers might lie ahead."

A shadow of a smile touched his mouth, brief but genuine. "Wise. Most owners do not take such care."

"Most owners," she said quietly, "are not widows of men lost beneath their own holdings."

His expression sobered at that, the fleeting curve of his mouth vanishing into thoughtful lines. He gave a small nod, one of quiet respect rather than pity.

"If it can't be made safe, it should be closed," she said quietly.

"And if it can?" he countered.

"Then we owe it to every man who's ever gone below to do better."

He gave a single nod. "Then that's our task."

"We'll not linger underground longer than necessary," he assured her. "I intend to speak with the foreman, inspect the damaged beam work, and confirm the air is fit to breathe."

She inclined her head. "Good."

He reached beside him and retrieved a folded garment, setting it gently upon the seat next to her. "I thought you might appreciate this. Mine dust is stubborn once it settles."

Georgina unfolded the coat. It was made of sturdy canvas, clearly intended for rough work, but clean and serviceable. She draped it over her knees with quiet gratitude. "Thank you," she said simply.

The carriage jolted as they left the smoother village lane for the rutted road toward the hills. Outside the window, the rising sun struggled through thinning clouds, casting pale gold light across the landscape.

"What else should I expect?" she asked, her gaze fixed ahead.

"Confined spaces," he answered. "The air will be still. The scent of coal is sharp. The men will be wary of our presence, but they know we come not to interfere, only to see with our own eyes."

She accepted this without hesitation. "Good. Let them see I will not flinch from what belongs to me."

His gaze flicked to hers, then, something unreadable moving behind his eyes. It wasn't a surprise, but perhaps a grudging admiration.

"No," he said at last. "I do not believe you will."

The wheels rolled over the rutted road, and as Ashdown Hill Mine came into view, a hush settled between them. It was not discomfort, but the quiet breath before stepping into the unknown.

The carriage slowed as they reached the mine road, the wheels crunching over loose stones and coal dust. Ahead, the black mouth of the Ashdown Hill Mine loomed against the slope, flanked by rough-hewn timbers and the sagging silhouette of a pulley system.

Weld stepped down first, extending his hand to assist her. She accepted, grateful for the solidness of his grasp, though neither of them spoke of it.

He helped her put on the white coat. She drew it more tightly around her. The weight of it was unfamiliar but oddly reassuring. Anticipation settled in her chest, steady and unmistakable.

A sharp wind tugged at the edges of her bonnet as she surveyed the scene. Miners moved like shadows between carts and scaffolding, their heads turning subtly at her presence. Though no man spoke a word, she felt their eyes marking her, sharp with unspoken questions.

"They weren't expecting you," Weld said quietly, reading the tension in the air as clearly as she did.

"Best they get used to it," Georgina replied, lifting her chin. "I suspect this will not be my only visit."

A flicker of something, approval, perhaps, crossed his features before he turned to greet a gentleman emerging from the dim light of the mine entrance.

"Foreman Archer," Weld called.

The man approached, cap in hand, his face lined and grim beneath the smear of coal dust. "My lord," he said, then glanced at Georgina with quick calculation. "Ma'am."

"This is Lady Ravenstock," Weld introduced evenly. "Co-owner of Ashdown Hill. She will be joining our inspection today."

If Archer was surprised, he masked it well. "As you say, my lord. We're ready for you."

Georgina nodded in acknowledgment, holding the foreman's gaze for a heart beat longer than necessary. He looked away first.

They moved toward the mine entrance, where lanterns were strung along the timbers, casting long shadows on the ground. Weld gestured toward a small rack near the opening, where spare lamps hung ready.

"Take one," he instructed her softly. "It's not as bright as the sun, but it will show you enough."

Georgina selected a lamp and tested its weight in her hand. The flame inside flickered, fragile yet defiant.

"Keep it close," he added. "The tunnels can turn upon you if you're careless."

Her pulse quickened, but she gave a brisk nod. "I'll stay close."

They crossed the threshold together, stepping from the crisp morning air into the dim, damp world beneath the earth. The chill of the tunnels coiled around her shoulders, seeping through the borrowed coat as if to remind her where she stood.

She had told herself it was a matter of duty, as simple as that. Yet as she lifted the lamp higher, casting its flickering light into the shadows ahead, she repeated the promise within her heart.

I will not flinch.

And she would not. Her borrowed coat was welcome now. She pulled it tighter around her shoulders as her lamp flickered to life, casting a modest circle of light into the gloom.

Ahead, Weld's lamp swayed steadily, sure and unhurried as he led the way. Shadows bent and stretched along the uneven walls, catching the glimmer of embedded coal seams like ink smudges in the rock.

"Mind your step," he said quietly, though she had already picked her footing with care. The uneven ground was damp beneath her boots, patches of water glinting like oil in the lantern light.

Georgina's heart pounded, not with fear, but with alertness. She absorbed every detail, the way the timbers groaned faintly overhead, the drift of dust in the air, and the scent of smoke from the miners' lamps mingling with the sharp tang of stone.

They passed a crew working to shore up a weakened section, their faces blackened with soot and concentration. Tools clanged against stone in a steady rhythm, filling the stale air with uneasy music.

Weld paused beside them, eyeing the angle of the newly

placed supports. His fingers brushed the timber, testing its give with practiced ease. A frown tugged at his mouth, but he said nothing as they moved on.

"This way," he directed, guiding her down a narrower passage. The air thickened around her shoulders, cool, dry, and still. It pressed like silence at a funeral, familiar, but no longer welcome. "We'll inspect the main beam and vent line before returning to the upper galleries."

Georgina followed without hesitation, her lamp held high. As they walked, she kept her gaze attentive, cataloguing the narrowing of the walls and the close press of earth above her head.

As they passed a side cut-off, a narrow passage branching from the main shaft, timbered but less heavily used, she slowed.

"Does the airflow run from this seam toward the main shaft?" she asked, lifting her lamp toward the opening, "or does it risk drawing firedamp back toward the working faces?"

Her voice was calm and steady, but it carried easily in the hush between hammer strikes.

Archer, who had been trailing them with dutiful silence, blinked as if she had spoken in a foreign language. He shifted, a flicker of discomfort crossing his soot-streaked face. "M'lady?"

Weld's gaze sharpened immediately, a quiet command glinting in his eyes. "Answer her, Archer."

The foreman cleared his throat, glancing toward the cut-off as though seeing it anew. "The flow runs toward the main shaft," he replied at last. "As it ought. Though with the new collapse, there's been… some disruption."

"Enough to cause accumulation?" Georgina pressed, her tone free of accusation, only genuine concern.

Archer hesitated, his fingers curling around the brim of his cap. "We've vented it well enough," he said, but his answer lacked conviction.

Weld's gaze lingered on the foreman a heartbeat longer, calm and assessing, before he turned to Georgina. No smile curved his mouth, but there was a light in his eyes, steady, quiet, and filled with something that might have been pride.

"You've studied well," he said, his voice low, meant only for her.

She could not look away. It wasn't the compliment, but the way he said it, without irony, without surprise, as though he had expected nothing less.

"I mean to do more than study," Georgina replied, lifting her lamp a fraction higher. "I mean to understand."

Her boot slid against loose stone, and she caught herself with a sharp inhale. A hand, his, brushed her back, steadying. Just enough. Then gone.

They moved on, though the question lingered behind them like an echo in the shaft. Georgina kept her silence, but her mind did not let the matter go. Archer's answer had wavered. His jaw shifted, just slightly, but Georgina saw it. He didn't trust Archer. Or the mine. Perhaps not even himself. She would follow his lead, for now, but she carried the ember of that concern. She'd seen enough ashes. This time, she would not wait for fire to become ruin.

Chapter Five

B Y THE TIME they returned to the carriage, light spilled across the lane, chasing off the last of the morning chill. Weld helped Georgina up first, his hand brushed her elbow, warm and steady, and sure for a breath longer than necessary. She didn't flinch. Didn't lean in. But how peculiar, that when he let go, the absence was oddly louder than the touch.

The warmth of midday filtered through the window as they settled into their seats, the rattle of the wheels a steady backdrop to their thoughts. Georgina kept her gaze trained on the hills slipping past the glass, reluctant to let him see how deeply the morning's impressions still unsettled her.

It was Weld who spoke first, his voice carrying the faintest thread of wry amusement. "I confess, my lady, I expected you to ask sharp questions in the mine. I did not expect you to ask Archer, the one that made him lose color beneath all that soot."

She glanced at him, a glimmer of mischief sparking despite herself. "I rather thought he paled because I managed to keep my footing in skirts."

"That too," Weld allowed, the faintest smile touching his lips. "You have a talent for unnerving men accustomed to ruling their domain."

"I should like them to remain unnerved," she replied briskly. "Keeps them from growing too complacent."

He tilted his head, studying her as if seeing her not merely as the lady of Ravenstock, but, in truth, as a formidable partner. "I believe they'll think twice before dismissing you now."

"Let's hope they think at least once before setting another poor timber," she replied. Then, after a beat, she added more lightly, "Though I expect Archer will lose sleep tonight wondering if I plan to return with a lamp in one hand and a lecture in the other."

A quiet laugh escaped him, low and warm. "It would serve him well if you did."

They settled into an easy rhythm, the tension of the mine loosening its grip. Georgina breathed more deeply, the stale air of the tunnels replaced by the honest scent of damp earth and wild thyme drifting through the window. The sunlight now carried the promise of afternoon warmth, gilding the fields in soft gold.

"And you, my lord," she ventured. "Was this morning everything you hoped it would be?"

His gaze flicked to her, sharp and steady. "No."

Surprise lifted her brows.

"It was more," he said simply. "I had not expected you to see so clearly what others miss."

She softened, just slightly, beneath the sincerity in his tone. "Perhaps because I have been blind too long myself," she admitted.

A quiet pause passed between them, not heavy but thoughtful. Then, with a tilt of her chin, she added, "And if I should take to carrying Mr. Hughes's papers beneath my arm, I trust you will not mock me too harshly."

"Never," Weld replied, his voice warm with quiet respect. "A lady armed with knowledge is the finest companion a man could hope for."

Georgina found herself smiling, not out of politeness, but something more genuine. She turned her attention back to the window, but not before she caught the slight lift at the corner of his mouth, as if he shared the unspoken thought between them.

The mine might hold its shadows, but here in the brightening day, there was something far less grim between them. Promise.

The carriage turned into the familiar drive, wheels crunching over the gravel as Ravenstock Manor came into view. In the clearing light of midday, the old stones seemed less imposing than they had in early morning mist.

As the carriage slowed, Georgina glanced toward Weld, her brow lifting ever so slightly. "I trust you are not too battle-worn from your time underground, my lord."

His answering smile was faint but real. "I have survived worse skirmishes, my lady. Though few as well-fought."

Before she could respond, the footman swung open the carriage door. Weld stepped down first, then turned to offer his hand. This time, she accepted it without hesitation, and as he steadied her descent, the warmth of his palm was solid and certain beneath her gloved fingers.

Once on firm ground, Georgina paused, her gaze sweeping the house front. Sunlight gleamed off the old leaded windows, and a faint breeze teased the ribbons at her throat. Without looking at him, she said lightly, "You may not yet know, but mine inspections tend to whet the appetite."

"I had hoped you'd say as much," Weld replied, with a shade more ease than before. He adjusted his coat, the smudge of coal dust on his cuff, an unspoken badge of the morning's work. "Though I suspect we have earned more than bread and broth."

She glanced at him sidelong, amusement curling at the corner of her mouth. "Fortunate, then, that Mrs. Hemsley believes in fortifying the body as well as the spirit. Will you stay for the midday meal?"

A pause, not hesitation, but consideration. "I would be pleased to."

"Good." She led the way up the steps, her stride brisk, though her heart beat an unexpected rhythm beneath her composed exterior. "Perhaps you might also spare a moment to glance at some documents. I'd welcome your opinion."

"I'd be delighted," Weld answered, falling into step beside her.

They crossed the threshold together, the house cool and shadowed after the brightness outside. Mrs. Hemsley awaited them in the hall, her expression professionally neutral, but her eyes quietly approving as they shed their outdoor garments.

"Mrs. Hemsley," Georgina said, a slight lift in her voice, "we find ourselves in need of sustenance."

"I anticipated as much, my lady," the housekeeper replied with the ghost of a smile. "The table is already laid out in the morning room."

"And perhaps some of your excellent pickled beets, if they are not too much trouble?"

"I shall see to it," Mrs. Hemsley assured her, departing with the efficient grace of long practice.

Georgina led the way to the morning room, a familiar comfort in the house that had, until today, felt anything but. The table had been laid with cold meats, slices of fresh bread still warm at the center, and a small jar of Mrs. Hemsley's prized gooseberry preserve. It was a modest meal, but honest and sufficient.

She untied her bonnet and set it aside, running her fingers over the brim before resting it on the sideboard. Weld, already out of his coat, glanced at the table and then at her, as if deciding between politeness and genuine hunger.

He helped her to her seat, waiting until she was settled before taking the chair opposite. Only two places had been set, a quiet acknowledgment that she had intended to share the table with no one else.

Mrs. Hemsley quietly placed a dish of pickled beets on the table and left.

"I confess," he said, settling into the chair, "I didn't expect to feel this famished after the morning's work."

"You expected the mine to take your appetite as well as your caution?" Georgina countered lightly as she unfolded her napkin.

His mouth curved, a subtle echo of amusement. "Something like that."

She reached for the bread, tearing a piece free with practiced ease. "Then it's a good thing Mrs. Hemsley had the foresight to keep us from fainting dead away."

"I owe her my thanks," Weld replied, helping himself to the cold meat, his movements unhurried but certain.

They ate for a moment in companionable quiet, the soft clink of cutlery filling the room. Through the window, sunlight warmed the pale drapery, and a small breeze stirred the lace at the edges.

As Georgina tore a piece of bread, she caught the easy rhythm of their meal, the absence of guarded formality. Once, this comfort between them had come without thought. Years had stretched the distance, yet here it was again, unexpected but not unwelcome. Perhaps they could find their way back to that ease, not as it was in youth, but as something steadier. Something earned.

"I would not have thought," Georgina said after a moment, "that such a dark, enclosed place could leave a person feeling more awake, not less."

He glanced up at her, something thoughtful flickering behind his gaze. "It sharpens the senses. Danger does that. You learn to notice every detail, every sound. The shift of a timber. The breath of air where there should be none."

Her expression softened, curiosity overtaking caution. "You notice everything, then?"

"I try," he said simply, meeting her eyes across the table. "Especially when the stakes are high."

Their gazes held for a heartbeat longer than polite conversation required, a subtle thread of understanding weaving between them.

Georgina was the first to look away, though a slight smile lingered at the corner of her mouth. She busied herself with pouring the tea. "Then I suspect you've noticed my determination as well."

"I have," Weld replied, his voice low, edged with quiet respect. "And I expect it will serve you better than most weapons in this fight."

"I do not care to be at war with my own holdings," she said, passing him a cup, "but I will not give them up easily."

He accepted the tea, cradling the warmth of it between his palms. "No," he said, with quiet certainty. "You will not."

They ate a little longer, a few easy comments slipping between them like old habits rediscovered. It wasn't laughter, not yet, but it was something close. A softening. A thaw.

"You will need stout boots, next time," he observed, nodding to her sensible but mud-spattered pair beneath the table.

She followed his glance and gave a wry twist of her lips. "So, it is to be next time already?"

His mouth quirked. "Unless today has deterred you entirely."

"Hardly." She tipped her head, the spark of challenge alight in her eyes. "Though I would appreciate fair warning if I'm to crawl through shafts like a coal rat."

"I'll see that you are forewarned," he promised. "Though I suspect you'd manage well enough, coal rat or not."

She laughed then, soft but genuine. "I suspect you're right."

Their meal drew to a close with no rush, no awkwardness, only a shared sense that this was the first of many conversations still to come. Outside, the day had turned brighter, as though the clouds themselves were taking their leave.

When Mrs. Hemsley returned to clear the dishes, she found both plates nearly empty and her mistress more at ease than she had seen since she had arrived.

As Mrs. Hemsley cleared the plates, Georgina glanced at her mud-spattered boots and then at Weld. "Next time," she said dryly, "you might also warn me to bring a stronger appetite."

He smiled, slow and genuine. "Consider this your first lesson in mining, Lady Ravenstock. It always leaves a person hungry for more."

Her answering laugh, quiet but warm, lingered between them as Mrs. Hemsley swept the dishes away. Even as the humor faded, her gaze drifted to where his hand rested near his cup, strong, steady, and capable. She wondered if he knew how much she had leaned on that steadiness today.

It wasn't his strength alone that unsettled her. It was the ease of it. The quiet way he carried responsibility, not as a burden, but as something he'd already chosen.

Perhaps he did. Perhaps, she thought, he had offered it on purpose, the same quiet assurance he'd carried underground when the shadows pressed close. There might be more to this partnership than obligation, though duty, she admitted, was not the worst place to begin.

Chapter Six

WELD ROSE AS Mrs. Hemsley swept away the last of the dishes. "Lady Ravenstock," Weld said, rising to pull back Georgina's chair, his voice even but a shade too formal for the warmth lingering between them.

Georgina placed her hand lightly on his sleeve. His gaze flicked to it, then rose to meet hers.

There was nothing improper in the gesture, yet the warmth of it lingered, as if her fingers had whispered something her lips could not.

He held her gaze a moment too long, enough to make her wonder if he felt it too.

"After this morning," she said, her tone both warm and steady, "I believe we've earned the right to set formality aside."

She let the moment stretch, holding his gaze. "You may call me Georgina."

A flicker of something, surprise, perhaps even quiet relief, crossed his features before he answered.

"I would like that very much," he replied, his voice low, the warmth in it feeling earned rather than assumed. "Then you must call me Alex."

Her lips curved, not quite a smile but near enough to soften her expression. "Alex," she said, tasting the name with quiet satisfaction. The sound of it was familiar, yet entirely new. "It suits you far better than *Lord Hawkesbury*."

She had said the name before, in other lifetimes, across chessboards, down quiet corridors at Ravenstock. But now it carried meaning. Not nostalgia. Not propriety. Just truth. And the faintest thread of something she wasn't quite ready to name.

A spark of dry humor touched his eyes. "So I've been told."

For a heartbeat, it was as though the years between them had faded away, leaving their footing less formal and more familiar.

They moved toward the window together, as if by silent agreement. Pale sunlight spilled across the floorboards, casting long shapes from the mullioned panes. Outside, the hills sloped gently toward the mines, shadows trailing from their ridges.

"You saw more in the mine today than most would have," Alex said, his gaze lingering on the horizon. "Archer won't sleep easy tonight."

"I rather hope not," Georgina replied, her tone edged with quiet resolve. "Too much has been lost already. If a sleepless night keeps him alert, so be it."

A glint of approval touched his features. "Good. Because I suspect there is more to be found beneath those timbers than bad luck."

They left the morning room and walked together along the corridor, their steps unhurried, though the quiet between them anything but empty. The hush of the house settled around them, broken only by the soft fall of their footsteps.

"Alex," she tried the name, soft but certain.

He glanced toward her, a subtle warmth in his expression, as though hearing his name from her lips after so many years kindled something dormant between them. "Yes?"

"I would like to understand more about the mine, the accounts, the holdings." She kept her gaze forward, though her attention was fully on him. "If I am to take my role seriously, I must see more than a single shaft and a set of ledgers."

He considered her for a moment. "You wish to see the accounts?"

"Not today." Her lips curved slightly, "Soon. I would rather begin with what you can show me, not what numbers might conceal."

A corner of his mouth lifted, not quite a smile but close. "Then I will show you."

They slowed near the doors to the gardens, where the late sun caught the leaves in a soft golden haze. Georgina's gaze swept over the tangled roses that had once been her mother-in-law's pride. Now, they were overgrown and wild.

"I left all of this for London," she murmured, almost to herself. "I thought I could turn my back on it, as if it had no claim on me."

His answer was quiet, but beneath the gentleness was something solid. "It was never the land that failed you, Georgina. Only the men who believed it belonged to them alone. You just weren't given a place in it until now."

She cast him a brief glance, surprised by the quiet conviction in his voice. There was no judgment in it, only understanding. And something else. A willingness to see her as she was, not as others expected her to be.

She turned to him then, fully, no longer glancing, no longer guarded. For the first time, she truly saw him. Not the title, not the role he played, but the man who had stood beside her in silence and danger and had asked for nothing in return. No deflection, no polite evasion. Only the truth between them.

"Not all men," she said, and though her words were soft, they struck clean and true.

He paused, then inclined his head, as if accepting the quiet challenge in her remark. "No," he agreed, his voice roughened by something more than mere conversation. "Not all men."

Their gazes held a moment longer, not as adversaries, not quite as old friends, but as two people seeing each other clearly at last, after too many years of shadows.

Then, with a slow breath, he turned toward the front hall. "I should leave you to the rest of your day," he said, though something in his tone suggested reluctance.

"I do have a house to tame," Georgina replied, allowing a

thread of humor to soften her words. "Mrs. Hemsley will have no patience for me wandering around idle."

"If you wish," Alex said, pausing as they reached the door, "I can send copies of the mining ledgers. You may read them at your leisure."

"I would prefer," she said, lifting her chin a fraction, "to read them with you."

His brows rose slightly, and there was a smile, not faint or fleeting this time, but real. "Then I shall bring them myself," he promised.

Her chest lifted slightly. It wasn't just what he said, but how easily he offered it. How naturally he included her now. Not a concession. A choice.

She watched him go. Only after the door had closed did she rest her fingers on the windowpane.

An invitation offered and accepted.

Georgina let her hand drop from the windowpane and drew a quiet breath. The stillness of the house was less oppressive now, as if the air itself had shifted. She turned from the front hall and made her way back toward the drawing room, her steps slow but steady. By the time she reached the doorway, her posture was composed, but the echo of that conversation still warmed her thoughts.

"Mrs. Bainbridge, my lady," Mrs. Hemsley announced from the threshold. "She's just arrived."

Georgina turned. "Show her in, please."

Mrs. Bainbridge entered with purpose, removing her gloves with practiced ease as she surveyed the room. Her gaze swept over the furnishings, the light, and finally Georgina herself. She missed nothing.

"I hope I'm not intruding." Mrs. Bainbridge's tone was light but purposeful. "I thought to stop by on my way to the seminary. My puzzle solver has taken a keen interest in that box, though it appears to have bested her for now."

Georgina offered a proper smile this time, genuine, if a touch surprised. "Come in. I was just—"

"—Thinking," Honoria filled in, settling into one of the chairs without being asked. "That's what your expression says. Thinking about what?"

Georgina eased into a nearby seat. "Sit with me. You've barely told me a word about your wedding."

"Oh, I have dozens of opinions and not a single final decision. Barrington is no help. The man would wed in his greatcoat if I let him. He thinks floral arrangements are a military campaign. And he's losing." She leaned back with a sigh. "And now the innkeeper is pressing us to rent the entire Rosalynde Bay Inn, lest the guests scatter into scandal before the cake is cut."

Georgina laughed, the tension in her shoulders easing slightly. "I suspect the scandal is half the reason some are attending."

Honoria's smile curved knowingly. "Naturally. Why else endure a weak punch and wilted roses?"

The warmth between them lingered a moment longer. An ease not often found in Georgina's days. But it ebbed as Mrs. Hemsley stepped into the doorway, her voice low but composed.

"Begging your pardon, my lady. This just arrived, delivered by one of the inspector's men."

Georgina accepted the folded paper. The wax snapped beneath her thumb, too loud in the still room. A tightness coiled behind her ribs before she read a single line. The parchment was heavier than it should have been, the seal pressed deep, as if meant to remind her who held authority here. She unfolded the letter and read.

Lady Ravenstock,

During my inspection this morning, I observed signs of instability in one of the secondary passages on your Ravenstock seam. Though the foreman assures me the risks are manageable, I would be remiss if I did not bring this directly to your attention.

Given the sensitivities of recent events and your own understandable vigilance, I advise immediate caution in that section.

*It may be prudent to restrict access until further reinforcement
is completed.*

*I remain at your disposal should you wish to discuss this in
more detail.*

In service of your safety and the mine's success,
Julian Everly

The words were measured, every line perfectly courteous. Too courteous. The sort of tone a man used when he wished to appear helpful while tightening the reins. It was not a warning she heard in those sentences, but control, politely veiled. Without a word, she handed the paper to Honoria.

"Julian Everly," Georgina read aloud. "Have you ever met him?" she asked.

"No. This is the first I've heard his name." Honoria read in silence, her brow furrowing. When she finished, she set the note aside with deliberate care. "Two men have already died," she said softly. "Rowland. And Hawkesbury's father. Does Everly think you would allow a third?"

"No," Georgina replied. Her voice was calm, but the edge in it was unmistakable. "I won't stand by."

"Good." Honoria's gaze sharpened. "The Ravenstock seam may carry your name, but it runs beneath Hawkesbury land. He has a stake in this and in you. You must tell him."

No more delays. No more caution masked as courtesy. "I'll draft him a letter at once." Georgina started to rise, but Honoria reached out and caught her hand, firm and insistent. Their eyes met.

"Mrs. Hemsley," Honoria said, never turning away, "send the coachman for Lord Hawkesbury. Now."

The housekeeper nodded once and vanished, her footsteps brisk and sure on the polished floor.

They returned to the window, standing together in silence. This time, they weren't watching someone go. They were sending for him.

Outside, the coachman swung into the saddle and took off down the lane. His coat snapped behind him as the wind rose, and in seconds, he was gone.

"If Everly, or whoever guides him, thinks I can be frightened into silence," Georgina said quietly, "they've chosen the wrong woman." Georgina glanced down at the folded note again, her fingertips brushing its edge. She shook her head. "I will not let them rob me again."

Honoria laid a hand on her arm, steady, grounding. "No," she agreed. "You will not."

The last echo of hooves faded into the wind. The house stilled again, but Georgina did not. Her resolve was no longer forming. It was set.

Georgina did not return to her desk. She could not sit idle. Instead, she and Honoria lingered near the window, their eyes drawn to the road as though sheer will might hasten Alex's return.

"He'll need twenty minutes, no more," Georgina said quietly, her gaze fixed on the bend in the lane.

Mrs. Bainbridge glanced toward the window and then rose, brushing her gloves clean of imaginary dust. "I ought to go before my pupils mount a full rebellion."

Georgina turned to her, a slight shake of the head. "Would you stay?"

That was all she said. Honoria held her gaze for a moment, then gave a single nod.

Honoria set her gloves aside. "Of course." She did not sit but moved toward the hearth to give Georgina the window and the quiet. No more words were needed.

The sun slipped westward, gilding the fields in brittle fading light. Shadows stretched long across the gravel drive, inching toward the door as though they, too, felt the urgency tightening in the air.

Georgina's hands folded over the note, smoothing the creases she had already worn into the paper's edge. Beneath her calm exterior, a storm gathered. It wasn't fear or hesitation. It was readiness.

A distant sound broke the hush, sharp and certain. The steady rhythm of hooves cut through the hush, faster than any casual traveler, and headed straight for Ravenstock Hall.

At once, Georgina crossed the length of the hall as the thunder of Alex's arrival filled the air. She did not wait for Mrs. Hemsley to announce him, nor for the servants to throw open the door. She opened it herself.

Outside, Alex swung down from his horse in a fluid, urgent motion, his brows drawn tight beneath the brim of his hat. Dust streaked his boots and coat, as though he had outridden the very wind.

Their eyes met across the threshold.

In his expression, she saw the sharp glint of unspoken questions, concern edged with something fiercer. Protectiveness, perhaps. Or the echo of their newborn partnership.

For a single breath, they stood in silence. No words may have passed between them, yet more was exchanged than any written letter could hold.

Georgina stepped back and held the door wide. He crossed the threshold, not as a rescuer, but as an ally. There was no time for hesitation now. Only action.

Chapter Seven

HE SWEPT OFF his hat, breath sharp from the ride, his eyes, and scanned her face as though to assure himself she was truly unharmed.

For a heartbeat, neither spoke. There was only the rise and fall of his chest and the faint tremor in her fingers, curled at her side.

"Georgina," he said at last. Her name caught slightly in his throat, rougher than she expected. His jaw flexed, and for just a breath, something raw flickered behind his eyes. Relief, sharpened by fear. "Are you hurt?"

"No," she replied, her voice steadier than her pulse. "No, Alex." She faltered, then found her footing. "Please. Come into the parlor. There's something you need to see."

Without waiting for a reply, she turned, the skirts of her gown brushing past him as she led the way. He followed at once, his steps heavy with the urgency of a man holding back more than speed.

In the parlor, she drew the letter from her pocket, smoothed the creases, and silently handed it to him.

He read it quickly, his eyes narrowing as he took in each line. When he reached the end, his fingers tightened, creasing the corners sharply.

"That arrived half an hour ago," Georgina said quietly. "I thought at first to send a reply, but when Mrs. Bainbridge read it, she insisted I send for you at once."

"You were right to," he said grimly, his gaze still fixed on the page. "Everly names the Ravenstock seam specifically."

"Yes." She drew a steadying breath. "And we were only there this morning."

He looked up, their eyes locking across the space between them. Behind his gaze burned a fire. Not yet a fury, but close, rising and hard to contain. Beneath it, something quieter. Fear, tightly leashed. Not for himself, but for Georgina.

"Archer hesitated over the ventilation," Alex said, not as a question, but as a truth laid bare.

"He kept glancing upward," Georgina added quietly. "As though evaluating more than the airflow."

Her fingers brushed the edge of the paper, as though the roughness might steady her thoughts. "I saw it too. And when we moved on, he lingered behind. Not to oversee the work. No, something troubled him."

Alex's jaw flexed, and a tight line formed at his temple. "Troubled enough to send a warning, once we were out of earshot."

"Or troubled enough to cover for someone else," she replied, her voice quiet but unwavering.

Their eyes met again, the truth settled between them with a quiet, unmistakable finality.

Silence followed, taut with recognition. If Everly meant to isolate her, to push her into acting alone, it had nearly worked.

"You're certain you're unhurt?" he asked again, softer this time.

"I am not so easily broken, Alex." She met his gaze full-on. Not a challenge. Not a plea. Just truth. And he did not look away.

He stilled. The moment hung between them, filled with all they hadn't said. Something flickered in his eyes, part approval, part something warmer, but it faded quickly into determination. He folded the letter crisply and tucked it into his coat.

"Then we act. At once."

She led him through the archway, motioning toward the

adjoining room. "She will want to hear what you think."

"Good," he replied, already moving. "She has a sharp mind. We'll need all the clarity we can gather."

Together, they crossed the threshold into the drawing room, their shared purpose trailing like the echo of a vow. Mrs. Bainbridge rose from the seat near the window, her gaze bright with expectation, her posture as commanding as any general's.

"Lord Hawkesbury," she greeted, her tone crisp. "I assume you've read the letter?"

"I have," he confirmed. "There's more in what it doesn't say than what it does. They are moving coal, likely through the older passages near the Ravenstock seam. And they're hurrying their work."

Georgina's pulse quickened. "Before we see it."

"Exactly."

"Then what must we do?" she asked, keeping her voice level.

His gaze lingered on her, not just for her question, but the calmness with which she asked it. "We move quickly. Tonight, if we must."

His eyes darkened, colder than fear. "If Archer is rattled, there's a reason. Either the collapse was no accident, or someone means for us to think it was."

Georgina's fingers tightened on the folds of her gown. "Everly's caution feels too precise. He is covering his steps, too neatly."

"He wants to appear cautious," Alex replied. "But his timing is too perfect. He's watching to see what we'll do."

"Then we must not act too quickly," she said, her determination settling deeper. "Not yet."

Approval flickered in his gaze, a spark against the gathering storm. "Agreed."

Outside the window, clouds pressed lower over the hills, shadows creeping across the land like a second skin. The air in the room was charged, drawn tight as a bowstring.

Georgina drew a breath, steady and sure. "They will not find me so easily moved. Whatever game they play, I will not be their pawn."

"You are no one's pawn," Alex said quietly, with the force of iron beneath velvet.

The words settle not as flattery, but as fact. He saw her clearly now. She was no longer a grieving widow or burdened title, but a woman worthy of standing beside him.

Honoria's gaze, keen and steady, swept over them. "I will make inquiries in the town," she declared, gathering her gloves from the arm of the chair. "If coal is being carted away, someone will have seen it. There are too many loose tongues in Sommer-by-the-Sea to keep it quiet."

Alex inclined his head. "Good. Any information will give us the advantage."

"And I will speak with Barrington," Honoria added, smoothing the fingers of her gloves with quiet precision. Her tone left no room for debate. "He'll want to be informed. I trust his judgement in such matters implicitly." A softer note entered her voice at the mention of his name, but it did not blunt her resolve.

A spark of approval lit in Alex's eyes. "Barrington has already voiced his concerns to me. He'll move swiftly if he knows the urgency."

Georgina felt then a subtle yet certain shift. The lines of defense were drawing together. "Then we will not be alone in this." She didn't say it with hope. She said it with certainty.

"No," Honoria replied, her gaze sharpening. "We will not."

Georgina turned and faced Alex. "And what of you?" Georgina asked, not as an afterthought, but with intent.

His answer came without hesitation. "I'll go back to the mine. Quietly, this time. I want to see for myself what Archer has not yet confessed."

Georgina's pulse thudded low and certain. "I'm coming with you."

His brows lifted, but there was no protest in his gaze. Only a moment's pause and then, quiet agreement. "You've already walked beneath those timbers once today," he said, "I cannot deny you a second time."

Mrs. Bainbridge, gloves in hand, regarded them both with a mixture of admiration and quiet determination. "If you're both going back into that mine," she said firmly, "then you will not go alone."

"I will have Lock, my mine foreman, accompany us," Alex confirmed. "And two men I trust without question."

Georgina straightened, a thread of steel woven through her spine. "Good."

For a moment, the three of them stood in shared understanding, not bound by rank or expectation, but by purpose. No longer solitary figures, but a line drawn firm against whatever forces meant to divide them.

As they moved to prepare, the clouds beyond the window shifted, casting pale light through the parlor once more. Georgina caught Alex's glance across the room. She felt the unspoken vow there and let it steady her.

It was not a vow made in words or touch, but it bound them all the same. She would not face this storm alone.

She was not a widow resigned to fear, nor a lady confined to the drawing room. She was a partner stepping fully into her role.

Into her future. And into the reckoning they would face together.

Chapter Eight

"THEY MEAN TO make a show of it," Alex said. He stood at the parlor window at Ravenstock Manor, his gaze fixed on the hills as dusk deepened.

Behind him, Georgina and Mrs. Bainbridge sat at a table. A tray of tea had gone cold between them, untouched. A list of wedding details lay forgotten at Mrs. Bainbridge's elbow, though she still held her gloves in one hand as if uncertain whether to stay or go.

"I expect that they will move under the cover of darkness," Alex continued. "Quicker. Quieter. Easier to claim it was always permitted."

Before Georgina could respond, brisk footsteps sounded in the corridor. Mrs. Hemsley opened the door to admit Jeremy Lock, Alex's mine foreman, his coat dusty from the road. He bowed with respect but without hesitation.

"My lord, my lady." He faced Alex. "I thought you'd want this information at once."

"Have a seat, Lock. Let me introduce you to Lady Ravenstock and Mrs. Bainbridge. You can speak freely here."

"You were right to suspect trouble at the Ravenstock side," Lock began, a flush creeping up his neck. He turned to Georgina. "I am sorry, my lady."

"That's quite all right, Mr. Lock." Georgina gestured. "Please go on."

He nodded and faced Alex. "I was in the stable yard getting

the cart ponies ready for the day. Behind me, two men from the Ravenstock side were checking their harnesses. That's when I heard them…*make sure the Ravenstock load is cleared before sundown, else it'll be too late.* The second man tried to hush him. *Keep your voice down, fool. He said. You want Lock or Archer to catch wind?* I kept my head down and my hands busy."

Mrs. Hemsley moved closer to the table.

"So, they plan to have the mine cleared before we arrive." Alex glanced at Georgina. "Was there anything else?"

"I deliberately stopped at the tavern. Two miners, thick with ale, were a bit free with their speech. *They'll come tonight and find nothing but dust,* one said. *We'll have the last of it out by then.* The other cautioned, *and mind you, don't leave tracks. If the owners find out, they'll bury us deeper than the seam.*"

Georgina glanced at her housekeeper. "Mrs. Hemsley?"

"I went to the market after you left this morning. I overheard two women speaking. At the time, I didn't understand their meaning, but now, I think it fits." Mrs. Hemsley paused. Her brows furrowed.

Georgina gently placed her hand on her housekeeper's arm. "Please, tell me what you heard. It may be nothing, or it may be exactly what we need."

Mrs. Hemsley nodded. "I was gathering some vegetables for the midday meal when I heard one say, *He's at it again, carting loads at all hours, like the devil's chasing him.* The other woman was just as piqued. *And what's so urgent, I ask you? It's just rubble, he says, but I know the glint of good coal when I see it on his sleeves.* I had no idea what they were talking about, but now it sounds suspicious."

"Well," Mrs. Bainbridge tapped the tabletop, her eyes bright with calculation. "Three reliable sources." She turned to Alex. "What do you intend to do?"

Alex didn't need long to consider his response. He had already made up his mind. "They want us to confront them, loudly and publicly, with accusations so they can claim they have nothing to hide."

"Are you going to try to catch them another day?" Mrs. Bainbridge asked with a mischievous twinkle in her eye.

Alex chuckled. "And disappoint them? Why would I ever do that?" He looked at Georgina. "We'll go to the mine as planned. But this time, we'll be watching." He let a grin touch his lips. "If they want a performance..."

Georgina smiled back, catching his meaning. "Then they are in for a show they never anticipated."

"I remember that look," Mrs. Bainbridge said.

"What look?"

"That innocent look that had your governess doing whatever you wanted."

"Ah, that look." Alex glanced at Georgina. "Well, yes. You used to—"

"I didn't do anything." Her voice made Alex think twice before he said anything else.

Alex cleared his throat. "I'll arrive first and look around for you. Let them think I've grown impatient for your company." He didn't hide the laughter in his voice. "It will give me time to look around before you make your entrance, without giving anything away."

Alex stood, and Lock rose with him.

"Thank you, Jeremy. You have been more than helpful. You'd best go home. I'll see you in the morning."

Lock nodded to the ladies. Mrs. Hemsley saw him out.

Alex rubbed his hands together, then turned to Georgina. "You don't have to go."

"Yes, I do." She was adamant. "It's my side of the mine that is being robbed."

She didn't flinch at the words. Not anymore. It wasn't grief that burned now, but the sharp heat of injustice. Of ownership. Of resolve.

He inclined his head, conceding the point. "Then I'll go

ahead. Give me a few minutes and follow afterward."

Georgina walked with him down the corridor and stopped at the door.

He turned and glanced at her.

"Alex… you will be careful."

"Of course, I will. They want us to see nothing. So we will accommodate them." He opened the door and was gone.

Georgina drew herself up, smoothing her skirts as she returned to the parlor. "If they expect to see me as nothing more than a lady out of her depth," she said, her voice calm but edged with quiet determination, "then I must look the part. Almost."

Mrs. Hemsley stepped forward at once, keen eyes narrowing as she took Georgina's measure. "Almost," the housekeeper repeated, with the faintest hint of a smile. She reached for the folds of Georgina's gown, adjusting the neckline by a careful fraction. "A little less governess… a little more…" She let the words trail off, but the meaning hung between them like a secret passed hand to hand.

Georgina arched a brow. "Temptress?"

"Temptation," Mrs. Bainbridge corrected smoothly, stepping in with a discerning glance over Georgina's ensemble. "Subtle enough to be accidental. Obvious enough to make them wonder."

Mrs. Hemsley fastened a loose strand of Georgina's hair near her temple, then, with a deft, knowing twist, let another curl fall deliberately free. "There," she declared. "Too hurried for propriety," Mrs. Hemsley said with a wicked little nod.

"I hope they choke on it," Georgina replied, though a hint of a smile touched her lips.

"They'll choke," Mrs. Bainbridge's gaze sharpened with approval. "And believe every last morsel of the tale we feed them."

Georgina exhaled a steadying breath, her pulse quickening beneath the quiet theatre of it all. "Then let's give them their performance."

As Georgina fastened her cloak and reached for her gloves,

Mrs. Bainbridge's voice followed her, low and steady with a spark of mischief beneath the steel.

"Remember, my dear," she said, like a final lesson before battle, "even a queen must let her crown tilt now and then, if only to keep her enemies guessing."

Georgina glanced back, a flicker of defiance lighting her eyes. "Then let them wonder which way it will fall."

Mrs. Hemsley, never to be outdone, gave a brisk nod of approval and added, "And may they be too busy watching your crown to notice your sword."

⤜⤜⤛⤛

DUSK HAD BEGUN to settle by the time Alex reached the mine. He dismounted at the edge of the yard, the air thick with silence and something just beneath it.

The mine looked no less grim by dusk, the shadows long and heavy across the yard.

He moved directly to the mine workings. Few men remained. This shift was nearly over. The rest of the men had already gone for the day. The carts, which were usually in the stable yard, were in neat rows close to the mine entrance. A few more stood empty just inside.

He stepped into the mine and glanced around. Several carts stood unattended. A quick glance showed them all the same, empty of coal, scrubbed of any trace.

Alex made his way into the shaft that Everly mentioned in his note to Georgina. Even from a distance, he saw the difference. The area was clearer than it had been that morning, emptied, swept, and disguised. But the braces remained. And the wood told the truth. It groaned above him.

He ran his hand along the beam's edge. The damp wood swelled beneath his palm. One careless step, one too-heavy load, and the beam would give way. This was what Everly had warned her about, and yet no workers repaired it. No hammering. No crew. It's been left to fail. Why? Were they too busy setting the stage?

Footsteps sounded beyond the shaft. Alex straightened, turning toward the mine's entrance.

Not hurried. Not panicked. Measured, as though time itself bent to their arrangement.

He stepped into the light just as the Ravenstock carriage rounded the bend.

The last of the daylight caught her first. It caught the strands of hair that had slipped from their pins, brushing gold across her cheek. It caught the delicate line of her collarbone and revealed, he suspected, by a gown, that Mrs. Hemsley had coaxed a fraction lower than custom, and with great calculation.

She stepped down from the carriage alone, her back straight, her chin lifted. Her bonnet hung by its ties in her hand, as if she hadn't bothered with it properly, or hadn't cared to.

He had expected her to come prepared. He had not expected her to be alone. Or to look like this, poised and unsparing and utterly unlike the woman he'd once known. Like determination and courage and, damn it all, like temptation wrapped in dusk and defiance.

His throat tightened, a slow, unwelcome heat coiled low beneath his ribs.

Georgina's eyes swept the yard before finding him. Whatever uncertainty she might have felt in her chest, she did not show it on her face. Her gaze caught his, steady, clear, and unflinching.

No falsehood between them. No performance. Only two people caught between danger and something far more dangerous.

Alex moved to meet her, his stride unhurried, deliberate. As he neared, his eyes skimmed her hair, the gentle lift of her shoulders, and the answering pull in his chest, as inevitable as the tide.

"You came," he said, his voice low, rougher than he intended.

She tilted her head, her lips curving with quiet audacity. "Of course I did."

For a moment, neither of them moved.

Then, drawn by something unseen, the space between them narrowed. Alex studied her, openly this time, not with haste, but with the attentiveness of a man who missed nothing. Especially not now.

"You shouldn't have come alone," he said, but there was no censure in it. Only something deeper. Quieter. Concern, yes. And something far more perilous.

"I didn't," she replied evenly, stepping closer so the space between them narrowed. "I brought my determination. And my patience, for whatever performance they've planned."

Her voice carried the same warm defiance as her earlier glance. Her chin tipped up a fraction higher, just enough to catch the wind as it teased another strand of hair loose from her pins.

Alex reached up, instinct outweighing caution, and brushed the curl back into place. His fingers grazed her temple, lingering a breath too long before he dropped his hand.

The faint hitch of her breath told him she had noticed.

As had he.

"We won't give them the show they expect," he murmured, his voice pitched low so only she could hear. "Then we'll give them something better."

Her brows lifted, curiosity sparking in her eyes. "Better?" She echoed.

"A distraction," he said, his meaning curling between them like smoke. "If they want to play at innocence, we'll let them believe we're too caught up in each other to notice the sleight of hand."

Her lips curved, not into a full smile, but into something far more dangerous: agreement.

"They'll think they've outwitted us," she said softly.

"They will," he confirmed, his gaze never leaving hers, "until it's too late for them to run."

The silence stretched between them, filled only by the wind stirring the coal dust at their feet and the distant creak of the pulley lines.

"Are you prepared for that, Georgina?" His use of her given name echoed with history. A quiet intimacy shaped by memory and something unspoken between them. "To play the part of the reckless widow meeting her lover at dusk? If they believe we're distracted, they'll move the coal."

A flicker of dry humor crossed her expression, but beneath it, a spark of something far warmer.

"I've played far less agreeable roles in my time, Alex," she replied. "This one, I believe, I shall enjoy."

Something shifted in his expression then. Not a smile, not quite. But the slow, inevitable gravity of a man drawn in, despite every warning in his blood.

"Then we must make it convincing," he said at last, his voice a shade rougher, the edges softened by the dusk. "For them."

"For them," she agreed, though her eyes held to his with a steadiness that made him wonder if, just this once, she spoke the truth of herself instead.

He offered his arm. She took it without hesitation.

Together, they crossed the yard, passing between the orderly rows of carts, walking as if they were blind to everything but each other. But Alex saw it all, every shift in the shadows, every whisper of coal dust on the breeze. So did she.

Together, they were far from blind. They moved across the mine yard as though it were a ballroom, the shadows drifting like columns of candle smoke.

The closer they drew to the Ravenstock seam, the more deliberate their steps became. Alex's hand, warm at the crook of her elbow, was steady and reassuring. She leaned into it just enough to sell the illusion, but the truth was, she didn't need to feign her awareness of him. It thrummed through her veins like a second pulse.

They paused near the stack of emptied carts, just as they'd

planned, the perfect vantage point for their charade, and for their scrutiny.

"Eyes," Alex murmured, low enough that only she could hear. "On the ridge. Watchful."

"I see them." Her lips barely moved, but her words curled into him all the same.

Beyond the mine entrance, shapes lingered in the half-light. Idle hands pretending to work. Shovels stirring dust rather than debris. And in the shadows above, a figure shifted too quickly to be part of honest labor.

"They're watching for a reaction," Georgina observed, calm and quiet.

"Then let's give them one to enjoy," Alex replied.

The dusk pressed close around them, the scent of coal and rain heavy in the air.

For a heartbeat, the world seemed to draw its breath, waiting.

The steadiness of his nearness, the familiar danger of it, and she wondered when pretending had become the truest thing between them.

He stepped closer, his gaze fixed not on the mine but on her, as though she were the only thing in the world worth his attention. His hand slipped from her elbow to her waist, a casual gesture, practiced perhaps, but not false. Not entirely.

"You're enjoying this more than you ought," she murmured, her voice pitched for him alone.

His mouth curved, the barest hint of a wicked smile. "I find I enjoy a great many things in your company, Georgina."

Their eyes held. The spark between them no longer kindling but burning steady and bright.

"You are not acting now," she whispered, her breath feathering against his cheek.

"Neither are you," he countered just as softly.

And then, as though it were the most natural conclusion to their charade, he lowered his mouth to hers.

The kiss was no accident. No hasty brush meant for watching

eyes. It was deliberate and dangerously real.

Her hand came to his chest to steady herself against the surge of sensation that shattered the illusion of pretense. His heart beat hard beneath her palm, as wild and relentless as her own.

For a moment, they forgot the watchers in the shadows.

For a moment, the mine, the risk, all of it blurred to the edges of their awareness. All of it eclipsed by the heat of something older than coal and more combustible than gunpowder.

Somewhere beyond the carts, a shovel clattered to the ground.

Alex didn't turn. He didn't need to. The sudden stillness told him all he needed to know. They'd been seen.

A breath of movement rustled along the ridge. Cloth brushed against stone. A boot shifted, too hastily placed. Whoever watched them was no longer just curious. They were caught off guard. Good.

He drew back from Georgina slowly, just enough to meet her eyes. Her gaze was steady, her pulse fluttering beneath his fingers where they still rested at her waist.

"They're watching," he murmured, low and pleased.

"And wondering," she returned, the corners of her mouth lifting in quiet triumph.

Then, before he could answer, her hand slipped to the nape of his neck, drawing him back to her, not roughly, not hurriedly, but with quiet intent. Her lips met his, soft and certain.

The second kiss was hers. And it was no longer just part of the performance. That, too, had consequences, ones they were no longer pretending to ignore.

It had nothing to do with their plan. Nothing to do with whoever watched. It was hers, unhidden, undeniable, and it changed everything.

For a breathless instant, his mind rebelled against the idea of control, of strategy. Her scent, her nearness, the deliberate grace of her mouth against his shattered all thought, scattered all reason. He responded without calculation, without caring who might see, one arm sliding around her back to gather her closer.

She sighed against him, a sound as old as longing itself. No fire had ever burned so hot, so close, and so impossible to leave untouched.

When they parted, it was by degrees, and only because the moment demanded it. Alex drew a breath that did little to steady him.

"If they weren't watching before," he said quietly, his voice roughened, "they are now."

Georgina's smile was slow, wicked, and more dangerous than anything the Order had yet devised. "Let them watch. Speculation is safer than suspicion."

She drew back, but not far. Just enough to turn her head and, with studied carelessness, glance toward the shadows at the mine's edge.

The figures watching them had stilled, like players caught mid-scene, uncertain whether they had been outwitted or simply entertained.

"Let them wonder," Georgina murmured, her gaze still fixed on their audience. "Let them think they've won."

Alex's reply was a promise: "They will, right up until the moment they understand they haven't."

As they turned toward the carriage, Alex's gaze swept once more across the yard. Near the stacked carts, the earth was freshly turned, darker than the soil around it. A faint glint caught in the lamplight, coal dust, far too fine to have come from today's work.

Georgina followed his glance. A few ledgers lay half-hidden on a barrel, the ink still damp as if tallies had been hastily changed. "They've been moving more than rubble," she murmured.

"And covering it with numbers," he said quietly. "Sloppy ones."

She met his eyes, a grim satisfaction beneath her calm. "Then we've found our proof—or the beginning of it."

Together, they stepped away from their tableau, leaving

behind the drift of coal dust and beneath it, the echo of a kiss that refused to be dismissed. What had begun as a strategy had ended as something far more dangerous. And she knew it.

Chapter Nine

"WE SAW EVERYTHING they didn't want us to," Georgina murmured as the carriage rocked into motion. "And nothing they thought we would."

As they turned from the mine yard, Georgina let her fingers trail lightly along the edge of Alex's sleeve, just enough to sustain the illusion, or perhaps the truth they had stumbled upon.

Her fingertips tingled with the memory, and her body caught in the echo of something too urgent to name aloud. It wasn't fear. Not anymore.

The eyes upon them remained. She felt them as keenly as the chill rising from the open shaft. But there was no pursuit, no shouted accusation. No sudden rush of miners scrambling to explain themselves. The Order's pawns had played their part and believed they'd witnessed the climax of this little play.

They had not. Alex guided her toward the carriage, the act of propriety now resumed. He helped her step inside, his touch lingering a heartbeat longer than necessity allowed.

As he started to close the door, she caught his wrist, not with alarm, but with something quieter. Calmer. Her gaze found him in the fading light.

Her voice was velvet over steel. "When we are alone," she murmured, "you will tell me if that kiss was only for their benefit."

She meant it as a strategy, but the question had teeth. She heard the edge in her own voice and didn't pull it back.

His eyes darkened, not with shadow but with certainty.

"When we're alone," he said, his voice low and unflinching. "I will tell you everything you already suspect. And more." Then, with deliberate care, he closed the carriage door with quiet finality, the echo of their conversation lingering in the air like the last line of a play. For a moment, he stood still, watching the soft sway of the curtains within, knowing she watched him too.

No words passed between them now. None were needed.

The moment was sealed, the illusion complete, and yet, something far more real had taken root.

He turned, crossing to his mount with the calm precision of a man who knew his role, even as the script began to change.

RAVENSTOCK MANOR LAY behind them, its calm façade guarding the women who had stayed behind to keep the illusion intact. This moment belonged to Georgina and Alex alone, and the final stitch in their tapestry of deception. Alex swung into the saddle of his mount, choosing to ride alongside rather than share the carriage, keeping with the pretense of a lover parting ways.

As the horses set off at a steady pace back toward Ravenstock, Georgina allowed herself a breath she hadn't realized she'd been holding. She settled back into the seat, her hands resting in her lap, the warmth of Alex's touch still echoing in her palms.

Through the small carriage window, she caught sight of him riding just behind the wheel, his posture erect, his jaw tight with thought, his gaze never straying far from her.

Neither of them spoke until they crested the ridge that offered one last view of the mine below. The yard lay shadowed beneath the lowering sky, the carts now idle, the workers slowly dispersing like actors after the curtain had fallen.

"They will report exactly what they saw," Alex called from his saddle, his voice cutting clean through the wind. "Nothing more, nothing less."

"They saw what we wished them to see," Georgina replied through the open window. Her voice held both pride and a quiet thrill. "Which is precisely the same as seeing nothing at all."

He met her gaze with a glint of shared satisfaction. "Let them think themselves the wiser."

"They won't suspect our next move," she added softly.

"No," Alex agreed. "They'll be too busy congratulating themselves."

The sun dipped lower behind them, casting the hills in amber light. The shadows lengthened across the road, stretching like fingers toward the horizon. But Georgina sat steady in the fading glow, her thoughts clear, her purpose sharper than ever. Determination. Possibility.

And the quiet certainty that what lay between them now was stronger than strategy, and far more dangerous to those who sought to divide them.

They rode on, leaving the hallowed ground of the mine behind them, but carrying something far more dangerous than any secret the Order could claim: Hope. And the unmistakable spark of a partnership forged not by necessity, but by choice, between two hearts no longer content to stand apart.

Chapter Ten

A STEADY DRIZZLE tapped against the library windows, the kind of rain that never quite stopped, that lingered like a question waiting to be answered. The air inside carried a damp chill, despite Mrs. Hemsley's best efforts to coax a fire into the hearth, but its glow did little to soften the mood. It was the sort of autumn morning made for unpleasant truths. Even the crate seemed reluctant, its wood swollen with moisture, as if it had absorbed the truth of what it held inside.

When it first arrived from the solicitor's office, it had seemed unassuming. Now, with its contents spread across the library table, it loomed, not in size, but in what it might reveal. A life reduced to papers and records, each scrap a breadcrumb on a path she had once refused to follow.

Georgina stood at the edge of the table, her fingers brushing a brittle sheet of paper, though her thoughts were far from ledgers and receipts. They lingered on last night. On Alex.

He had looked at her as if she were not merely part of this fight, but essential to it. His kiss, steady, certain, utterly unguarded, had left no room for doubt. She had wanted it. She didn't regret it. No. She wanted more.

Not flirtation. Not indulgence. But the kind of desire that was honest, undeniable, and lasting, if they were brave enough to name it. The kind of desire that didn't vanish with the daylight.

The memory warmed her now, unexpected in the morning's gloom, a quiet ember that refused to fade. There would be time, later, to decide what it meant. To ask what came next. But now was not for longing. It was for reckoning. Quiet, necessary, and overdue.

She drew a breath and looked down at the pile before her. This time, nothing would escape her.

The table was covered with papers and ledgers spread out in messy layers. A life once carefully ordered, now taken apart, sheet by sheet. Receipts curled at the corners, trade notes faded. Yet while the rest lay scattered and worn, Rowland's methodical records sat in a neat stack on the edge of the library desk, just as he'd left them nearly a year ago, as if they were still waiting for him.

She shifted closer, her fingertips grazing the paper, the parchment, and the brittle edges of the past. She crushed aside the invoice from the grocer and picked up a folded paper with Rowland's careful handwriting. Her breath caught, not from grief, but recognition. But the sweep of his handwriting brought him back for a moment, quiet, meticulous, and calculating as ever.

She unfolded the page, expecting to find the receipt she meant to send Mrs. Bainbridge for the silver tea service Rowland had ordered the winter before the accident. But instead, her eyes landed on the heading: *Iron delivery—Hawkesbury account.*

Her brow creased. That didn't make sense. Rowland had dealings with the Hawkesbury accounts. But those transactions ended months before his death. This entry is dated after he passed away.

She traced the line with one finger, half-hoping the letters would blur or shift, offer some hint of a mistake. But the handwriting held steady. It was Rowland's, or a copy so precise it made her skin crawl. She turned the sheet over but found nothing on the back but dust and a faint smudge near the corner.

She reached for the ledger and flipped through the brittle pages until she found another slip from the same supplier. This one was dated alarmingly close to the day Rowland died.

A chill slid down her spine, not sharp, just there. Creeping in. Steady. Like a draft through a closed door.

Her fingers tightened on the folio. Not fear. Not even surprise. Just a rising certainty that whatever innocence she'd once given Rowland, and the mine, was gone.

"This can't be a coincidence," she said under her breath, but part of her already knew the truth.

Her pulse quickened. She brushed the dust from the cover, as if it would clear her thoughts, too, and tucked the folio under one arm. Somewhere in the corridor, she heard Mrs. Hemsley's voice, carried softly, part of the house's quiet rhythm.

Georgina's course was set. There would be no hesitation. She could have sent word and asked Weld to come to her, but no letter would convey the gravity of what she held. Or the unease curling in her chest. She needed to see him herself. Only then would she know whether her instincts had betrayed her.

The rain had begun in earnest by the time Georgina arrived at Hawkesbury. It spattered the carriage windows with a relentless rhythm that did little to calm her racing thoughts. Rain blurred the outlines of the manor, turning the stones to silver. Mist clung low to the ground, rising like breath over the earth. As the carriage slowed, a chill seeped through her gloves, and she tightened her hold on the folio, as though the damp might steal it from her grasp. She didn't wait for the step to be lowered. Gathering her skirts, she descended on her own.

The stone was slick beneath her boots, the wind sharp for autumn. But her spine remained straight, her stride certain. She would not let the rain undo her resolve.

A footman hurried forward, surprise flickering over his face at the sight of an unexpected visitor. But before he could speak, Georgina did, her voice clear, steady, and edged with purpose.

"I must speak with Lord Hawkesbury at once. It is a matter of some importance."

The footman hesitated only a fraction before bowing and hurrying inside.

Left alone on the doorstep, the rain needled her shoulders. Georgina's thoughts tumbled ahead of her faster than her breath. Would Alex take her discovery seriously? Would he see the danger in it?

Several heartbeats later, Weld emerged from the great hall, his coat unfastened, and his brow furrowed in thought. He appeared, his expression sharpening with concern the moment he saw her.

"Lady Georgina," he said, striding forward. "Are you alone?"

"I came at once," she said. "There was no time to lose." She held the folio toward him without further explanation. "I believe you'll want to see this."

He took it, his fingers brushing hers briefly before he opened the worn cover.

"We're in the library. Come with me."

She followed without hesitation.

Inside, the library was dim, the fire banked low. A scattering of maps and ledgers lay across the wide table. Barrington was already there. He looked up as they entered, setting aside his reading while Georgina crossed to the table. Alex handed her the folio without a word, and she opened it to the page she'd marked.

The scent of damp wool and old paper lingered in the air, but none of them noticed. All attention was focused on the open page.

"I found it this morning," Georgina said, leaning in to point at the entry. "I was searching for something else entirely. Then I saw the date."

Alex bent over the page, his eyes narrowing. He traced the line with his thumb, reading it twice. His jaw set.

Alex glanced at her. "This is dated after Rowland's death."

She nodded. "And the handwriting is Rowland's. Or meant to be," she added.

Barrington leaned closer. "Forged," he said grimly. "A clever one, but still a forgery."

"A deliberate falsification," Alex agreed, his voice low with contained fury. "And likely not the only one."

Georgina felt the flicker of grim satisfaction she'd been holding at bay. "Then it was worth bringing."

"It was more than worth it," Alex said, closing the folio with deliberate care. His gaze lifted to hers, steady and unreadable except for the faintest flicker of something deeper.

"You've done more than bring us a clue. You've confirmed everything we feared."

Their eyes met, and in that moment, Georgina saw something behind his calm, respect, yes, but also something heavier. A quiet alignment. A shift.

Georgina looked at the folio. Her thoughts moved quickly now, lining one truth beside another.

"It said the delivery was from Hawkesbury," she murmured. "But that makes no sense. Rowland had no dealings with your mine, Alex."

Alex's brow furrowed. "No. He didn't."

She glanced up. "Then why use the name? Why forge a record tying my husband to your estate? Perhaps they wanted to make it harder to untangle the truth."

Barrington straightened, catching the thread. "Or to cast doubt. If someone started asking questions, they could point to a shared transaction and muddy the waters."

"They used Hawkesbury's name," Georgina said, her voice gaining strength, "to hide the trail. And Rowland's to validate it."

Alex nodded grimly. "They've folded both of us into the same deception. That's not a coincidence."

They had scarcely begun to sift through the remaining pages of the folio when footsteps echoed from the hall beyond the library doors.

Barrington turned just as Kenworth, his valet, entered, shoulders still slick with the autumn drizzle. His boots left a trail of water on the polished floor, and rain-darkened gloves clutched a single folded note, sealed in blue wax. He looked as though he'd ridden hard, and harder still to contain whatever message he carried.

"A message for you, sir," he said, crossing the room with practiced efficiency. "Delivered from Mrs. Bainbridge, with the request that it reach you directly."

Barrington took the note. His brow tightened as he broke the seal and scanned the page.

Alex stepped to his side, eyes narrowing as he read over Barrington's shoulder.

Barrington turned the note so both could see the familiar, tidy script.

My lord,

While reviewing the ledgers for the seminary household accounts, I encountered an entry that does not correspond with any authorized disbursement. It concerns a purchase of coal from Hawkesbury Mine, dated several weeks after Lady Georgina's loss. Yet the payment was directed to an unfamiliar account name, one I cannot trace to our suppliers. I thought it best to bring it to your attention without delay.

—H. Bainbridge

Barrington exhaled a slow breath. "Another posthumous transaction."

"A familiar hand at work," Alex added grimly, his gaze lingering on the letter. "They've extended their reach into the seminary's accounts."

Georgina stepped closer, reading over Barrington's arm. "It means they've been at this longer, and in more places, than we feared." Her pulse thudded in her ears as her eyes fixed on the unfamiliar account name. Whoever had orchestrated this scheme had done so with precision, weaving their deceit through corners no one thought to question, until now.

Alex's eyes met hers, steady and clear. "It does."

A thoughtful silence followed, thick with what they now understood. This was bigger than any of them had wanted to admit.

"We'll need to see those ledgers for ourselves," Barrington said, folding the note and tapping it against his palm.

"I can arrange that," Georgina offered without hesitation.

Alex closed the folio with deliberate care, gathering the documents as though bracing for the battle ahead. "No more surprises. From this moment on, we search with purpose."

Georgina said nothing at first. His words did not startle her. They settled slowly, like truth often did, without drama, but with impact. She was no longer just Rowland's widow sorting through the past. She was in this now, not by chance, but by choice.

She met Alex's gaze, her voice calm and certain. "Then let's begin." No longer the widow uncovering her past, but the woman claiming her future.

Chapter Eleven

"WE BEGIN HERE," Alex said, his voice low but firm, "reviewing each document."

Alex's finger paused at the column of figures again. "This entire shipment is misdated," he said, tapping once. "And not just by days. It's weeks out of step with the others."

Georgina leaned in, brow furrowed. "Then it's more than forgery. It's an orchestration. Someone wanted that entry to be seen at a glance and accepted."

Barrington joined them at the table, eyes scanning the spread of documents with practiced scrutiny. "This one too," he said, drawing out a slip Georgina hadn't yet noticed. "Coal. Same supplier. Different recipient."

He held it out for Alex, who frowned as he read. "Hawkstone Holdings," he muttered. "We've seen that name before."

Georgina nodded. "In Rowland's accounts. Once. A single mention, and I remember it because he corrected it in the margin. He crossed it out and wrote 'error.'"

Barrington exhaled through his nose, setting the slip beside the others. "It wasn't an error. It was a thread they meant to snip before anyone noticed."

Alex looked between them, something cold settling in his chest. "Then we scrutinize everything. From this point forward, nothing is too small. Nothing is assumed."

The room fell quiet for a beat, the rain offering its steady rhythm as the only sound.

Georgina reached for another page, sliding it across the table. "If we follow the names, the shipments, the payments, you can see the pattern. It's not clear yet, but it's there."

Alex glanced at her. "We're not chasing shadows anymore. We're building the map."

Barrington stepped back, eyes on the growing line of papers. "And when we've got it?"

Alex didn't hesitate. "Then we start pulling threads."

Alex glanced at her, meaning to study the page, but his gaze caught instead on her mouth as she read. She licked her lips in concentration, and his body betrayed him before his mind could take hold. He forced his eyes back to the ledger, the neat columns his only refuge from thoughts he had no business entertaining.

And yet the memory caught hard, her mouth beneath his, warm and certain, nothing held back. She had kissed him back. No pretense, no caution. A woman certain of herself, and, for that moment, certain of him. But this was not the time.

He dragged his attention back to the ledgers, as neat columns and cold ink might cool the heat in his veins.

"This supplier name," he said, his voice rougher than he meant, "we've dealt with them before."

"Legitimate dealings?" Barrington asked, his arms folded, his gaze leveled on the page.

Alex pressed his mouth into a grim line. "To my knowledge. But Bexley manages most of the estate's transactions. He should have caught this."

Georgina's gaze sharpened. She knew Bexley by reputation, buried in paperwork and apologies, known for his diligence yet forever scrambling to keep pace with the estate's needs. Overwhelmed, perhaps. But complicit? She tucked the thought away.

"We'll speak with him," Barrington said quietly, as if reading her thought. "Discreetly."

Alex's eyes narrowed on the ledger. "We've also had trouble with Tom Carver. Refused to fill a coal order last quarter. Said it was an issue of stock from his mine, but I wonder now if there's more beneath it." Alex rolled his shoulders once, a tight, unconscious motion. "Could be coincidence. But it doesn't smell like one."

"Could Carver be at the center of this?" Georgina asked.

"If he is," Barrington replied, "he's played it well. Either his refusal is genuine, or someone's using his name to muddy the trail."

Georgina frowned as she traced the supplier's name with her fingertip. "Then they're using Carver's name to conceal the real transactions."

"Exactly," Alex said grimly. "Carver would never cooperate willingly. But his name provides convenient cover."

Barrington squinted at another entry. "Here. Trentham & Clegg. They're legitimate and reputable. They're large enough to handle multiple contracts without raising questions."

"Didn't they supply the iron railings for the garden enclosure?" Barrington asked.

"They did," came Mrs. Bainbridge's voice from the doorway. She swept into the room like a general, a second ledger balanced in one hand. "And household coal for the seminary. Reliable enough, though not flawless. We've had to chase them over missing invoices more than once. Their clerk has a most inconvenient habit of disappearing the moment answers are required."

She tipped her head toward Georgina, adding wryly, "You recall the poor fellow, Lady Georgina? Pale as milk, sweat beading on his brow, and all too eager to blame the post."

Georgina allowed herself a tight smile. "As I recall, he nearly bolted when you produced the accounts book."

"Only nearly," Mrs. Bainbridge replied, a touch of pride in her voice.

A flicker of amusement passed between them, a brief spark that lit the room. Barrington glanced up, the faintest smile tugging at his mouth, though his eyes remained fixed on the ledger. "Fear of you, madam, may yet keep the honest men from straying."

"Fear and accuracy," Mrs. Bainbridge answered smartly, running a finger down the page before her. "Both serve their uses."

Alex's expression darkened. "Which makes their name the perfect cover to mask illicit payments."

Barrington tapped a line in the account book. "Except this payment didn't go to them."

Alex leaned in and swore softly. "No. It went to an unaffiliated account using their name. It's a false trail. Deliberate misdirection."

Alex closed the folio carefully, pressing his palm against the leather as though sealing it. "I want every account. Every name. Every shipment that passed through these hands."

"We'll find them," Barrington agreed. "But we'll need Mrs. Bainbridge's ledger to cross-reference." He turned to Mrs. Bainbridge. "Did you bring the household ledger?"

She gave a small nod. "I brought it but left it in the carriage. I wasn't certain if you'd need it."

He turned toward the door. "Kenworth."

The valet appeared almost immediately, still carrying the damp from outside.

"Please retrieve Mrs. Bainbridge's household ledger from the carriage."

"I left it under the forward seat, Mr. Kenworth. It's wrapped in oilcloth," Mrs. Bainbridge added.

"At once, ma'am." He disappeared down the corridor. As the door closed, the quiet deepened.

The fire had burned low, embers pulsing in the grate as shadows stretched long across the walls. Outside, the rain picked up, drumming harder against the glass.

Alex paced the length of the room, restless. His gaze drifted to the scattered folios and finally to a stack of Rowland's letters. He picked one up, scanning the familiar, uneven script.

Georgina watched him a moment, then asked softly, "Were

you close? You and Rowland?"

Alex hesitated, then answered honestly. "We respected each other. That's not always easy."

Georgina's mouth curved. Her smile was soft, genuine. "No, it isn't."

They returned to the ledgers. Georgina and Mrs. Bainbridge bent together over the figures, the rhythm of their work quiet but purposeful, the storm outside echoing the reckoning taking shape.

Mrs. Bainbridge traced a finger down one column. "Here. A coal delivery, paid to an unfamiliar account."

"Not one of our suppliers," Georgina noted, her pulse quickening.

Alex leaned in. "Same name as in Rowland's transaction."

Georgina squinted at the slip, something prickling at the edge of her thoughts. The date had troubled her since morning. Could it have been an innocent mistake?

But then her eyes drifted lower, catching the word that made her breath catch. Commision.

Her hand came to her mouth before the laughter burst out, bright and unrestrained, until tears stung her eyes.

The men stared at her, startled.

"Georgina?" Alex's concern cut through the room.

She waved a hand, breathless. "Don't you see it, Alex? The date was bothering me, yes, perhaps just an error, but this," she pointed, her eyes alight, "look at the word. Read what's there. Not what you expect to see."

Alex took the slip, brow furrowed. Then comprehension bloomed across his features. Slowly, unmistakably, his mouth curved into a grin. He passed it to Barrington.

"Rowland's signature," he said, his voice rich with realization. "It was always the double s in 'commission.' He never spelled it correctly."

Silence held for a long moment. Then, relief. Laughter. The sharp, sweet kind that comes not from joy, but from finally *knowing.*

Barrington's eyes narrowed. "But this one is."

"There's your proof," Alex said grimly. "It's a forgery."

Georgina wiped her eyes, her breath coming in short, triumphant gasps. "And not even a clever one."

At that moment, the library door creaked open. Kenworth stepped in, shoulders beaded with rain, holding a leather-bound ledger and wearing a look of long-suffering patience that couldn't quite hide the humor beneath.

"I retrieved the ledger from the carriage," he said, crossing the room. "Mrs. Bainbridge, I found it precisely where you said it would be."

He set the book on the table with care, then added, more to the room at large than to her directly, "I remain grateful that she accompanied me earlier today to collect it. I gave her my best arguments for staying behind, but I suspect she could out-debate Parliament itself."

Already at Georgina's side, Mrs. Bainbridge arched a brow. "A good thing you didn't waste your breath, Kenworth. We saved time."

"And discussed the entire wedding seating arrangement while we were at it," he added, deadpan. "I fear the guest list may haunt my dreams."

"You shall be well prepared, then," Barrington said, dry as dust as he closed a ledger. "If this investigation proves less treacherous than wedding preparations, we shall count ourselves fortunate."

Georgina's lips curved despite the tension still coiled beneath her ribs. She brushed a damp curl from her cheek, her gaze sweeping the room, where scattered ledgers, rain-damp coats, and quiet resolve bound them not just in purpose, but in partnership.

"Better our investigations than our nightmares," Mrs. Bainbridge replied, tapping the ledger with a crisp finality.

Alex let the moment of levity settle, then straightened. "At first light, we go to Trentham & Clegg directly. Barrington, have the Brigade ready to move. Mrs. Bainbridge, I ask you and Lady Georgina to continue combing the seminary accounts. Any irregularities, no matter how small, must be found."

Georgina inclined her head, meeting his gaze squarely. "We'll not overlook a single line."

"And Bexley?" Barrington asked.

"I'll handle him," Alex replied, his voice clipped with resolve.

A pause followed, thick with understanding.

Georgina's eyes swept over the ledgers once more, the impact of their findings settling in her chest. They had moved beyond chance discoveries now. What lay ahead was deliberate, dangerous, and no longer hidden.

She could feel it, thrumming beneath the surface of the quiet room: not fear, but determination. A tether of purpose binding them. Barrington with his steady command, Mrs. Bainbridge sharp-eyed and unflinching, Kenworth ready at a moment's notice, and Alex.

Alex, whose gaze met hers across the scattered ledgers. In his gaze, she saw not only determination but something deeper, something unsaid yet unmistakable. Respect, yes. Admiration, perhaps. And beneath it all, a flicker of something unspoken, far harder to name, and far more dangerous.

Heat bloomed in her chest, warmer than the fire's glow. She did not look away.

For so long, she had lived as though her story had ended with Rowland's death. As though her purpose had been buried alongside him. But here, now, with the evidence spread before them and Alex's steady gaze holding hers, she felt the unmistakable stirring of something new. Not an ending. A beginning.

"You told us how to begin," she said, her voice clear and sure. "Now, when do we begin?"

His reply was a promise, quiet and fierce. "At first light."

Outside, the shadows deepened as the storm thickened beyond the windows, but within the library walls, their purpose held fast, no longer scattered fragments, but a force. Ready to fight.

And beneath his words, she heard something else. Not spoken, not yet, but present all the same… Not spoken. Not yet. But they threaded beneath every plan they'd made. A promise waiting to be named. With you.

Chapter Twelve

"WE WON'T GET far if you grind your teeth to powder," Barrington said, his tone dry as ever.

Alex didn't respond. Next to him, Georgina watched with the calm of a woman who had already made her choice and dared anyone to question it.

Alex's gaze tracked the passing landscape, though the blur of the rain gave him little to study but the tightening knot of his own thoughts. The countryside blurred beneath the gray hush of dawn, hedges and fields washed in pale light, puddles rippling beneath the carriage wheels. He had ridden into battle beneath clearer skies than these, and yet, nothing had felt so uncertain. His jaw worked, tight with the unspoken tension that had coiled since Georgina first declared she would join them. He had half a mind to argue further, but he knew when a battle was already lost.

Georgina sat poised, her hands folded atop a leather case of notes, her expression steady despite the chill seeping through the air. She had not come as a bystander. She had come as a participant, an investigator in her own right, and the quiet strength in her bearing left no room for doubt. He hadn't wavered once in her determination to accompany them, no matter that he had advised against it. No matter that his concern for her had knotted in his chest like a tightened noose. She would stand beside him, come what may, and her quiet strength only fueled the conflicting churn of pride and worry rising in him.

The carriage jolted over a rut in the road, and her shoulder brushed his. She did not pull away. Neither did he. The warmth of that brief contact lingered longer than it ought.

She stole a glance across the dim interior. He looked out the window, quiet but alert, and something in his stillness steadied her. They had once exchanged confidences over coffee and ink-stained maps. Now they shared silence, and somehow, it meant more.

The tension between them simmered, quiet, steady, and alive. A current beneath still waters, waiting. He felt it, keen and insistent, as if the very air between them carried its own charge.

The city crept closer, the rhythm of hooves muffled in the wet road. Smoke from nearby chimneys threaded the damp air as they pulled into the yard of Trentham & Clegg. The coal merchants' yard bustled with the usual grim efficiency. Laborers hauled crates, clerks hurried between deliveries, their arms cradling ledgers and correspondence beneath their coats to shield them from the drizzle. Wagons rattled across the cobblestones, iron rims flashing dull in the watery light. Rain dripped steadily from the eaves of the main office, tapping an almost impatient rhythm.

Georgina's gaze swept the yard as they stepped down from the carriage. She marked the hurried steps of the clerks, the soot smudged across crates, the pale slip of paper that fluttered free from a stack and was snatched back before it could fall to the wet ground. Nothing seemed amiss, yet a chill crawled along the base of her spine, not from the weather, but from the knowledge that appearances were too easily arranged.

Crates lined the yard, stamped with destinations across the region and stacked like quiet sentinels to industry. It all appeared orderly enough, but beneath the surface of legitimate trade, someone had twisted these familiar names into tools of deceit, shields behind which the real work was done. The unease in Alex's chest came not from the merchants at work, but from the shadowy figures hidden behind their ledgers. The person who had forged the invoice had made a wise choice. A reputable firm would attract less suspicion.

Mr. Clegg, a stout man with an efficient manner, looked up from his ledger as they approached. He wiped a damp hand against his waistcoat and offered a courteous nod, though his brow lifted in mild surprise at the sight of their party. His eyes, alert despite the early hour, flicked from Alex to Barrington and Georgina with a businessman's practiced curiosity, assessing, not alarmed. His uncapped pen bled a small pool of ink onto the corner of the ledger, forgotten in his moment of observation.

"My lord," Clegg said, addressing Alex directly. "What brings you out in this weather?"

Alex stepped forward, rain beading on his coat. "Mr. Clegg, a moment of your time. We've come regarding a recent payment made to you."

Clegg's frown deepened. "Of course, my lord. Please, come inside."

He led them through to a cramped office that smelled of damp stone and ink, motioning toward the chairs near the desk. His movements were brisk, practiced. He was clearly a man who spent his mornings poring over figures and receipts.

"May I see the invoice in question?" Clegg asked, settling behind his desk and gesturing to the cleared space before him.

Alex withdrew the folded document from the inner pocket of his coat and placed it between them. The paper, softened from handling, showed faint smudges where his thumb had pressed the corner. He left it untouched on the polished desk.

Clegg unfolded it with professional ease. His brow furrowed as he read, deepening into lines of unease. He lifted the page to the rain-streaked window, angling it toward the light to catch the watermark's faint impression.

His lips compressed to a line. "If anyone else were sitting across from me," he said at last, his voice low and flat, "I'd take this for a poor joke."

Barrington's gaze sharpened. "Joke, Mr. Clegg?"

Clegg didn't answer immediately. He rose, crossed to a shelf lined with bound volumes, and ran his fingers along the cracked spines. Selecting one, he flipped through with efficient precision until he found the proper section. His finger stopped on a line of numbers.

"You'll note our numbering system," he said, turning the book for their view. "Sequential, without exception. TC-1198, TC-1199, TC-1200..." He gestured to the forged invoice. "This one, TC-0381, is a full series behind. That sequence passed through our books last year."

He held the forgery to the light again. "And our watermark, a crossed hammer and pick, should be deeply pressed into the parchment. This mark is faint. Almost stamped rather than embossed."

Clegg returned the document with quiet finality. "My lord, this is not my invoice. The name is ours, yes, but the document is not."

Alex's mouth tightened. "Then it's a forgery."

He turned to Georgina, his gaze steady. "Do you see anything further, my lady?"

Georgina accepted the document and turned it in her hands, her fingers grazing the rough edge where the false seal had been pressed.

"The seal," she said softly, running her fingertip over the embossed mark. "On your proper invoices, Mr. Clegg, the press leaves a deeper impression. Whoever forged this worked quickly, but not well."

Clegg inclined his head, a glimmer of grim appreciation flickering in his eyes. "You have a keen eye, my lady."

"They're using reputable names to mask their trail," Barrington said, still studying the forgery as if he might extract more truth by sheer will. "Clever enough to pass a cursory inspection, but not clever enough to withstand a close look."

"A rushed forgery," Alex agreed, sliding the document back into the inner pocket of his coat. Already, his thoughts turned to the necessary steps, a campaign not waged with cannon or sword, but with ledgers and quiet shadows. The Brigade would need to move. Not with force, but with precision. Questions asked in the right places, by the right men.

"Some months ago," Clegg recalled, thinking aloud, "a gentleman inquired about our invoice formats. Claimed he was auditing estate accounts."

Barrington's mouth pulled into a flat line. "Then we've confirmed at least one method of deception."

Alex exhaled, low and steady, feeling the shape of the battle settling into place. "We widen our net," he said firmly. "Barrington, reach out to the Brigade's informants. Quietly. If someone is operating this deeply in our territory, they must have left a trail."

Barrington gave a sharp nod. "I know the men for it."

"And I'll speak to Bexley," Alex added, a clipped edge in his tone. "If there's been talk among the suppliers, he may have heard it."

Georgina closed her case of notes with deliberate care. Her thoughts had already turned to the seminary's ledgers. She pictured Mrs. Bainbridge's steady hand, her unerring eye for inconsistencies, and felt a spark of renewed purpose.

"I'll return to Mrs. Bainbridge," she said. "We'll comb through every ledger, every slip of correspondence. If they've hidden the truth in the shadows, we'll shine a light on them."

There was no moment of doubt. No need for reassurance. She knew what had to be done. She no longer waited for permission to do it.

Alex caught the resolute line of her jaw, and something fierce twisted in his chest. Not fear. Not even worry. A fierce rush of admiration twisted in his chest. Undeniable, proud, and entirely his undoing.

By the time they stepped back into the yard, the rain had softened to a fine mist, delicate as silk thread and just as persistent. It beaded along the crate edges and pooled in shallow dips across the worn cobblestones. The air hung heavy with the scent of wet stone and coal dust, the quiet hum of honest industry persisting around them.

Alex offered Georgina his hand as she stepped toward the carriage. Her gaze met his, steady, unreadable. For a moment, she hesitated, not from uncertainty, but from what had passed between them, unspoken. When her gloved fingers curled around his, her grip was sure, warm despite the chill.

The moment stretched, not quite lingering, but not hurried either. Not hesitation. A promise passed without words, quiet as breath, certain as dawn.

Barrington mounted behind them with the practiced ease of a man who had long ago mastered both horse and carriage. His expression remained unreadable beneath the brim of his hat, though Alex caught the slight tilt of his head. It signified approval, perhaps, or quiet expectation.

Alex settled opposite Georgina, the forged invoice secured once more within his coat. His eyes found hers across the narrow space, and for the first time that morning, he allowed himself a breath not steeped in urgency.

"Then we force them into the light," he said, steel beneath his quiet voice.

The carriage rocked into motion, wheels splashing through the rain-polished yard, their course set into the oncoming storm.

Neither spoke, but both understood that there was no turning back.

Chapter Thirteen

Alex had seen Bexley flustered before, but never with quite so much paper and perspiration competing for dominance.

He pushed open the door to the steward's office without ceremony, his entrance muffled by the lingering damp in the air. Bexley, bent over a spread of ledgers, didn't hear him at first. The steward's lips moved in a silent tally as his finger chased figures down a page, utterly absorbed in his task.

Alex took the moment to observe, his gaze sweeping the room with a soldier's precision. Disordered stacks of account books teetered precariously, some marked with hastily folded notes, others bearing the blots of spilled ink. Sheets of correspondence lay curled at the edges where they had been hastily dried by the hearth. It was not the chaos of deceit, Alex thought grimly, but of drowning.

Bexley turned a page too quickly, and the motion disturbed a loose slip of parchment. It slid free, fluttering toward the floor. He lunged to catch it, and in the same motion became aware of Alex's presence. He startled, rising abruptly, his chair scraping back against the floorboards with a screech. His arm clipped the corner of an unsteady pile, sending it listing dangerously before he managed to right it with a flailing hand.

"My lord!" Bexley managed, cheeks flushing as he attempted a bow amidst the clutter.

Alex's expression remained cool. He had entered prepared to confront a man complicit in deceit. Instead, he found chaos, honest, desperate chaos.

"Leave the courtesies, Bexley," Alex said, his tone edged. "Tell me what you've found."

"Yes, my lord," Bexley rasped, tugging his sleeves down to his wrists as though it might restore some semblance of order to himself, if not the office. He shuffled through the nearest pile of ledgers and opened one to the marked page. His finger, slightly ink-stained, trailed the line of entries with nervous precision.

"I've been reviewing the suppliers' accounts as you instructed. There are... there are gaps, my lord," he admitted, his voice tight with strain. "Payments issued, but no matching delivery receipts. And," he swallowed visibly, "some letters I had set aside for follow-up have gone missing."

Alex narrowed his gaze. "Which letters?"

"Most notably, the correspondence from Mr. Tom Carver," Bexley replied. He drew a shaking breath. "I had flagged them for irregularities, but when I returned to the file, they were gone."

Alex's jaw tightened. "When did you last see them?"

"Two days ago, my lord. Before I turned to the estate accounts. I cannot explain their absence." Bexley's brow furrowed deeply, his genuine confusion evident in the furrow between his brows. "No one should have had access to those files. At least, I believed so."

The sharp edge of suspicion dulled. Georgina would have told him to look twice before condemning the man. The thought steadied him more than the ledgers ever could.

Alex watched him closely, measuring his words, his demeanor, the restless motion of his hands. He saw no guile in Bexley, no subterfuge, no confidence trick. Just a man sinking under the weight of honest failure.

The sharp suspicion that had carried Alex into the room cooled, tempered by recognition. This was no conspirator standing before him, but a steward overwhelmed, swamped beneath a tide of deceit not of his making.

He drew a breath and let it out slowly. "You are certain of

that?"

"To the best of my knowledge, my lord. I swear it." Bexley met Alex's gaze squarely, and though his shoulders sagged beneath the strain of the confession, there was honesty in his eyes.

Alex inclined his head once. "Very well."

Relief flickered across Bexley's features, though it did little to ease the deep lines of fatigue carved into his face. "Anything I can do to assist further, my lord?"

Alex's gaze swept once more over the disarray of ledgers and papers. His mind ticked through the estate's resources, assessing what little could be done to bolster Bexley's failing defenses.

"You'll need help to untangle this," Alex said at last. "Speak with Mr. Hughes, our solicitor. He'll know someone reliable to assist you."

Bexley's brows rose, and for the first time since Alex had entered, a glimmer of hope flickered through him. "Yes, my lord. I will."

Alex fixed him with a final, steady look. "Choose carefully."

"I will, my lord," Bexley promised, drawing himself up with a semblance of his former diligence.

Alex turned to the door, the line of his shoulders set, the thread of urgency pulled tighter still. The trail they followed had not yet gone cold, and he would not allow it to do so.

⇒⇒⇒⇐⇐⇐

GEORGINA STEPPED DOWN from the carriage at the Sommer-by-the-Sea Female Seminary. Damp mist clung to the stones of the courtyard, curling around the iron railings like a reluctant guest unwilling to depart.

Georgina drew her cloak closer against the chill as she crossed to the main hall. Despite the grey weather, a quiet energy filled the seminary grounds. Students flitted between lessons, voices low beneath the patter of rain, while Ellen supervised from beneath a sturdy umbrella with military precision.

Inside, the warmth of the familiar office greeted her like an old friend. Lamplight softened the edges of the high-ceilinged room, casting golden pools over the ledgers spread across the broad oak table. Mrs. Bainbridge was already there, her sleeves neatly turned back, her spectacles perched at the bridge of her nose as she bent over the latest column of figures.

"Lady Georgina," she greeted without looking up, "I trust Hawkesbury Manor proved instructive?"

"It did," Georgina replied, settling across from her. "Though I suspect this task may prove more fruitful."

Mrs. Bainbridge gave a wry smile. "At least these ledgers do not argue with me. The bakers for the wedding, on the other hand, seem determined to drive me to distraction.

Georgina's lips curved. "They still debate?"

"Endlessly. Marmalade enthusiasts against sugared rose loyalists." She sighed, though amusement softened her exasperation. "One might think I were convening a royal court rather than ordering cake."

"You could assign them ledgers instead," Georgina suggested with a small laugh. "It might distract them."

"I am not convinced they would not begin debating sums and margins instead," Mrs. Bainbridge retorted, though her eyes glinted with humor. "At any rate, I far prefer the company of these numbers over the squabbles of bakers. At least here, the falsities can be proven."

They fell into quiet industry, the soft scratch of quills and the muted patter of rain filling the room as they worked through the entries. Georgina's attention sharpened, her focus narrowing to the columns of amounts and suppliers.

Her thoughts, however, drifted more than once to Alex. She imagined him across the estate, pacing the steward's office with the same restless determination he had carried since the moment she arrived at Hawkesbury Manor. He would not sit idle. She knew that now with certainty. He would drive toward the truth with the same fierce energy he had shown in every encounter between them. She pictured the quiet steadiness in his gaze, the warmth that always reached her first. The memory stirred her pulse, unwelcome for its timing, but impossible to dismiss.

Perhaps Mrs. Bainbridge read something of Georgina's unspoken thoughts, for she murmured without lifting her gaze, "Lord Hawkesbury strikes me as a man who will burn through every wick of daylight if left to it."

Georgina smiled despite herself. "He does not yield easily."

"A useful trait," Mrs. Bainbridge replied, her tone approving. "And a dangerous one, if pointed in the wrong direction."

Georgina returned to the ledger before her, pressing past the warmth that bloomed in her chest at the observation. "Fortunately, he is pointed in precisely the right one."

They bent over the ledgers once more, the rhythm of their search resuming.

Georgina paused, her brow knitting as she studied a particular entry. The amount struck her first, unusually high for even the seminary's considerable needs.

"This sum is too large for household use," she observed, her finger trailing beneath the line.

Mrs. Bainbridge adjusted her spectacles and leaned closer. Her eyes narrowed. "And the supplier?" She exhaled slowly, her voice cooling. "Not one of ours. Nor anyone I would entrust with so much as a bundle of kindling."

A coil of unease tightened in Georgina's chest. "That makes two irregularities. Different names, same strategy."

"They're weaving a careful pattern," Mrs. Bainbridge agreed, "but we've caught the thread."

She reached for a slip of paper and marked the entry with decisive strokes. The impact of their discovery settled over them like a gathering storm.

Georgina closed the ledger, her pulse steady but quickened by purpose. "We take this to Lord Hawkesbury."

Mrs. Bainbridge stood, smoothing her skirts. "Without delay."

As they crossed the office to retrieve their cloaks, Georgina allowed herself one final glance at the ledgers spread across the table. The pieces were aligning, the shadows thinning.

They were no longer chasing whispers. They were closing in.

THE FIRE IN the Hawkesbury study had burned low, casting long shadows across the papers strewn like fallen leaves over the desk. Outside the rain had eased to a sullen mist, clinging to the windows in thin, wavering lines. The room carried the scent of damp wool and woodsmoke, and beneath it all, the faint sharpness of ink left uncapped for too long.

Alex stood before the hearth, one hand braced against the mantelpiece, the other holding Kenworth's latest dispatch. The paper, still creased from its hurried folding, bore the unmistakable marks of haste. Ink smudged in the margin where the messenger's hand had slipped in the wet.

"A stranger asking after Carver's operations," Alex read aloud, his voice tight with tempered urgency. He lowered the paper to the desk, weighing its meaning. "It seems we are not the only ones following this trail."

Barrington, standing at the opposite side of the room, gave a grim nod. "They're watching their loose ends."

"Then we'll see them unravel faster than they can tie them," Alex replied.

Footsteps sounded in the corridor beyond, brisk and purposeful. Moments later, Georgina and Mrs. Bainbridge entered the study, cloaks still damp from their ride. Rain pearled along the edge of Georgina's hood before she pushed it back, revealing eyes alight with determination.

"We found a second irregularity," Georgina announced,

moving directly to the desk. Her pulse ticked at her throat. This was no coincidence—no clerical oversight. It was too clean, too intentional. A false thread sewn into truth. She set the seminary ledger between them with practiced efficiency and opened it to the marked page. "Another payment routed through dormant accounts, buried so neatly it might have been missed entirely."

Mrs. Bainbridge stood beside her, her expression as firm as the inked annotations on the ledger. Her voice cooled, the edge of steel replacing civility. "Not one of ours. And not one I'd trust with a paper lantern in a rainstorm."

Alex stepped closer, scanning the entry. The pattern emerged at once. It was a clever concealment masquerading as a routine expense. His jaw tightened. "They're using legitimate channels to mask their diversions."

"And counting on chaos to hide them further," Mrs. Bainbridge said with a note of contempt.

Barrington leaned over the desk, studying the figures with a soldier's eye. "It's a careful construction," he agreed. "But not without cracks."

Georgina met Alex's gaze across the table. "And we have found them." For a heartbeat, the firelight flickered between them, catching in his eyes. He trusted her judgment. It was evident in the quiet stillness between their words. That knowledge settled through her like warmth after a storm.

For a moment, Alex saw nothing but her and the fire's reflection flickering in her eyes, her posture steady despite the damp chill of her cloak. She had not come this far to falter, and the certainty of it settled in his chest like the first true breath after a long climb. Something fierce twisted in his chest. Not fear. Not worry. Rather, a quiet awe, sharp as it was steady.

His voice, when he spoke, carried the weight of decision. "Barrington, have the Brigade prepare to move. Quietly."

"Already done," Barrington replied, a faint trace of approval beneath his customary steadiness.

Kenworth stepped forward from the shadows near the door,

clearing his throat. "My lord, word from our informants near Carver's holdings. Unfamiliar riders, seen twice at the far ridge."

Alex's gaze sharpened. "They're moving their pieces."

"And so must we," Georgina said, her tone crisp.

Alex's attention lingered on her a heartbeat longer, the corners of his mouth easing from grim tension to something nearer respect, perhaps even admiration. "You've proven yourself invaluable in this, Lady Georgina."

She inclined her head, but there was no modesty in it. Only resolve. "We will see it through."

Alex looked at Barrington, then back at the ledger where their discoveries lay bare. No more half-measures. No more shadows unchallenged.

"Then we go to Carver," Alex said. The silence that followed wasn't hesitation. It was an agreement, forged in urgency and trust.

Chapter Fourteen

"YOU CANNOT EXPECT me to remain behind," Georgina said, her arms folding tightly as Alex tightened the saddle girth with grim finality.

His hands stilled on the leather strap. He had braced for her resistance, but the clarity in her tone struck deeper than he cared to admit. "No," he said, keeping his voice level, "I expect you to do something that no one else can accomplish but you."

Beside him, Barrington stood, his steady gaze tracking the preparations in the yard. "We need to know what passed between your late husband and Tom Carver," Barrington added. "There's history there, and it's buried deeper than the mines themselves."

Georgina's lips pressed together, her chin lifting. She had no intention of being pushed aside, not after everything they had uncovered. "Then let me hear it from Carver himself," she challenged.

The steadiness in her voice caught him off guard. Pride stirred, tempered by the quiet ache of knowing she would never again yield to anyone's protection, least of all his. Alex's mouth tightened. He wished he could give her that freedom, but not this time. "Carver is too unpredictable. He may not be involved, but as a mine owner, he has his own stake in this. I will not risk you walking into a trap."

She drew a breath. "You think this is a trap?"

"I hope not, but we're not certain. Barrington and I must be prepared."

"Very well," she allowed. Her mind had begun to race with thoughts on how to obtain the information they needed. "I won't disappoint you."

"I didn't think you would," Alex agreed. "Find out everything you can about Rowland's dealings with Carver. Mrs. Hemsley will have kept a close eye on household matters."

Georgina nodded, already turning over possibilities. "Mr. Titus," she added aloud, thinking swiftly. "Rowland's valet. He might have kept letters or notes. He knew the rhythms of Rowland's dealings better than anyone."

Barrington's expression shifted slightly. "Titus sailed for Canada shortly after your husband's passing."

Her mouth tightened, but she pressed on. "Then, Mrs. Hemsley, it shall be. She will remember. She always remembers."

Alex could not help the trace of admiration that flickered in his gaze. "You will see what others have missed. I will be at Barrington's after seeing Carver."

Before she turned away, he reached into his coat and drew out a small pistol. It was light but reliable. He held it out without ceremony.

She raised a brow at the sight of it. "You cannot be serious."

He wished, for one reckless moment, that he could keep her out of harm's way with words instead of weapons. "I am very serious," he returned. "You'll carry it because I won't risk losing you, not to them. Not to silence."

She accepted it without hesitation, her hand steady. There was no bravado, only the quiet assurance of someone who understood the importance of such things.

He leaned in slightly. "Breathe. Never rush the shot."

A flicker of something warmer stirred in her eyes. Not amusement, but a quiet respect, perhaps even trust. She accepted the pistol and tucked it beneath her cloak without further comment.

Alex helped her into the coach, closing his hand over hers a heartbeat longer than necessary as she settled into her seat. He lowered his voice. His words were meant only for her ears. "Trust me to keep the road clear."

Her answer came soft but certain. "I trust you."

The words landed deeper than she could have known. In the hush that followed, trust was perilously close to confession.

Their eyes held for a breath longer, then he closed the door firmly behind her.

As Alex swung into the saddle beside Barrington, Georgina's coach rolled forward, wheels crunching over the damp gravel as it turned toward Ravenstock Manor.

"We may be riding in different directions," Barrington said, "but we're still fighting the same battle."

Alex nodded once, eyes narrowing toward the uncertain horizon. "And no ground left uncovered."

❯❯❯❰❰❰

As THEY RODE into Carver's yard, the sound of hooves drew attention long before words were spoken. A few miners glanced up from their tasks, wary eyes tracking Alex and Barrington as they dismounted. Carver emerged from beneath the timbered lean-to, a rag in one hand, wiping coal dust from his fingers as he watched them approach.

He hadn't been waiting, but he was not caught unprepared either. His posture spoke of a man accustomed to hard labor and harder decisions, guarded but not openly hostile.

"My lords," Carver greeted, with a nod first to Alex, then to Barrington. His gaze shifted between them, cool but not insolent. "To what do I owe the pleasure?"

Alex met the miner's eye steadily. "A few questions about your recent orders." His tone was calm and steady. "We've reason to believe your name has been used in some irregular dealings."

Carver's jaw tightened subtly, and he glanced back toward

the men behind him. "I run an honest mine, my lord. Orders come and go. Some I fill, some I decline."

Barrington stepped forward slightly, his gaze sweeping the quiet yard. There was no sign of outward trouble, but there was something in the way the workers lingered, watchful, cautious, as though deciding whether to stay or slip away.

"You've turned away orders, then?" Barrington asked, keeping his voice even.

Carver folded the rag between his hands. "Aye. A few lately. Materials that didn't suit, or requests that came from unfamiliar quarters."

Alex studied him closely. Carver's responses were careful, not evasive. He was not a man accustomed to explaining himself, but neither did he seem surprised by the line of questioning.

"You didn't think to raise any concern?" Alex pressed gently, a prompt, not an accusation.

Carver's mouth pulled tight. "With respect, my lord, a man in my position thinks twice before accusing gentlemen of misconduct. Especially when the orders come dressed in proper accounts and fine seals."

Alex absorbed that quietly. It was an honest answer, and it told him more than if Carver had blustered.

"What did these gentlemen look like?" Barrington asked.

Carver shifted his weight. "Respectable. Well-fed. Fine coats. You know the sort." His gaze flicked to Alex, not as an accusation, but as a grim acknowledgment.

Barrington's eyes narrowed slightly. "Did you recognize any names?"

Carver shook his head once. "Names were not given." He paused, then added, "But their eyes were sharp as razors. They knew what they were about."

Alex held his gaze a moment longer, seeing the truth beneath the caution. Carver would not say more, but it was clear enough. The man had seen trouble coming and chose to stand aside rather than risk himself.

"You've done the right thing to refuse them," Alex said at last. "And if they return?"

Carver's expression hardened. "I'll do the same."

There was a quiet moment as the words settled between them. Alex inclined his head slightly, a gesture of acknowledgment and, perhaps, quiet respect.

"Good," Barrington said simply.

With that, they stepped back, allowing Carver to return to his men. As they turned toward their horses, Barrington spoke low to Alex beneath the creak of harness leather.

"He knows more."

Alex's eyes stayed on the mine yard as he replied, his voice low and sure. "He does. But we've planted the seed. He'll come to us when he's ready."

"And if he doesn't?"

Alex swung into the saddle with practiced ease. "Then we'll be ready when he slips."

He trusted her. Respected her. But the part of him that had walked battlefields also knew that not all courage went unpunished.

>>>><<<<

THE CARRIAGE HAD scarcely stopped before Mrs. Hemsley appeared at the front door, her shawl clutched tightly against the wind. She was not a woman easily flustered, yet beneath her usual composure flickered a hint of unease.

"My lady," she said as Georgina stepped down from the coach. "There's a visitor to see you. She claims to have information about the mine."

Georgina's pulse quickened. "The mine? Who is she?"

"A tradesman's wife by the look of her. She wouldn't give me her name nor be turned away, not even when I said you were at Hawkesbury." Mrs. Hemsley lowered her voice slightly. "She asked after Baron Ravenstock."

That settled it. Georgina gathered her cloak tighter around her shoulders and strode into the house, her mind already piecing together questions before she reached the study.

The woman rose as she entered, twisting her hands in the apron bunched at her waist. Her clothes were modest, neat but worn, and her eyes were rimmed red from worry and sleepless nights.

"My lady," the woman began, her voice frayed at the edges. "I…I thought it right to come myself."

Georgina gestured to the chair opposite the hearth. "Please, have a seat. We'll have tea."

The woman glanced at the seat as if it were a strange thing. "No, thank you, my lady. I'll stand. I cannot stay long. My boy is waiting for me by the gate."

"I understand. Then tell me why you're here."

Mrs. Hemsley lingered just long enough to ensure their guest was settled before retreating toward the doorway, where she kept to the shadows, attentive but discreet.

"My husband," the woman began, clutching her hands tightly together. "He's a carrier by trade. Last fortnight, he began receiving parcels from a man I'd never seen before. Orders, he claimed. But not from anyone he trusted."

Georgina's brow drew together. "And this man, did you see him clearly?"

The woman hesitated, then nodded. "Pale as milk, dark hair combed too fine for a laborer. He looked like a clerk, but he had the manner of someone used to giving orders. He lingered in the village longer than he needed to, watching."

"And your husband?" Georgina pressed.

The woman's eyes filled with a troubled sheen. "He's been restless. Unsettled. I fear he's caught in something neither of us understands."

Georgina's voice softened, threading reassurance into her words. "You did well to come to me. Does your husband still carry for this man?"

"No, my lady. Not since last week. He found reason to turn him away, saying the work was too thin to waste the effort."

A measure of relief, but not enough to ease the tightness in Georgina's chest. "And the man, did he give his name?"

"No, my lady," the woman said. "But he watched our house for days after."

Georgina's expression hardened. "I will see that no harm comes to you, your husband or your children," she promised quietly.

Tears pricked at the corners of the woman's eyes. She bent her head in a silent, grateful nod.

Mrs. Hemsley stepped forward then, gently taking the woman's arm. "Come, we'll see you to your boy," she said, her tone kind.

Georgina waited until the door closed behind them, her gaze fixed on the hearth where the shadows played over iron and stone. She let out a breath she had not realized she'd been holding, her mind already chasing the threads the woman had offered.

When Mrs. Hemsley returned, Georgina turned to her at once, her voice firm.

"What do you know of my husband's dealings with Mr. Carver?"

Mrs. Hemsley folded her hands and took her time gathering her thoughts. "They spoke now and then, my lady, but rarely at the house. Most of their dealings were kept to letters or at the mine. His lordship was a careful man." She hesitated, then added, "Mr. Titis kept all his lordship's personal correspondence. Before he left, he tucked it away in the crate you've not yet finished going through."

Georgina's gaze sharpened. "Show me."

Mrs. Hemsley led the way to the corner of the study, where a crate sat beneath the window, half-sorted papers spilling from its top. "When I shifted it earlier, there was a folio tucked beneath the ledgers. I thought it odd at the time."

Georgina knelt beside the crate, pushing aside a stack of estate receipts to reach the bottom. Her fingers brushed over folded vellum, then caught on a familiar ribbon. She drew it out, her pulse quickening.

Rowland's hand. Slanted, precise. His private notations marked the margins of payment routes, suppliers, and dates. Names she had seen in the Hawkesbury ledgers. Names she had seen today, including Tom Carver.

Her breath caught, not in surprise, but in confirmation. The truth wasn't hidden. It had been there all along. She was simply the one willing to see it.

"This is exactly what I was looking for."

Mrs. Hemsley's voice became quiet but sure. "You always did have an eye for the truth, my lady."

Georgina rose, clutching the folio. "Call for the carriage. I'll take this to Barrington and Alex."

"As you wish," Mrs. Hemsley said, already turning to the bell.

As the servant left the room, Georgina allowed herself one final glance at the papers in her hands. The threads were beginning to gather, not yet a noose, but close. And this time, she intended to tighten it.

THE APPROACH TO Sommer Chase stretched ahead, the hedgerows dark with lingering mist, and the lane still damp from the day's rain. Alex guided his horse at a steady pace, Barrington riding beside him in thoughtful silence.

Carver had given them little, but little was not nothing. Shadows clung to his words, just enough to confirm their suspicions. And enough, too, to confirm that the man was not yet an enemy, but neither was he a friend.

Alex's mind, however, had already turned toward Georgina.

He had given her a task suited to her talents, and he knew well she would not treat it lightly. Still, a tightness lingered beneath his ribs. He could not deny that part of him didn't want her near any danger.

As they crested the final rise, hooves drummed behind them. Alex twisted in the saddle, just in time to see a second carriage turning up the lane. It was familiar, elegant, and unmistakably Georgina's.

His breath caught, not with surprise, but with a sharp spark of anticipation. She had found something. He could see it in the firm set of her shoulders, the way she leaned forward as if eager to close the distance between them.

Barrington's gaze flicked toward him, then to the carriage, his eyes sharpening. "Looks as though your lady has not been idle."

"It certainly does," Alex replied, already swinging down from his mount.

The coach drew to a halt almost alongside them, and before the footman could descend, Alex was there, opening the door himself.

Georgina met his gaze, her chin lifting in quiet triumph. Without a word, she placed the folio in his hand.

Alex's eyes fell to the bundle, its worn ribbon barely holding its contents. He didn't open it. There would be time for that once they got inside. But he felt its significance as surely as if the pages burned in his palm.

Their gazes held, something unspoken passing between them.

"You've found the trail," he said softly.

"No," she said. "*We* did."

Chapter Fifteen

T HE FOLIO LAY between them on the desk at Sommer Chase, its worn edges softened by time and travel. The desk itself bore the faint scent of lemon polish and old parchment, its surface dappled with late afternoon light that filtered through the tall windows. Dust motes swirled lazily in the golden shafts, as if unwilling to settle where decisions were being made.

Georgina kept her hands clasped in her lap, resisting the urge to smooth the parchment or press it flat, anything to fill the silence. The dark leather chair beneath her creaked softly when she shifted, a sound quickly swallowed by the hush of the room.

Alex stood behind the chair, neither sitting nor moving, only watching the folio as if it might reveal its secrets without being opened. His silhouette was still against the fireless hearth, framed by the worn stone mantle and a wall of books so orderly it bordered on severe.

It struck her then how still he could be, how his restraint was not cold but practiced. A man used to standing ready for orders. For danger. For truths that came with a cost. Something in that quiet steadiness drew her more than any charm could have. He hesitated not because he doubted her, but because he understood the importance of what they were about to uncover.

"I suppose we ought to begin," she said, her voice steadier than she felt.

Alex nodded once, then opened the cover with a soldier's calm. He turned the first page slowly, as if rushing might alter what was written. Georgina leaned in. Barrington remained a quiet presence at the window, letting the importance of the moment settle before he spoke.

There it was. A line halfway down the page, a familiar format, a common enough entry, and a word that snagged her attention before she fully read it.

"There. It's spelled 'commision.' Just like the other one."

Alex leaned over the document for a better view. "The same mistake?"

"Commision," she murmured, narrowing her eyes. "It's spelled incorrectly."

She paused, a small catch tightening in her throat. Rowland had once misspelled it, but after correcting himself, he became almost obsessive about getting it right, even overcorrecting others, especially his aunt. He'd circled her error three times in red ink, unforgivable, he wrote next to it, along with a silly sketch of a hangman's noose in the margin. She'd thrown a cushion at his head.

No, he would never let that error stand.

"And," Barrington looked over the document as well, "they almost got away with it. Twice."

She nodded slowly. "The same spelling error. The exact same one as before. This isn't a coincidence. It's a pattern. Someone's trying to make this look like Rowland's doing and doing it badly."

Barrington stepped in beside them. "That confirms it. Two separate documents with the same flaw? Either someone's careless… or confident no one would notice."

Georgina nodded. "He didn't write this. But, if it wasn't Rowland, then someone else wanted it to look as though he had."

Alex glanced toward her then, the faintest trace of something softer beneath the discipline. "You see what others overlook."

The quiet praise sent a warmth through her that had nothing to do with the fireless hearth.

A quiet knock interrupted them.

Kenworth stepped in, bearing a porcelain tray and an apologetic expression. "Forgive me, but Mrs. Bainbridge insisted I not let the tea grow cold."

"Tea for four seemed insufficient," Mrs. Bainbridge said as she swept into the room with a tilt of her head. "I assumed you'd be deep in something unpalatable. Forgery, was it?"

Georgina blinked, caught between admiration and exasperation. "You always arrive at the perfect moment."

"I try," Mrs. Bainbridge said smoothly. "And I brought lemon cake. No one thinks clearly on an empty stomach. Besides, I need your opinion about the cake."

Barrington glanced at his bride-to-be. "More wedding cake tasting."

"The baker sent this along and asked for our opinion. I couldn't refuse." Mrs. Bainbridge sliced the cake while Georgina poured the tea.

"Is Mr. Carver the traitor?" Mrs. Bainbridge asked as she held out a plate. "He appears so trustworthy."

"It's always the ones you trust that do the worst of it." Barrington took a plate of lemon cake from Mrs. Bainbridge. "Like that major during the war, turned faster than Benedict Arnold."

"Rowland used to say, He brings gloves to every handshake," Georgina said, setting her cup down with care. "I always thought it was just one of his odd little sayings, clever, but harmless."

Everyone paused and glanced at her.

"It meant they never showed their true skin," she continued. "They always kept a layer between themselves and everyone else."

She smiled faintly, a small tilt of her head. "He used it once at a dinner party, when a magistrate spent twenty minutes praising a bill he'd voted against only the week before. Rowland just nodded, then leaned toward me and whispered it, gloves on, even for handshakes. I thought it was a comment on fashion. It took me a year to realize he was warning me."

Mrs. Bainbridge finished stirring her tea, placed the spoon on the saucer, and raised her cup. "Then half the House of Lords must be suspects." She sipped her tea while a soft chuckle filled the room.

"Even so," Alex said, setting his cup aside, "I think we'd better keep an eye on the gloves."

The warmth of the moment faded into thoughtful silence, and Georgina set her teacup down with care.

"Before I came to Sommer Chase," she said softly, "I received a visit from one of the tradesmen's wives."

Everyone gave her their attention.

"She didn't ask for anything. She only wanted to be heard," Georgina said softly. "Her husband had come home shaken. He told her there'd been talk about deliveries gone missing, men being warned to keep quiet."

She hesitated, her voice gentling. "She didn't even sit. Just stood in the hallway, wringing her hands in her apron. I offered tea, but she refused. Said she couldn't stay long. Her little boy was waiting just outside the gate."

Barrington's expression darkened.

"She said her husband wouldn't speak of it again. Not even to her. Said he didn't want trouble. He said that he'd already seen what happened to others who asked questions, but she did mention that the man watched their house for days afterwards. I told her that she would be protected.

"She didn't give her name at first. She just said her husband was stationed at the southern shaft. But I recognized her. Mrs. Kellett. Her boy attends the Sunday lessons. She's a quiet woman, and always the last to leave."

Georgina drew in a breath and looked between the three of them. "This isn't just about money or records. It's pressure. It's fear. Someone is making sure the truth stays buried by any means."

"It's too organized," Barrington said, jaw set. "Too methodical. Too Order-like. It confirms my fears that the subversion extends beyond management and into the workers and their families."

He moved toward the hearth, resting one hand on the mantel as if grounding himself. "You've heard me mention them before, the Order of Shadows. A name that sounds like superstition to some, but make no mistake. They're real. A network buried deep in the corners of government, trade, and industry. They don't seek attention. They seek control."

He turned to face them, his expression sharp. "This mine, our region's entire coal supply, isn't just valuable. It's strategic. Whoever controls it controls transport. Commerce. Power. And if the Order wants that control, they won't stop at forgeries and whispers. They'll bury anyone who gets in their way."

Georgina exhaled slowly. The weight of the woman's trust settled heavily on her shoulders. She had given her word that Mrs. Kellett would be protected. But how? Against whom? Her promise had been instinctive, but now it felt perilous. Truth was a fragile shield when power hid in shadows.

"You may be correct." Alex moved to the edge of his chair. "We need to plan our next steps. We revisit Trentham & Clegg and look further. Whoever forged that invoice used their name for a reason. I want to know if it's happened elsewhere."

Barrington crossed to the sideboard and unrolled a worn map of the region. "We'll start with Carver again. I want a second conversation, one where we don't let him set the tone. If he's hiding something, it ends now."

Georgina leaned in beside them. "And the mine ledgers. We need to see how much damage has already been done."

Alex glanced toward her, something unreadable flickering behind his eyes. She'd stepped into this fully, not with hesitation, but with clarity.

"Are you with us?" he asked quietly.

She met his gaze without flinching. "Reporting for duty."

The corner of his mouth lifted, not a smile, not entirely, but enough to tell her he'd heard more in those words than agreement. For once, she didn't look away.

It wasn't said lightly. Those three words held the weight of her name, her grief, and her choice to stand beside them. She had crossed an invisible line. She was no longer a widow sorting papers, but a woman stepping into the heart of something larger, more dangerous, and far more personal than she'd ever anticipated.

Alex held her gaze for a beat longer. Then he nodded, once, short and sure. Not as a commander giving orders, but as a man recognizing a comrade.

They weren't soldiers. Not really. But at that moment, they might as well have been.

A rustle at the doorway broke the moment. Kenworth stepped in again, this time without a tray.

"Apologies, sir," he said quietly. "This was found by the side entrance. No one saw who left it."

He held out a plain envelope. No seal. No name.

Alex opened the envelope and found a single sheet of folded paper. He unfolded it.

The ink was smudged, the message brief. The paper was coarse, folded twice, and still damp at the edges as if it had traveled far through rain or sweat.

Some things buried are best left that way.

No signature. No threat. And yet the air shifted, colder than before.

Georgina stepped closer, reading the words over Alex's shoulder. She didn't say anything. She didn't need to.

They'd been noticed.

Chapter Sixteen

THE AIR THICKENED the closer they came to Carver's land. It wasn't the weather. The day was clear enough, the sky was low and gray but dry. No, it was something else. The stillness of the trees. The hush of animals gone to ground. A kind of breathless silence.

Even the horses seemed to sense it. There was a shift in Alex's mount's gait, a wariness in its steps, as though the very earth had turned cautious. Somewhere in the brush, a bird called once and then fell silent.

He adjusted the reins with one hand, the leather familiar and grounding beneath his fingers. Every muscle in his body was alert, not from fear, but from readiness. The kind honed over years of campaign, when the land itself whispered of danger, and silence pressed too tightly around the edges of thought.

Alex had felt it before. Before battle. Before loss. He didn't like it.

He glanced sideways at Georgina, though he already knew what he'd see. Her posture was straight, her chin set. Not stiff, not defiant, just determined. She wasn't here with his permission, but by her own decision.

He tried to remember the last time someone had made a decision like that. A decision that was rooted not in duty or fear, but in conviction. She had no obligation to be here. No promise to keep. And yet she'd stepped forward anyway, into danger, into uncertainty, into something even he couldn't name.

He'd always admired her intelligence. Her ability to listen without interrupting, to notice without seeking attention. But this, this calm, steady resolve, was something different. Something rare.

She didn't belong in a world of forged ledgers and shadowy threats. And yet she did. She saw what others missed. She heard what men ignored. She brought clarity to things he'd trained himself not to feel.

He knew what he felt for her. He didn't question it. Admiration had long since turned to something deeper, quieter, and far more dangerous. What troubled him now was how much he needed her to stay safe, and how little control he had over that here.

The path to the house was muddy from yesterday's rain. The ruts were deep and careless. No one had come through with a wagon. No one had cared to smooth the way.

When they reached the front gate, Alex dismounted first, scanning the yard with a soldier's instinct. The stables stood quiet. A shutter on the second floor hung crooked on its hinge, tapping gently in the breeze.

Carver opened the door before they could knock.

He looked worse than before, drawn, sweat-damp, and hollow-eyed. His shirt was buttoned wrong, and there was a smear of coal dust across his collarbone, as if he'd scrubbed himself clean but hadn't bothered to check the mirror.

Alex didn't speak. Neither did Carver.

"Where is your family?" Georgina asked, breaking the silence.

Carver blinked, the question landing like a stone in a pond. "They're not here," he said after a heartbeat. "Went north."

"Why?" she asked gently. Not accusing, not prodding, just asking.

Carver's mouth pulled tight. "Safer that way."

Alex stepped forward. "Safer from what?"

Carver's gaze dropped to the porch boards. He didn't answer.

Wordlessly, Carver stepped back and let them in.

The interior was dim. One lamp burned low on the table. A child's boot sat beneath the table, half tucked under a chair. Forgotten. Or maybe left on purpose. A reminder.

The air held the musty scent of old coal and ash. It wasn't filth, not exactly, just abandoned. It was as if the soul of the place had left with the people who had once made it a home.

They didn't sit.

"We know someone's using the mine records," Barrington said, stepping beside Alex. "Forging documents. Covering tracks."

Carver said nothing.

"The subversion goes beyond accidents," Alex added. "And we think you know who's behind it."

Carver's jaw flexed. "I don't."

Georgina moved past both men, quiet as breath, and rested her gloved hand on the back of a worn chair but made no move to sit. "Tom," she said gently.

He flinched at the sound of his first name.

"You said Rowland once helped you," she continued. "Do you remember what he said?"

Carver's gaze flicked toward her, then he looked away. "Said I should watch my accounts more closely. That some numbers didn't add up."

"Did he tell you why?"

Carver swallowed hard. "He thought someone was watching my shipments. The coal that left my mine didn't match what reached the docks."

"And did it?" she asked.

He nodded once. "No. He was right. I just didn't want to believe it."

"Who else knew?"

Carver hesitated. His eyes met hers again, and this time, held.

His throat worked as if he were forcing the words past something bitter. "I don't know their names," he said finally. "But I saw one of 'em. Came to my house late once. Said if I didn't keep quiet, my wife might fall down a flight of stairs. My boy, too."

He looked away again, jaw clenching. "My boy's only seven. Thinks he's off on an adventure. Doesn't know why he can't write home."

Georgina's hand tensed against the chair, but she didn't speak. She gave him space, and that quiet filled the room like breath after drowning.

Carver's voice dropped to a rasp. "I sent them north with a friend I trust. Didn't tell them why. Didn't say how long. Just... gone."

Georgina's voice was barely a whisper. "That's why you sent them away."

Carver nodded. "They don't know where they are. No one does. And I'm not about to tell anyone."

Something shifted, not in Carver, but in himself. He'd come here prepared for denial. For evasion. He hadn't expected fear. Real fear.

And Georgina, she hadn't just uncovered it. She had carried it like it was hers.

Carver didn't offer more. He didn't need to.

Barrington gave a short nod, jaw tense. "We'll speak again."

Carver didn't answer. His silence wasn't defiance anymore. It was exhaustion. Survival. He looked like a man who'd bartered away every piece of peace he had left just to keep the people he loved alive.

Barrington gave Alex a glance, then stepped back toward the door. "I'll keep watch." The click of the latch behind him left the room quieter than before.

"Thank you, Tom," Georgina said softly. "I hope your family will be able to come home soon."

They stepped back into the fading light. The sun was low now, throwing long shadows across the path. Georgina didn't speak. Neither did Alex.

Not until they reached the edge of the gate.

"You did well," he said quietly.

She looked up, brow furrowing. "I didn't do anything."

"You got through to him. That's more than I could've done."

Georgina shook her head, a half-smile tugging at the corner of her mouth. "No. He just needed someone to ask the right questions."

Alex stopped walking.

She turned to face him.

"I saw the way he looked at you," he said. "Like you were safe to speak to. Like you weren't going to use what he said against him. That's not something you can fake."

Her gaze dropped, just for a moment. "You're not angry I came?"

"Angry? No. I needed you here. More than I knew."

The silence between them held more than the fading light could contain.

She wanted to speak, to thank him, to scold him, to ask if he still dreamed of her, but every word was perilously close to a confession.

Instead, she looked at his hands, steady at his sides, and thought how easily strength could disguise tenderness.

That surprised her. Not the words, but the way he said them. Like, there was no space left for pretense.

He stepped closer.

"I knew what I felt for you before we came here," he said. "But seeing you in there, not backing down, not looking away, made me want you in a way that doesn't fit the life I've known."

Her breath caught.

"Then maybe that life was never meant to hold this," she said. "You don't have to make it fit. You just have to choose it."

His hand brushed hers, lightly, reverently, and for a long moment, neither moved. The wind caught her hair and tangled it across her cheek, and he reached to smooth it back. Not urgent. Not possessive. Just… present. For a heartbeat, the world held its breath with them, the air between their faces carrying the faint scent of rain and coal dust, something ordinary turned sacred.

"Then I'll build the life that can hold it," he said. "With you."

For an instant, she couldn't breathe. The words were simple, but they carried the kind of promise that remade the air itself.

She saw in him not the soldier or the earl, but the man who had finally stopped running from duty, from desire, from her.

And the knowledge settled in her chest like warmth breaking through frost.

A hush passed through her, not from surprise, but from recognition. From the sound of something solid settling into place.

She didn't answer him with words. She stepped forward instead, closing the last inch between them, and kissed him.

It wasn't rushed, or questioning, or bold. It was quiet. Certain. A seal on something that had already begun to live between them, wordless and real.

When she pulled back, she didn't look away. And he didn't let go.

For a moment, there was only the sound of their breathing. The world held still. The hush was different now. It was no longer the silence before battle, but something gentler. The kind that came after the truth had been spoken.

Alex brushed his thumb along the side of her hand. He didn't speak. He didn't need to. Everything that mattered had already passed between them, unspoken but undeniable.

Georgina's gaze softened, her lips still tingling, her heart steady in a way it hadn't been in years. The steadiness frightened her almost as much as the kiss itself. It meant she could no longer pretend this was temporary. She didn't feel swept away. She was anchored.

And then the air shifted.

The sound reached them a heartbeat later. The distant rhythm of hooves, fast but uneven, echoed off the ridge. Hoofbeats on packed earth, too deliberate for a casual rider.

Alex's jaw tensed. He turned, scanning the tree line, every instinct coiled. The hoofbeats were too steady, too sharp. Not a merchant's sway or a messenger's clatter. A searcher's rhythm.

Intentional. "Someone's coming," he said.

Georgina stepped back just enough to adjust her gloves, her voice calm but sharp with awareness. "Let them."

They walked back toward the horses in silence, not awkward, but full. Full of what had been said, and what didn't need to be. Alex glanced down once as their shoulders brushed. His hand hovered for a moment, then settled at the small of her back, a simple gesture that said: you're not alone in this.

Georgina didn't flinch from the contact. If anything, she leaned slightly into it.

Then came the second echo of hoofbeats, louder this time, carrying speed and urgency.

Alex's hand fell away, replaced by instinct. He turned to face the sound head-on, listening for weight in the stride, for familiarity in the rhythm. It wasn't one of theirs. The tempo was wrong by half a beat. A single rider. Not charging but not meandering either.

"They're not lost," Alex murmured. "They're looking for someone."

Chapter Seventeen

THEY RODE IN silence until Georgina's gate came into view. The lanterns were already lit against the gathering dusk. Alex dismounted first, offering his hand as she stepped down from her saddle with more grace than he had any right to expect after such a day.

"I'll study the receipts and ledgers," she said, her voice low and steady.

He didn't answer right away. He watched as she slipped inside, the folio still tucked under her arm. When the door closed behind her, he turned back to Barrington.

"We'll need her insight on the rest of it," Alex said as he mounted his horse.

"And ensure she is out of harm's way," Barrington said. "There is much to discuss. Let's get to Sommer Chase."

A soft glow shone from one of the upper windows of Ravenstock Manor as they turned from the gate. Alex lingered a moment, glancing back. He couldn't see her, but he pictured her at her desk, head bent over the folio, sleeves pushed up, determination set in every line of her.

"You've seen that look before," Barrington said as he nudged his horse into motion.

"On you," Alex replied. "Just before we breached the southern wall at Ciudad Rodrigo."

Barrington gave a dry grunt. "That ended with a limp and three days unconscious. Let's hope she's smarter than we were."

The ride to Barrington's estate passed in near silence, the kind of silence that settles between two men already thinking in the same direction. The sun had slipped low by the time they turned off the coastal road, casting long shadows across the frost-dusted hedgerows. Alex let his horse fall into pace beside Barrington's.

"Carver wasn't just afraid," Alex said quietly. "He'd already surrendered."

Barrington gave a single nod. "That kind of fear doesn't come from one man with a ledger. It comes from the kind of pressure you don't talk about. The kind they used during the war."

Alex glanced at him. "You think it's the Order."

"I'd stake my commission on it." He guided his mount through the open gate. "They isolate, threaten, then wait. They watch a man ruin himself to protect his family."

Barrington added another log to the fire and settled back into his chair.

"This isn't just about stolen coal," he said, eyes fixed on the flame. "It's too deliberate."

Alex looked over. "You think it's orchestrated."

"I think someone's pulling strings we haven't even seen yet. Quiet hands. Patient ones."

Alex's brow tightened. "You have a name?"

Barrington shook his head. "Not yet. But if I ever meet the man behind this, I'll recognize his methods."

Alex thought of Carver's stiff posture, his clipped answers, the way his eyes kept darting toward the empty yard. It hadn't been resistance. It had been resignation. And he'd seen it before. It had been in his father's eyes, just before the estate began its slow decline. The silence after his father signed away his shipping contract had been heavier than any raised voice. And he had missed it entirely, too young to see what fear looked like in a man who had run out of options.

Barrington didn't bother removing his coat once inside. Instead, he led Alex straight to the study, where a fire already smoldered low. He crossed to his writing desk and pulled out a fresh sheet of parchment.

"Edward needs to know what we've found."

Alex dropped into the leather chair opposite. "Will he listen?"

"He's been listening for years. He just hasn't had proof." Barrington dipped his pen, scrawling in a tight, decisive hand. "There's a rot in government, and Edward means to dig it out. I just need to give him the spade."

Alex watched the ink pool into clean lines. "You trust him?"

"With my life." He paused. "And with Honoria's."

Alex looked up. Barrington gave a wry twist of a smile. "He's been telling me to marry Honoria for years. Said I was wasting her time, and mine. I asked her more than once."

"She said no?"

"She said I was more fun unmarried." Barrington set down the pen. "Until this last time. I knew the minute I looked into her eyes that she would say yes."

Alex let out a low breath, not quite a laugh. "He'll be unbearable when you tell him."

"Delirious with triumph," Barrington agreed. "He'll probably demand a seat at the planning table. He already gave Honoria a list of people for the wedding."

Alex gave a half smile but didn't respond. He rose, crossed to the fire, and stood watching the flames.

"You're thinking of Georgina," Barrington said.

Alex didn't deny it. "She's in it now. No more questions. No more hesitations. She's too clever not to see what this is becoming."

Barrington added another log to the fire and settled back into his chair. "There was a man I knew once, Lieutenant Wade. Clever as anything. Saw subversiveness where none of us did, except one time, and then it was too late. He trusted a supplier we shouldn't have. Cost twenty men their lives."

Alex looked toward the flames, jaw tight. "We won't let that happen here."

"No," Barrington said. "Because we have Georgina Ravenstock. And we won't let her carry the burden alone."

"And we make damn sure she never stands alone."

The two settled into quiet contemplation.

The door creaked open not long after, and Georgina stepped in without knocking, the folio under her arm.

Kenworth brought tea and vanished, leaving behind a neatly folded note beside the pot.

If you're planning treason, sirs, at least let me iron my coat first.

Alex smirked and handed it to Barrington, who shook his head and tucked it into his pocket.

"You're not sleeping," Alex said.

"Neither are you," she replied. "I couldn't rest until I was certain we hadn't missed something." She set the folio on the desk and opened it. "I went through everything again, this time tracing the pattern from the invoices forward instead of backward. Rowland had marked several entries twice. The same date and phrase were used, with delivery scheduled for offshore cargo, but no location was listed. It's repeated in two different hands. One looks like Rowland's. The other, I can't identify."

"Different slope, different rhythm," she said. "Rowland wrote decisively. This... this looks like it was added in haste. Or in secrecy."

Barrington joined them, studying the page. "That's not local delivery language. That's shipping."

"I agree. What struck me was that there's no port listed," Georgina said. "Nor a recipient. Just a mark and an abbreviation. R.T.S."

Alex leaned in, tracing the edge of the ink with one finger. "Then we need the port records. Sommer-by-the-Sea's dockmaster logs. That will tell us what ships came in, which ones left, and what the cargo they carried."

Barrington gave a thoughtful nod. "Or we contact Mr. Seaton. He was nearly killed for uncovering false freight entries. The

Order wanted his daughter married to their puppet so they could control the entire Seaton fleet."

"Didn't they hold Viscount Hollingsworth in prison to keep him out of the way?" Georgina asked.

"Three years," Barrington said. "The marriage plans failed, thanks to Seaton's stubbornness, his daughter's spine, and the viscount's determination."

"Is Seaton still at the docks?"

"In Portsmouth now," Barrington replied. "But he'll help us. If those shipments were bound for a port he's touched, he'll know what to look for."

She looked back at the folio. "And he might recognize *R.T.S.*"

"If it's a route or a code, yes," Barrington said. "We'll send him word tonight."

"If they're shipping stolen coal, it won't be in plain sight." Barrington looked at both of them. "But the gaps will be there. You don't move that much weight without someone noticing."

"Unless someone was paid not to notice," Georgina murmured.

There was a brief silence. The only sound was the crackling of the fire.

Alex looked at her, not the folio. She stood with her arms crossed. She was determined, brilliant, and unshaken. And for the first time, he didn't fear losing her heart, but rather the sharp, hollow fear of losing her entirely.

He'd spent years guarding what was left of his world, his estate, his name, the ghosts of men who had trusted him. But this was different. Georgina wasn't something to preserve. She was someone to stand beside, someone who turned quiet deduction into revelation, someone who made him believe that not all was lost. And suddenly, what he wanted most wasn't the protection of what remained. He wanted to protect what could possibly be their future together.

"We start with the ships," Alex said.

She nodded. "If Rowland saw this, he knew it was bigger than one mine."

Alex met her gaze. "Then we follow the shipments. And we find out who's been profiting."

He didn't move right away. The room had settled and become quiet once again, but his pulse had not. Slowly, he reached across the desk and drew the folio closer, brushing her fingers as he did. Her hand remained where it was, steady and unflinching, the faintest warmth lingering between them.

Barrington cleared his throat, but the sound was not entirely necessary.

"Kenworth can be ready within the hour," he said, his voice dry. "He'll ride for Portsmouth with a sealed message for Seaton. We'll ask for shipping records from the past six months, flagged for any coal-related entries and anything marked *R.T.S.*"

Georgina withdrew her hand and turned to Barrington with a nod. "And if he finds nothing?"

"Then we dig deeper," Alex said. "This time, we know where to look."

Barrington moved toward the door, calling for Kenworth to prepare the dispatch. Georgina remained where she was for a moment longer, her eyes still on the folio.

"You'll tell me the moment you hear from Seaton?" she asked.

Alex nodded. "You'll be the first."

The fire popped in the grate. She reached forward and turned one of the documents slightly, aligning it just so. It wasn't nerves, more like precision. Or ownership. She was part of this now. No less than either of them.

Barrington paused at the door and glanced back. "My men used to say the ones with the questions were the most dangerous." He offered her a smile, the kind that left you feeling uplifted and appreciated. "You ask the right ones, Lady Ravenstock."

She met his gaze, neither flattered nor dismissive. "I was married to a man who trusted quietly and died anyway. I'd rather ask questions."

A flicker of approval crossed Barrington's face.

Minutes later, Kenworth returned in full riding gear, the sealed letter in hand. "Any message for Seaton besides what's written?" he asked Alex.

Alex handed him the folded folio copy. "Tell him this one's not forged. And take the fast route. But not the obvious one."

Kenworth gave a half-bow and a wink. "Always do. Back before dawn if the wind's in our favor."

They watched him go in silence, the door closing softly behind him. The only sound was the fire, and the quiet rustle of paper as Georgina turned another page.

"Rowland used to keep a list," she said softly, almost to herself. "Not of partners. It was a list of names he wouldn't do business with. He said it wasn't worth the coin if he couldn't trust the weight."

Alex turned back toward her. "Do you still have it?"

"It might still be in his desk," she said. "Or the safe. I haven't gone through everything yet."

Barrington crossed to the fire and nudged the logs. "Then you'll look. Carefully. We'll follow the manifests, and you chase the names."

She nodded once. "Agreed."

Alex moved to her side. "I'll walk you out."

They crossed the hall in silence, the shadows longer now, but less heavy. Outside, her carriage stood, lamps lit, the horses shifting gently in the cool night air.

At the step, she turned.

She hadn't said anything, hadn't reached for him, and yet there was a shift in the air between them. It was familiar and charged, like the moment before a storm that might cleanse instead of destroy.

"There are times you amaze me, Georgina. How did I not see this before?"

As they continued to the carriage, she tilted her head, a smile catching at the corners of her mouth. "Perhaps you weren't looking."

That smile lingered in his thoughts. It wasn't flirtation. It was confidence. She was a woman who no longer asked to be seen, but rather a woman who decided who was worthy to see her.

The carriage door was already open. Alex offered her his hand, steady and sure, as he guided her inside. She didn't release it right away. She just held his gaze for a moment longer, and something quiet and unspoken passed between them.

It wasn't a promise. Not yet. But it was a possibility, and that might be rarer still.

"Be careful," she said.

"You too," he answered, and for once, meant every word.

He closed the door with care and remained there as the driver snapped the reins. The carriage rolled forward, the gravel crunching under the wheels. He didn't move until the glow of lamps vanished beyond the trees. The night was colder for her absence, though the warmth she'd left behind refused to fade.

He had faced down rifles, traitors, betrayal, but nothing had left him so still inside as the space she left behind.

Chapter Eighteen

GEORGINA TRIED ONCE more to open the middle drawer of Rowland's desk, biting the inside of her cheek as she jiggled the lock. It was stubborn, resistant, and increasingly personal. She had been working on it for over an hour. She went into the dining room, removed a butter knife from the table, and went back into Rowland's study. She sat down, ready to try one more time, when the unmistakable clamor of two determined women echoed through the front hall.

A moment later, Mrs. Hemsley appeared in the doorway, her expression equal parts resigned and amused. "You have company, my lady. The spirited kind."

Before Georgina could stand, Mrs. Bainbridge swept into the room in a flurry of purpose and silk trim. Eliza Langford followed, her cheeks pink from the wind and eyes bright with mischief.

"There you are!" Mrs. Bainbridge declared. "Exactly where I feared you'd be, elbow deep in receipts."

Georgina raised an eyebrow. "Good morning to you as well."

"No, no. Absolutely not," Eliza said, moving to confiscate the nearest folio. "We are abducting you. Tea. Cake. Perhaps scandal, if we're lucky."

"I was in the middle of something." Georgina put down the knife and tried to suppress a smile.

"And you will be again," Mrs. Bainbridge said smoothly. "But for now, you are coming with us. You've been entirely too industrious of late, and I won't have you turning into Honoria Two."

Georgina glanced at her. "You are Honoria."

"Precisely," she replied. "And no one needs two of me. Come along. I have lemon cake to discuss."

Georgina hesitated, glancing back at the half-open folio on the desk. She had made real progress that morning, and part of her complained about the idea of abandoning the thread. But the warmth in Mrs. Bainbridge's eyes and the spark of mischief that trailed behind Eliza like a scarf on the wind softened her resistance. She missed this. She missed being seen for more than her responsibilities.

"I suppose it won't do to turn into Honoria Two," she said, rising.

"Perish the thought," Mrs. Bainbridge said dryly as she took Georgina's wool cloak from Mrs. Hemsley and helped her into it. "There. We are ready to leave."

Georgina allowed herself to be ushered out, the sounds of Eliza and Honoria already sparking ahead like the opening notes of a lively overture.

The Rostov Tearoom in Sommer-by-the-Sea was bustling with quiet energy, its blue damask wallpaper catching the golden lamplight as the sun gathered beyond the windows. Painted panels framed each section with white wainscoting, and every table was dressed in crisp white linen, a lace overlay catching the light like frost. Small vases of late-autumn blooms sat neatly at the center of each table, red quince, dried lavender, and dusky orange rose hips gave the room a warm, russet glow.

Georgina paused just inside the entrance, breathing in the comforting aroma of black tea and something earthy, mushroom barley soup. A favorite in colder months. She hadn't realized how taut her shoulders had become until the scent reached her, loosening something inside.

They were shown to a table beneath the large front window, where the last of the morning light met the flicker of a table candle. Georgina slipped off her gloves and let her fingers rest against the smooth linen. Tatiana Rostov passed by with a welcoming smile and a glint in her eye, whispering something to a server who promptly vanished in the direction of the kitchen.

Eliza leaned in, already unwrapping her scarf. "You have no idea what you've missed. Mrs. Penworthy's cat has now taken up residence at the Milliner's, and young Mr. Tattleton is courting both seamstress sisters with alarming success."

"Only one of them knows it," Mrs. Bainbridge added, lifting a menu. "So far."

Georgina laughed, the sound catching her by surprise.

Within minutes, tea was served, along with warm bread and a plate of sweet scones that looked almost too pretty to eat. Tatiana Rostov returned with the lemon cake, setting the tray down with a flourish.

"I've never seen three more determined women in my tea-room," she said with a wink. "If the cake fails, I'll have to add you to the menu to keep the customers coming."

Mrs. Bainbridge patted her hand. "If we make it to the wedding without a public scandal, it'll be a miracle."

Georgina smiled. "Tatiana, have you changed the tea blend?"

"A touch of orange peel," she said proudly. "Autumn demands something a little brighter."

The proprietor disappeared again, leaving behind a thread of citrus and steam in her wake. The air was full of the scent of honey, spice, and freshly steeped leaves. It was impossible to hold on to anything heavy.

"The lemon cake," Mrs. Bainbridge announced, cutting a square with precision, "is the clear winner. Edward agrees, and that man eats like a bishop on a fast day. I have declared the matter closed."

Georgina took a bite and hummed in agreement. The lemon was vivid and sharp, the cake delicate beneath it. "Rowland hated lemon," she said idly. "Once, he pretended to enjoy an entire tart just to impress a visiting solicitor. I don't think his mouth ever forgave him."

Eliza grinned. "That's love."

"Or politics," Georgina said, amused. "But it was kind, in its way."

"If someone ate something revolting for you, would you marry them?" Eliza asked suddenly. "Or at least give them a second dance?"

Mrs. Bainbridge gave her a look over her teacup. "Is that how you're measuring affection now?"

"And the gown?" She asked rather than answer the question.

"Madame Pembroke has outdone herself. Rose blush silk, fitted bodice, embroidery so fine I wept a little. Quietly. In private."

"And the venue?" Georgina ventured.

Mrs. Bainbridge's smile faltered. "Rosalynde Bay is… intimate. Which is to say, insufficient. I refuse to be married in a barn, no matter how charming."

"You could try the Assembly Rooms," Eliza suggested.

"I will not," Honoria said flatly. "But I may have to."

They laughed, and for a long while, the world beyond tea and satin and lemon glaze simply didn't exist.

Eliza said, too casually, "I've met someone."

Georgina arched a brow. "Have you?"

"I have. He's charming. Clever. Not entirely alarming."

"That's a very specific kind of praise," Georgina said, smiling. "Who is he?"

"Julian Everly," Eliza replied, lifting her cup. "And before you ask, yes, he is handsome. I wouldn't waste our time otherwise."

Mrs. Bainbridge's fingers paused ever so slightly on the cake knife. A flicker, gone too quickly to name, crossed her expression before she smiled.

"Everly?" Georgina repeated the name, snagging oddly in her thoughts. "I've seen that name before."

"Eliza," Mrs. Bainbridge said carefully, "where did you say you met him?"

"At the bookseller. He recommended a dreadful novel and a delightful play. I liked his voice. And his coat."

The moment passed lightly but not unmarked.

"I should like to meet him," Georgina said.

"Oh, you will," Eliza promised. "Unless I've scared him off by being exactly myself."

Mrs. Bainbridge reached for another slice of cake. "If he survives that, he might be worth keeping."

Eliza laughed and leaned back in her chair. "Tell me something, either of you. What does it feel like when it's right?"

The smile on Eliza's face shifted, touched now by something more thoughtful.

"Just curious," Eliza said lightly, but there was something behind the question, some shadow of her own wondering. "Were you jealous of Celia?"

Georgina blinked, startled by the question, then laughed. "Not in the least. We all knew each other well, Alex, Celia, Rowland, and I. Celia was lovely. Alone and with him. There was no need for envy."

She sipped her tea. "And before you ask. Yes, he grieved her properly. And quietly. That's the kind of man he's always been."

Mrs. Bainbridge gave a small, approving nod. "Grief doesn't always need trumpets."

Eliza looked faintly chastised. "I didn't mean—"

"I know," Georgina said gently. "But I think it's important to say." She set her cup down. "You mean the kind that leaves a mark."

Eliza nodded slowly, her smile softened by something quieter. "Exactly that. Not convenient. Not polite. Not a match on paper. I mean the kind that leaves a mark."

Mrs. Bainbridge looked briefly toward the window. "You don't notice right away. At least, I didn't. I just found myself breathing easier around him."

Georgina stirred her tea, watching the leaves settle. "You stop defending the parts of yourself you thought you had to protect.

And you realize someone saw them before you did."

They lingered through the noon hour, letting time stretch. When the server returned with a final pot of tea and a plate of candied lemon peel, Georgina realized with quiet wonder that she was smiling more easily than she had in days. Not politely. Not as a defense. But from something nearer contentment.

When they parted at the carriage, Eliza kissed her cheek and whispered, "You haven't vanished, you know. You're just a little misplaced. We're glad to have found you."

Mrs. Bainbridge added, "And don't pretend you didn't need cake."

Georgina laughed again, not because she meant to, but because something inside her had shifted loose. Something she hadn't known was held so tightly. She returned to Ravenstock Manor warm from laughter, her cheeks tingling from the cold and the long-forgotten exercise of smiling.

The laughter still clung to her like warmth from the fire, a small ember she carried home.

The house felt different now. It was less like a monument, more like a home. She paused in the front hall, where the warmth of the day followed her inside. The sunlight spilled through the transom windows and caught in the polish of the banister like light caught in memory.

The air carried the faint scent of lavender from Mrs. Hemsley's morning efforts, and somewhere in the distance, the clock in the front parlor gave a single, decisive chime. Her gaze flicked to the framed etching that had always hung by the staircase. It was Rowland's taste, precise and humorless, and then she glanced at the vase on the console table, perpetually crooked and still just so.

Her hand brushed the doorframe as she crossed to the study. For a moment, she paused there, looking in. The desk was no longer a barrier. It was an invitation. A place waiting for something to begin.

Her boots clicked softly on the stone as she crossed the

threshold.

She set her gloves on the desk, hesitating for only a breath. Her fingers hovered above the drawer that had resisted her earlier, as if the desk itself had finally decided to relent. It opened without resistance. She smiled, pleased with herself, reached inside, and removed the household expense ledger.

Her fingers closed around it before her mind caught up. It was a slip of paper folded with intention, worn thin at the creases. As she opened it, she remembered not the document but a moment. It was last autumn. Rowland was standing by the window, folding something just like this and sliding it into a ledger with quiet finality. She'd asked what it was, and he'd smiled faintly, said, 'Something for later.'

At the time, she thought he meant a debt. Now she wondered if he meant a warning. This time, she found the list.

She brushed her fingertips over the folded paper tucked inside the household ledger as a place marker. She gently unfolded the paper. It was a list of names. No one would have thought to look for anything that important in the household ledger. But she knew Rowland's habits. He'd always trusted his own codes over a locked drawer.

There were twelve names on the list, most of which she didn't recognize. But one stopped her cold.

S. Mallory.

She had seen that name before. Her breath caught, the air around her suddenly still. A memory surged. Alex's tone, a passing mention weeks ago, and a flash of parchment in Rowland's journal. She'd dismissed it then. She wouldn't now.

This time, she would not ignore it. She let the paper settle on the desk and rested her hand beside it, steady now.

The room was quiet, but it welcomed her.

She hadn't been hiding, only waiting to remember who she'd always been. And now, she had found the path forward and the woman willing to walk it.

Chapter Nineteen

THE LAMPLIGHT HAD barely begun to stretch across the floorboards when Georgina returned to the desk. She hadn't expected the list to shake her, yet it had, not for what it revealed, but for what it demanded.

Rowland's desk held the familiar sprawl of the folio, its pages spread open and visibly marked by Georgina's hand with lines drawn, names circled, and margin notes drawing conclusions and clarity. She had marked each reference to S. Mallory with a red pencil line, careful and deliberate. Three transactions, two different signatures, and a delivery firm she'd never heard of: *R.T.S.*

Beside the folio sat Rowland's refusal list, the page she had found tucked between old ledgers, as though even in death he'd wanted her to find it on her own terms. She lifted it now with a kind of reverence, not for the paper itself, but for the decisions it represented. Mallory's name appeared fourth from the top, written in Rowland's strong, deliberate script. She tapped the edge of the list with the ends of the pencil, her brow furrowed.

Rowland had trusted too few, spoken even less. But when he struck a name, he did so with reason.

She remembered Samuel Mallory, but just faintly. She thought he was a quiet man with a stiff collar and fingers stained from ledger ink. He'd come to dinner once, years ago, back when Rowland still hosted investors and tradesmen. There was tension even then. She recalled entering the study late one evening to find the door not quite closed, Rowland's voice low but tight with restraint. Mallory's tone had been smoother, too smooth, as if veiled in courtesy while issuing some kind of demand. Georgina hadn't caught the words, only the scrape of Rowland's chair as he rose and said, "This conversation is concluded."

After that, Rowland never spoke of him again. He'd simply struck Mallory's name from the accounts and locked away the ledgers for a fortnight.

That memory settled now beside the false signatures and vanished records.

She sat straighter as footsteps approached. A shadow moved in the hallway, followed by the familiar creak of the study door. Alex entered without ceremony, his coat still dusted from the road, a folded note in one hand and an unreadable look in his eyes.

"Seaton sent this by courier," he said, but he didn't hand it over immediately. Instead, he scanned the desk, the open folio, and the scattered annotations. He took in the careful chaos she'd created, the evidence of hours spent chasing truth, and something softened behind his eyes. It was the kind of look that reached her before his voice ever could—a wordless acknowledgment that she had become the steadiness he hadn't known he needed.

When he finally passed her the letter, their fingers touched. He didn't draw back. Neither did she. For a moment, the study held its breath. The air was alive with the quiet pulse of recognition that had nothing to do with ledgers or lies. How easily his nearness unsettled the order she prized; it was a disturbance she no longer wished to correct.

Georgina unfolded the page and scanned the contents.

"Nothing on *R.T.S.*," she murmured. "He's never dealt with them, never heard of them, and says no reputable port he's worked with lists it in their ledgers."

Alex moved to stand beside her, looking down at the folio. "Then it's not a company. It's a mask."

She nodded, her voice quiet. "And someone is using it to

move coal."

A stillness passed between them. Not empty, not hesitant, just full of mutual recognition. The kind that came when two minds reached the same place without speaking.

He studied her, the lamplight brushing gold into the edges of her hair. "Mallory?"

"Possibly," she said. "But if so, it isn't with his own hand. These signatures don't match. And Rowland refused to do business with him."

Alex's mouth tightened. "So, either Mallory's cooperating, or someone is using his name."

Georgina reached for her pelisse. "Let's find out which."

Before they left the study, she rolled the folio with care and fastened it with the blue ribbon she had kept nearby. Alex crossed to the window, watching the clouds move fast over the rooftops. "We won't get every answer today," he said, "but we'll see who flinches when we start asking."

Georgina smiled. "It would be easier if they'd stop lying outright."

His answering glance held the faintest curve of amusement, and something warmer beneath it, the kind of warmth that made truth seem far more dangerous than deceit.

He offered his arm, and when she took it, there was no ceremony, only shared purpose.

Alex watched her with something close to admiration. "You always plan to go charging into the unknown, or is that just this week?"

She smiled faintly. "Only when the unknown dares to forge my husband's documents."

THE DOCKS OF Sommer-by-the-Sea bustled with late-afternoon trade. Crates clattered against cobblestones. Voices echoed over the water with commands, bargains, and greetings. The scent of salt and coal dust clung to every surface.

Georgina walked at Alex's side, her gloves folded neatly in one hand, the folio tucked under her arm. Now and then their sleeves brushed, and the accidental contact grounded her more surely than the cobblestones beneath their feet.

Ships rocked gently against the current, ropes creaked on wet moorings, and gulls circled overhead like idle gossips. The autumn breeze carried a metallic tang of coal, sea, and tarred wood.

Despite the bustle, she noticed the irregularities, the hurried gestures, the brief glances that lingered too long, the sense that eyes were moving ahead of them rather than away.

The harbor might appear chaotic, but it moved with a rhythm. Any disruption would stand out.

Dockmaster Dilling met them by the warehouse office, the same man who had hedged through their questions once before. He offered a stiff bow, wiping his hands on a kerchief that looked long overdue for retirement.

"Lady Ravenstock. Lord Hawkesbury. Didn't expect you again so soon."

"We've questions about Mallory," Georgina said. "And a firm marked *R.T.S.*"

Dilling's eyes flicked to the folio. "Mallory hasn't moved shipments through here in weeks."

Georgina opened the folio and turned it toward him. "And yet he's listed here. Three times in the past month. Including last Thursday."

The dockmaster's jaw shifted. "Could be a clerical error. Maybe one of the lads—"

"I'd like to see your outbound manifest for that date," Alex said calmly.

Dilling hesitated, his gaze flicking once toward the ledger shelf. Then, with a grunt, he motioned them into the office.

The space was cramped and smelled of spilled ink, damp

paper, and the faint acrid tang of tobacco. Georgina took it in at a glance. There were half-rolled charts, worn seals, and the frayed edge of a dispatch from Bristol pinned askew behind the desk. A brass weight lay on the window ledge, streaked with soot. He rifled through a thick binder and laid a single page on the desk. Georgina leaned in.

Mallory's name appeared, but the ink looked fresher than the others. Wrong pen, wrong pressure.

"May I?" she asked.

Dilling hesitated. "That stays in the ledger."

Georgina didn't touch the page. She simply studied it. "This isn't Mallory's handwriting. Not the one I know."

Alex pointed to a corner stamp. "That's not the original registry seal. It's been overlaid."

Dilling bristled. "I record what I'm given. If you're suggesting—"

"We're not suggesting anything yet," Georgina said coolly. "But someone is using a name they shouldn't, and a company that doesn't exist."

She straightened and turned to leave. "When was the last time Samuel Mallory signed in himself?" she asked, pausing near the door.

Dilling hesitated. "Months ago. Maybe longer."

"Then why does his name keep appearing?"

He rubbed the back of his neck, suddenly interested in the floorboards. "Could be his partner. Used to work through a firm, Shaw & Mallory."

Georgina's eyes narrowed. "You didn't mention that before."

"Didn't seem relevant."

"It is now," Alex said, his voice low and final. He lingered just long enough to give the dockmaster a look that required no words at all.

Outside, the wind had picked up. The tide dragged the scent of wet rope and coal along the shore. Georgina pulled her pelisse tighter. She cast a glance back toward the office door as it closed behind them. Something about Dilling's expression as they left her unsettled. Not outrage, it was expectation. Like a man who'd already lit the fuse and was simply listening for the sound of the explosion. As though he had known they would come, and now that they had, some unspoken clock had started. The folio pressed against her arm like a reminder of what she'd seen, and what still eluded her.

As they reached the edge of the warehouse row, Alex paused.

"What is it?" she asked.

"Warehouse two," he said quietly. "A man in a grey coat. He's been watching us since we arrived."

Georgina didn't turn. She adjusted her grip on the folio, pretending to straighten her glove. "Do you recognize him?"

"No. And he doesn't mean to be recognized."

They continued walking, unhurried. Georgina focused on each step, keeping her stride measured. Her thoughts were not as steady. Her pulse had quickened, and Alex's hand had shifted slightly, as though prepared to catch hers at the slightest stumble.

Behind them, the gulls shrieked above the masts, and a cart rattled over a dock plank. She resisted the urge to glance over her shoulder. If the man followed, they'd know soon enough. If he didn't, she wasn't sure that it would be better.

They didn't speak again until the harbor was behind them. The road ahead narrowed, and Georgina let the silence stretch a little longer, her mind mapping out what they had and what they still didn't. The documents. The name. The false company. What they lacked was certainty. And time. A gust of wind tugged a strand of hair loose, and Georgina let it go, her mind still circling the names, the ink, and the dockmaster's evasion.

"Rowland would've followed it quietly," she said after a moment. "Without confrontation. But he wouldn't have let it lie."

Alex glanced her way. "You're not following quietly."

She shook her head. "There's no time to remain quiet anymore. Not when names are being used like coin."

He didn't answer, but his gaze lingered on her face. And for the first time since they began this, she wondered if he was more worried for her welfare than the outcome.

"No," she agreed. "I'm not following quietly." She didn't need protection. He knew that. But still, something in him braced against the path she'd chosen. Not to stop her. Just to walk beside her.

They walked in companionable silence, their steps falling into natural alignment, as if each pace forward steadied what the conversation had unsettled.

"If they're trying to erase Mallory," Georgina said, "they should have done a better job of forging his signature."

Alex gave a low, thoughtful hum. "Then we follow the signature."

Georgina nodded. "And every place it doesn't belong."

They didn't speak again until the turn in the road, where the sea slipped out of view. But the tension it left behind remained, like coal dust caught beneath the skin. Between them, silence no longer created a distance. It had shape, and the unspoken promise of what neither dared name. Yet even that dark shadow couldn't quite smother the spark between them, the kind that turned shared danger into trust.

Chapter Twenty

THE FOG HAD begun to lift by the time Georgina reached Sommer Chase. The grounds, still damp from the morning mist, glistened in patches along the gravel path, the hedgerows etched with dew. Her arrival was not expected, but she suspected it wouldn't be a surprise either.

Kenworth opened the door with his usual poise, though his coat still clung with the sharp scent of the road and salt air. "They're in the study," he said, stepping aside. "Tea's not yet on, but a situation is." He offered her a dry look, but there was warmth beneath it. He'd always had a sense for when something serious was afoot, and when Georgina Ravenstock appeared before luncheon, it was rarely a social call.

The hall carried the familiar scent of hearth smoke and waxed pine. As Georgina passed through, she registered the low murmur of voices, the soft thud of footsteps overhead, and the ever-present rhythm of a house run efficiently, but alert.

Barrington was standing near the fire, a small stack of papers in one hand and a coal pencil in the other. Alex leaned over the desk, reviewing a page marked with Seaton's tight, deliberate script. The tension in the room wasn't explosive. It was coiled. The kind that made every sound more noticeable.

"Late morning post," Barrington said, gesturing with the pages. "Kenworth rode out early to meet the courier halfway."

Georgina removed her gloves and stepped beside them. "What did Seaton send?"

Alex looked up, meeting her eyes. His expression was serious, but it eased the moment she spoke. It was the smallest shift, a softening at the edges of a man who spent his life braced for impact. She hadn't meant to become his reprieve, yet here he was, breathing easier because she stood beside him.

"More than expected," he said, handing her the top page. "A manifest. Shipments flagged with *R.T.S.*"

The paper was slightly damp at the edge, but the names were clear. Cargo: timber, raw commodity, and coal. Her eyes traced the margins. Beside each entry, smaller than the cargo listings, was an initial, a single letter in this case: D.

Alex leaned closer, his sleeve brushing hers, and she caught the faint scent of rain still clinging to his coat. Focus demanded she look at the paper, not at him.

"It's the same abbreviation," she murmured. "And now… just the one initial."

Barrington stepped beside her. "No full names?"

"No," Alex answered. "But Georgina brought a list yesterday. Names of men Rowland refused to do business with. All three of them had ties to coal, and their last name began with the letter D."

Georgina nodded, lifting the manifest slightly. "Michael Dane. Charles Denholm. Jonathan Drexler.

She reached into her satchel and withdrew a folded journal page, smoothing it on the desk beside the manifest. "Last night, I compared Rowland's list to several records, an old investment ledger, the port registry, and a merchant's directory." She tapped the annotations scrawled beside each name in her own hand.

"Dane is tied to Greyline Holdings through a silent partnership. No official record, but his solicitor has handled transactions on their behalf. Denholm funds customs infrastructure, though he's pulled out of two major projects without explanation. Drexler's name is attached to three coal contracts and four legal complaints that disappeared quietly. All of them have patterns. All of them know how to hide behind someone else's ink."

Barrington gave a low grunt. "I've heard of Drexler. Denholm's name came up once, when the East London port nearly collapsed."

"And Michael Dane?" she asked.

He was silent a moment longer. Then: "He's on Honoria's guest list. I remember frowning at it."

Alex's brow furrowed. "So, we've got three names. One initial. And no solid direction yet."

Georgina stepped closer to the desk and laid the paper down gently. "We don't guess," she said. "We narrow. The *D* may not be Dane. But all three deserve a closer look."

Barrington crossed to the map pinned to the far wall, where pins and threads marked coastal activity. He marked the ports where *R.T.S.* had surfaced, Portsmouth, Dover, and Lowestoft. Then he linked them. A triangle. A network.

"Same points," Barrington muttered, retracing the threads with a pencil. "Same shape. Just tighter now."

Alex followed the line with his eyes, then looked back at Georgina. There was no triumph in his gaze, only trust, deep and certain, the kind that was more intimate than any touch. "If Rowland flagged Mallory, and this *D* is connected to the same shipment chain, then he was chasing something bigger than a forged invoice."

"He was tracing it to its source," Georgina said. "And someone knew it."

The fire gave a soft pop, and no one moved to speak. Outside the window, the haze still hovered low, reluctant to fully clear.

"We verify the D," Barrington said at last. "All three. Backgrounds, associates, shipping ties. Seaton can help with that."

Alex nodded. "And once we know who *D* is, we find out who gave him cover."

After she left Sommer Chase, Georgina didn't return to the docks or the merchant's hall. She went home. There were papers she'd skimmed and set aside, notes she'd copied without context. Something had slipped past her attention, and she meant to find it.

The gate creaked softly behind her as Georgina stepped into the quiet of Ravenstock Manor. The air inside carried a slight chill, touched by the fog that had seeped in at dawn and never quite lifted. She didn't call Mrs. Hemsley, nor did she remove her gloves. The quiet was different now. Once it had been loneliness; today it was expectancy, as though the walls themselves waited for her to bring something, or someone, back within them. Her steps carried her straight toward Rowland's study.

The room smelled faintly of cedar and old ink, with a trace of sea air that always seemed to linger along the northern windows. Light filtered through the drawn curtains, and dust floated lazily in the shafts that cut across the desk. The folio still lay open where she'd left it, flanked by ledgers and folded notes, her world for the past several days.

She moved with quiet precision, checking each note again, as though expecting something new to appear now that the morning had reshaped her perspective. She reached into her coat pocket and drew out the folded slip of paper, the one she had found in the crate days ago and tucked away ever since.

Unfolding it slowly, she let her gaze settle on the handwriting. The same careful script she had once teased Rowland for was too neat, too measured, like a man afraid the ink might misbehave.

If you find this, you'll know why I didn't say more.
You were always better at following silence.

She didn't smile. Something in her chest tightened, not from grief, but something quieter. A steadiness. A direction.

Rowland hadn't written that for comfort. He had written it as an instruction. And she'd been following it ever since, even without knowing it.

She turned to the corner desk where Rowland had kept his shipping records. Among the scattered receipts and marginal notes was the list she'd begun the night before. There were three initials, each containing the letter D. She'd written notes beside each one in a tight, slanted hand.

Michael Dane was linked to Greyline Holdings through a silent partnership. He had influence at court and was rarely seen at port.

Charles Denholm was an investor in East London's customs yards. He was known for his abrupt withdrawals of funding.

Jonathan Drexler was a coal merchant with shifting addresses and three lawsuits buried under as many trade disputes.

None of them were innocent. All of them were plausible. She folded the list with steady hands. There was no question anymore, only direction. Sommer Chase was waiting.

She folded the paper again and slipped it into her sleeve, close to the pulse point beneath her wrist. As she turned toward the door, movement in the corner of her eye made her glance toward the hallway.

Mrs. Hemsley stood at the threshold, holding a tray with untouched tea. "You'll be going out again, my lady?"

Georgina gave a single nod. "Soon."

"Shall I have your coat brushed?"

She almost said no, then reconsidered. "Yes, thank you." She handed the coat off, and watched as Mrs. Hemsley vanished down the hall, then collected the folio and the list of names. She did not linger.

When the door closed behind her moments later, it was with the same soft hush that had greeted her upon entry. The house did not press her to stay. It understood.

By the time she returned to Sommer Chase, the mist had thinned to ribbons along the hedgerows, and the path was drier beneath the carriage's wheels. She didn't stop to greet anyone this time. The folio was in her hand, and the name on the list was no longer speculation. It was a place to start.

Georgina stepped through the study doorway at Sommer Chase just as the clock chimed once on the quarter hour. She carried the list and the folio in one hand, but her presence announced itself long before she spoke.

Alex looked up the moment she entered. His expression didn't change much, but something eased behind his eyes. The tension that had lived in her chest since morning loosened in answer, the unspoken recognition passing between them like a shared breath. He straightened slowly, as though her return had restored something unspoken.

Her presence didn't fill the room. It was rooted in it. Quiet, focused, unmistakable. It was not that she made others smaller. It was what made the work matter more.

"I found this," Georgina said, crossing the carpet and extending the page. "It was among Rowland's notes. Tucked between ledger entries. It matches the abbreviation Rowland flagged, *R.T.S.*, and again, only a single initial, *D.*"

Alex took the page without hesitation, his fingers brushing hers briefly. The contact wasn't prolonged, but it steadied something between them.

He unfolded the sheet and studied it in silence. Barrington leaned over his shoulder.

Georgina watched the line of his profile in the lamplight, the stillness of a man listening as much with instinct as intellect.

"Only the one initial," Alex said. "No context?"

Georgina shook her head. "But I cross-referenced the names. There are three possibilities, Michael Dane, Charles Denholm, and Jonathan Drexler. All of them have surfaced in trade conversations before."

Barrington gave a low whistle and stepped to the map. "That list narrows the pool, but not enough to draw blood. We need confirmation."

"And caution," Alex added. "If Rowland didn't name the man directly, he must've had reason to hold back."

Georgina crossed to the desk and laid the folio beside the manifest. "It's not proof. But it's pressure. Someone wanted this trail hidden. Rowland tried to preserve it."

Barrington looked at her, something softer in his gaze. "And you've uncovered it."

Alex's voice was quiet, steady. "You always knew how to read what wasn't said."

No one said anything after that. They didn't need to.

The fire cracked once in the hearth, and the warmth of the study wrapped around them not like comfort, but clarity.

Barrington picked up the list. Georgina reached for the folio. And Alex stepped toward the window, watching as the last of the low clouds rolled back toward the sea.

Georgina let the quiet settle around her. She didn't need a declaration or a plan. Still, some part of her wished the stillness would break not with words, but with the sound of his voice saying her name, low and certain, a promise shaped in air. This moment, standing shoulder to shoulder with men who respected her mind, was its own kind of reckoning. She hadn't just followed the silence. She'd broken it. And in that breaking, the room breathed with her.

Chapter Twenty-One

IT WAS NEARLY noon by the time Georgina stepped back into the study at Sommer Chase. The sun had burned off most of the lingering mist, and the household had already settled into its steady rhythm. Fire crackled. Ink dried. And no one seemed particularly surprised to see her again.

Alex stood at the desk, sleeves rolled to the forearm, eyes sharp with thought. The folio lay open in front of him, a neat ring of annotations in his hand. Georgina joined him without fanfare, slipping her gloves into her pocket as she scanned the open manifest beside him.

The quiet between them had evolved. It had become a kind of language between them, fluent in pauses and glances, where meaning lived not in words but in the steadiness of being seen. It was no longer the silence of strangers working toward the same goal. It was familiar, undistracted, fluid, and unspoken.

"I would've overlooked it," Alex said, tapping the margin. "The *D* here is subtle. Almost meant to blend in."

"That's what makes it dangerous," Georgina murmured. "It's a pattern. One meant to be invisible until it isn't. If this were a network, there'd need to be shorthand, a way to communicate without spelling things out."

They both looked up at the same moment. The mirror of it made Barrington, sitting in the armchair near the hearth, chuckle softly into his tea.

Before Alex could reply, footsteps approached. Kenworth

appeared in the doorway with a sealed note and the faintest crease to his brow.

"Courier from the village," he said, handing the envelope to Alex. "Left this with one of the stable boys just after breakfast. No return address."

Alex accepted it with a nod of thanks, broke the seal, and unfolded the single sheet inside. His brow lowered in concentration as he read. Then, without a word, he passed it to Georgina. His fingers brushed hers, and she felt the faint tremor beneath the control he wore like armor. He was steady for her sake, but she recognized the effort it cost him.

The paper was coarse, folded roughly. But the handwriting was deliberate.

Denholm's not your man. The others? Too much smoke to see clearly. Greyline's where it starts.

No name. No signature.

"Carver," she said quietly.

Barrington looked up from his chair near the hearth. "How can you tell?"

"The handwriting. He signed the ledger at the shaft office once while I was there," Georgina said. "It's him."

Barrington rose, frowning. "He's watching from the edges, then."

"Or still too scared to come in," Alex added. "But it narrows the field."

Georgina read the message again. "Denholm is eliminated. That leaves Drexler and Dane."

"And Greyline," Barrington said, walking toward the wall map. "It's always been the quiet ones. The firms with no face."

"I want to trace Greyline's structure," Georgina said. "Not the public one. I want the real names behind it."

"That may take some doing," Alex said. "They use substitutes."

"But not perfect ones," she replied. "There's always a slip. A letter. A pattern."

Alex's gaze lingered on her. "Then we'll find it."

There was promise in it, quiet and deliberate, the kind that reached further than words. She met his gaze and, for an instant, forgot the map, the names, the risk. She only saw the man who refused to stand apart from her fight.

Barrington had already reached for a clean sheet of parchment. "Edward will know where to start. I'll send word through his private channel."

Georgina rested a hand on the desk, eyes flicking back to the folio. "I want to be useful, not cautious."

"You're already more than that," Alex said. "You've moved us further than we'd ever have gone without you."

His voice was even, but something deeper hummed beneath it. The sound of it settled through her like warmth through cold stone, a reminder that belonging could come in the shape of belief. She didn't answer with words, only glanced down at the message again before folding it and slipping it into the back of the folio.

Alex stepped around her to the window, then turned back. "What do you propose?"

"Listen to what isn't said," she replied simply.

That made him smile, faint and private. "We're good at that, apparently."

She returned the smile, just a flicker, and looked to Barrington. "I want to find out who owns Greyline Holdings. Not what's in the public record. Who truly controls it?"

"You won't find that on a letterhead," Barrington said.

"No," Alex agreed, "but Edward might. If anyone has access to the financial webs behind these shadow firms, it's the Home Office."

Barrington crossed to the writing desk. "I'll send word. I'll phrase it carefully."

Georgina leaned one hand on the edge of the table, watching them both. "I want to do more than wait."

"You will," Alex said. "We'll track the shipping from Seaton's end. You'll take the documents we flagged and dig through Greyline's history. And we'll meet again this evening."

"This isn't just courtesy, is it?" She said softly. "I'm not being allowed in—"

"No, you are not," Alex said, his voice clear. "You are needed."

His voice wasn't commanding. It was collaborative. Inclusive. It landed in a way that made her straighten, not from pride, but from purpose.

Something unspoken sparked between them, a knowing that trust, once given, could be its own form of intimacy.

Barrington was already writing. Kenworth had disappeared to prepare the dispatch. The fire snapped behind them.

But it was Alex's gaze that lingered a moment longer, silent and sure. He didn't reach for her hand. He didn't need to. The space between them didn't feel empty. It was charged.

Ravenstock Manor stood in its quiet stillness, the afternoon light filtering through gauzy curtains that caught the breeze from the sea. Georgina stepped into the study and removed her gloves. The day had already folded around her like a set of instructions, and she had no intention of deviating from them.

She went straight to Rowland's desk.

It had become a familiar dance, papers reshuffled, corners lifted, ledgers checked and checked again. But today her eye was drawn to the right-hand drawer, the one that stuck slightly when she pulled it. She opened it and withdrew a slim folder that she'd marked before but hadn't read in full.

The pages were thin, lined with faint blue ink. Trade accounts. Holdings. Investments. And something else, an envelope tucked in the back.

She slid it free.

Inside, a note in a stranger's hand. The penmanship was elegant, practiced, but unfamiliar. It bore no greeting, only a single sentence.

Greyline will cover the discrepancy. M.D. will see to it.

Georgina stilled. No signature. But those initials. A chill slid beneath her skin. Not just because of what it implied, but because of what it *confirmed.* Rowland had known. He had tried to protect her. Even in silence. Michael Dane. It had to be. But why would Rowland involve the Viscount Albury?

She scanned the accompanying page. It was an inventory list with a notation beside a set of entries: *R.T.S. – October 10 – see* enclosed.

She glanced at the envelope. So, this was the enclosed. She folded the paper carefully, returned the rest of the file to the drawer, and moved to the window. Beyond the hedge, the path to the lane was empty, the sky above shifting to amber with the first whisper of sunset.

She didn't feel triumphant. She felt closer. And she was ready to return to Sommer Chase.

The lamps were just being lit when Georgina returned to Sommer Chase. The study glowed with firelight and low conversation, its corners touched by the softness of approaching evening. She stepped through the doorway and found Alex and Barrington where she'd left them, though both now stood at the hearth, their postures alert.

She didn't need to announce her discovery. The folio was already open again, waiting.

"I found something," she said quietly, holding out the letter.

Alex took it, scanned the line, and exhaled through his nose. *M.D.*

"Michael Dane," Barrington said flatly.

"Not proof," Georgina said. "But close."

The letter was passed back and forth, studied, and compared to the manifest from Seaton. Notes were made. Plans considered. And then, the door creaked.

Kenworth entered without a tray for once. No tea, no sardonic remarks. Only a folded sheet of paper in his hand, sealed in wax.

"Another courier," he said. "This one from Portsmouth. He arrived not five minutes ago. Said to put it directly into your hand."

Alex accepted the note and studied the seal. There was no crest, only a single pressed mark. A circle with no center, like something watching, without ever being seen.

His brows lifted.

He broke the seal and opened the page. As his eyes moved down the paper, his jaw set.

He handed it to Barrington. Georgina, standing just beside them, leaned closer.

You're following ghosts. Step back. Others have vanished for less.

The handwriting was sharp and tidy but unfamiliar. Barrington flipped the sheet and looked for more. Nothing.

"That's not a warning," he said. "It's a threat."

Georgina stepped closer to the fire. "It's anonymous. No seal. No sender. No signature."

Alex met her eyes. "But someone knows what we're doing. And they want us to stop."

Barrington set the paper on the mantel and watched the edges curl in the heat.

No one spoke for a long moment.

Then Alex turned to Barrington. "We shift to Ravenstock. Fewer eyes, more control."

Georgina glanced between them. "It's not fortified."

"No, but it's less exposed politically," Barrington said. "And you'll be more comfortable there. We'll bring Kenworth and two of my men. They'll assist Mrs. Hemsley with the household and keep watch."

"I won't be coddled," Georgina said.

"You won't be," Alex replied. "But you'll be protected. That's not the same thing."

She didn't argue. Not because she agreed with the reasoning, but because she could sense it wasn't truly negotiable.

Kenworth cleared his throat from the doorway. "In that case,

I'll tell the men to start packing. I assume we're taking the good teapot?"

That broke the tension, just enough.

"I'll follow after sunset," Barrington said. "There's one more message I need to send."

Georgina nodded, already turning toward the door. "I'll prepare Mrs. Hemsley for guests."

Alex walked her to the threshold. Outside, the last of the sun caught the edge of the horizon. The quiet stretched between them again, but it carried purpose now, anticipation threaded with care. She could feel the words he wouldn't say settle in the space just before the door.

"You're not alone in this," he said.

She nodded once. "Neither are you."

He didn't watch her go. He went with her.

By the time the carriage was ready, Kenworth had issued orders, and two of Barrington's men were already mounting up. Georgina stepped inside, her folio pressed to her chest, and Alex followed without hesitation.

The ride to Ravenstock was quiet. Not the silence of uncertainty, but of understanding. Of readiness. When the wheels found rhythm over the road, their shoulders brushed once. Neither drew away. The quiet between them was less like distance, more like promise, an unspoken pact sealed in motion.

And as the lamps were lit at the manor, and Mrs. Hemsley appeared in the doorway with a furrowed brow and a warm welcome, the wheels of their plan were already in motion.

Ravenstock had once held only memories. Tonight, it held the future.

Chapter Twenty-Two

THE TRANSFORMATION OF Ravenstock Manor had been swift but subtle. The drawing room was no longer a space for formal callers or idle embroidery. Ledgers lay open on the long table beside trade maps and shipping manifests. The fire in the hearth burned low, and candlelight pooled in glass dishes to hold back the creeping dusk. What had once been a house of grief now moved with quiet purpose.

Georgina sat at the corner of the long table, sleeves pushed up, a stack of notes at her elbow. Across from her, Alex read through a report from Seaton, his brow furrowed in concentration. He hadn't spoken in some time, but she didn't mind. Their silence had settled into something companionable. The rhythm of paper, ink, and breath.

She reached for the teapot and refilled his cup without asking. He looked up briefly and murmured, "Thank you," his voice low, as though the moment deserved quiet. Then he returned to the report.

Her gaze lingered a moment longer. The firelight cast him in amber, drawing out the blue in his eyes and the sharp lines of his jaw. He looked tired. But not in the way he had before, this was not the weariness of battle or loss. This was a different kind of weariness. The kind born of doing what mattered. She recognized it because it mirrored her.

Sometimes, she thought she could almost see the boy he must have been, the one she had missed knowing, and the man war had shaped in his place. The thought made her chest ache.

"You missed supper," she said quietly.

"Did I?" He glanced at the clock and frowned. "You didn't eat either."

She offered a wry smile. "Mrs. Hemsley left us both a tray in the library. It may be cold by now."

He set the report aside. "Let's see if anything survived."

They left the drawing room and crossed the hall together. The house was quiet, the kind of quiet that came from being watched over. Barrington's men kept to the periphery, their presence not seen. Kenworth had lit the sconces and vanished.

As they passed the corridor, Mrs. Hemsley stepped out, wiping her hands on a linen towel. "I've put dinner in the library," she said, pausing only briefly. "The dining room was too… formal tonight."

Georgina nodded. "Thank you."

Mrs. Hemsley gave her a small smile, then turned to Alex. "I've also moved your things into the east wing, my lord. Lord Barrington's valet insisted on arranging the boots himself. I locked the cabinet just in case."

"In case, Mrs. Hemsley?" Alex asked.

"In case he gets an idea that the rest of the cabinet needs rearranging, my lord." She nodded respectfully.

Georgina raised an eyebrow. "You're assuming they're staying?"

"They didn't say it," Mrs. Hemsley replied with a knowing glance, "but I heard it just the same."

She disappeared down the hall, leaving behind the scent of lavender and a faint sense that everything was now properly in motion.

In the library, the tray waited on a sideboard, the lids still warm to the touch. Bread, cheese, and a stew that had gone tepid but not unpleasant. Georgina poured fresh tea while Alex uncovered the plates.

The smell brought with it an odd sense of comfort. A domestic moment was stolen from war planning.

They sat at the low table beside the hearth, and, for a while, they ate in silence.

Then she said, "You were right. About moving operations here. I feel safer."

He looked at her, not in surprise, but with something closer to relief. "Good. That was the intent."

She reached for a slice of bread. "And yet, there's something about this that doesn't feel like hiding. We're not retreating. We're… concentrating."

He gave a quiet laugh. "Exactly."

Their eyes met. She didn't look away.

A knock shattered the calm.

Alex was on his feet in an instant, every muscle taut, moving before his thoughts could catch up. Georgina rose more slowly, her instinct alert but shaped by the closeness to danger, not training. At the door, Kenworth stood with one hand on the knob, the other resting lightly near the pistol at his belt.

"It turned out to be harmless," he said. "A loose shutter in the west corridor. It sounded worse than it was." He gave a small nod. "The grounds are secure."

Alex didn't immediately relax.

"I checked it myself," Kenworth added. "There's no cause for concern."

"Thank you," Alex said.

Kenworth nodded once and withdrew. The door clicked softly shut behind him.

Only then did Georgina let out the breath she'd unconsciously been holding.

Alex crossed to the hearth and paused there, his back half-turned. "You should get some sleep."

"So should you," she said.

But neither moved.

He looked past the window, then back at her. "I need some fresh air. Come walk with me?"

She pulled her shawl around her, moved toward him, and placed her hand on his arm. "It would be my pleasure."

They stepped out into the cool night. The air was clean and still, stars pushing through the mist like promises. They crossed the stone path behind the manor, passing the hedgerow and the edge of the stables. The land sloped gently beyond the garden wall, opening toward the sea. Moonlight silvered the field beyond.

Alex stopped beside an old yew tree, his hands at his back, eyes scanning the horizon.

She stood beside him, her cloak wrapped tight.

"What are you thinking?" she asked.

"That I don't like not knowing who's watching."

She looked up at him. "You think someone is?"

"I'd be a fool not to."

She nodded, then hesitated. "Does it ever get easier? The waiting? The watching?"

He looked down at her. "No. But it gets clearer. You start to see what matters more than fear."

"And what matters to you?" She asked, the question soft.

He took a breath, long and steady. "You."

She blinked.

"You matter," he said again. "Not just because you're brilliant or brave or infuriatingly certain when I'm not. You matter because when I look at you, I see the one thing that feels steady in all of this."

The wind stirred her hair. She didn't step away.

"I knew it before Sommer Chase," he continued. "But here, now, I can finally say it without wondering if I've presumed too much."

Her voice, when it came, was barely above a whisper. "You haven't." The words were both surrender and truth.

He reached out, his fingers brushing hers, a tentative question in the form of a touch. She didn't speak. She didn't need to. Her hand closed around his.

For a long moment, they stood that way, the space between them thinning like breath on glass.

He leaned in. Not quickly, not boldly, but with the certainty of someone who had waited for the world to stop shifting. And she met him there.

His mouth touched hers, soft and steady. Not seeking permission but answering something that had long gone unspoken.

She responded in kind, her fingers finding the edge of his coat, not to pull him closer, but to stay grounded as the moment unfurled around them.

There was no urgency, no pretense. Just warmth, and truth, and something that felt a great deal like home.

She tasted warmth and wind, safety wrapped in the unraveling tension. He kissed her like he had always known what she meant to him and had only now earned the right to show it.

When they parted, it wasn't because they had to, but because they both wanted this to last.

His forehead touched hers. "I wanted that for longer than I can say."

"So did I," she murmured, the words quieter than the breeze.

They didn't speak for a long moment. The breeze moved gently through the yew's branches, and their hands remained loosely joined. Georgina's voice broke the quiet. "And now, Alex?"

Alex looked toward the horizon, then back at her. "Now we don't look away."

She drew a slow breath, leaning slightly into him. "I'm not afraid. But I'm also not used to wanting something this much."

His hand tightened gently around hers. "Then we'll get used to it together."

She laughed softly, the sound curling like smoke in the still air. "That almost sounded like optimism."

"Don't tell Barrington," he said, and she laughed again.

When they turned back toward the house, they didn't rush. The night was quiet, and for the first time in weeks, so were they.

Later, after the house had gone quiet, Georgina stood by the window of her room, her cloak still on and her hands resting on the sill. She hadn't lit the lamp. There was comfort in the shadows tonight. The kiss didn't replay in sensation, but in stillness. The peace in her chest startled her more than his touch. Love had once arrived as a negotiation. This time, it asked for nothing. And she let it stay.

There had been no hesitation in his hands. And in his eyes, nothing but quiet certainty. It was real. She hadn't meant to fall so easily. And now that she had, she didn't intend to let him go.

A knock sounded faintly below, boots on the stone floor, and voices too low to decipher. Then nothing. She stayed at the window for a moment longer. Finally, she turned. There was work to do. She changed out of her cloak, lit the lamp, and gathered the remaining pages of Rowland's ledger. When she stepped into the study an hour later, the scent of ink and coal dust met her like a memory.

Now, she knew what she was working toward.

Alex and Barrington stood shoulder to shoulder over the long table. Georgina had laid out the folio's newest contents, duplicate manifests, mismatched delivery stamps, shipping logs that led nowhere and everywhere.

"This is more than concealment," Alex said, tracing a trade route that looped back on itself. "This is choreography. Elegant. Ruthless."

"And sprawling," Barrington added. "They've built a network under our noses."

Georgina moved beside them, eyes narrowed. "It's not just about hiding. It's about control."

Alex caught the way Barrington's eyes shifted toward Georgina for the briefest moment. He didn't comment, but the line of his jaw softened as if something had clicked into place for him. Alex felt it too. The shift, the certainty. Not just strategy anymore. Something closer to belief.

A long moment passed. Then Barrington looked at Alex. "We

can't keep bouncing between houses. This war's being fought here." He paused, eyes scanning the ledgers again. "Rowland left behind more than clues. He gathered intelligence, organized, detailed, damning intelligence." He turned to Georgina. "And he put it all in your hands. The Order has no idea what he gathered and what we have. And we dare not move it. Not now. Not with eyes watching."

"Then stay," she said, quietly but without hesitation. "We'll hold the line from here."

"She was right," Alex replied.

"We're fortunate it's the weekend. It will look like any other country house party, though our entertainments may run more to ledgers than lawn games." Georgina chuckled and turned to Barrington. "We'll have to ask Mrs. Bainbridge to join us."

Barrington gave a dry huff of agreement. "If she isn't already on her way."

Alex allowed himself a half-smile. The war might still be coming for them, but tonight, they had a plan, a home base, and the beginnings of something more than strategy.

And just outside the library window, the dark settled softly around Ravenstock Manor, keeping its quiet vigil over the future they had begun to claim.

Chapter Twenty-Three

THE SUN DIPPED just low enough to cast the drawing room in honeyed light, long shadows sliding across the floor like quiet sentinels. Georgina stood near the hearth, one hand resting lightly on the mantle, the other curled around a cup of cooling tea.

As the day unfolded, the rhythm surprised them both. There were shared tasks with notes deciphered, ledgers compared, and timelines aligned. Barrington retreated to the study with a frown and a stack of papers, muttering about inconsistencies in shipping ledgers.

"If I'm not back before dinner, send a search party," he'd said dryly, disappearing behind the study doors. "And bring tea. Strong. Or I'll be asleep with my eyes open."

"We'll send Kenworth in full armor," Alex had replied, earning a rare snort from Barrington.

Mrs. Bainbridge swept through the room moments later, cheeks pink from the wind, a portfolio under her arm. "Don't mind me," she said breezily. "I've brought three decisions Barrington needs to make before sunset. If he refuses, I'll declare war. With lemon cake." She winked and vanished into the study.

Kenworth moved through the house with quiet efficiency, ensuring the perimeter was secure. Neither Alex nor Georgina had requested that he stand guard, but they silently appreciated his efforts. At some point, he reappeared with news from the village. "The outer roads are quiet. One of the stationers reported someone asked about freight routes. They described him as a tall man, with a dark coat and heavy boots, but no one matching that description has returned," he said. "No signs of watchers, but I've doubled the patrol."

Georgina thanked him, and Alex nodded his approval. "Keep a sharp eye, Kenworth. And let us know if anything feels off."

The valet inclined his head. "Always, sir. Does that include when Mrs. Bainbridge arrives? I have it on good authority that she is coming armed with receipts, triumph, and a poorly veiled agenda."

Alex raised a brow. "Should we prepare for battle?"

"I already warned Cook," Kenworth said dryly. "She's doubled the lemon glaze." He paused, then added, "Shall I let Cook know the two of you will be dining here or in the library again? She's determined not to repeat last night's confusion with the tray."

Georgina glanced up from the folio. "The library, I think. But perhaps let her know to keep something warm. We may lose track of time again."

Kenworth bowed. "Very good, my lady. And if I may add, if there's to be another walk after supper, I suggest you take one of the lanterns. Last night's misplaced candlestick caused quite a stir among the footmen."

After Kenworth departed, Alex caught Georgina watching him over the edge of the folio.

"If you keep frowning like that, you'll crease the parchment," Alex said at one point, glancing over at Georgina with a sideways smile.

"And if you keep sighing like that, you'll wear out the ink," she shot back, lips twitching.

He leaned in. "You have a remarkably sharp tongue for someone who mislabeled two entries this morning."

She feigned offense. "I was testing you."

"And I passed?"

"Barely."

They shared the long table for most of the afternoon, tracing the links between suppliers, decoding abbreviations, and occasionally debating the merits of Alex's penmanship.

Somehow, decoding ledgers with him was like learning a language she hadn't known she missed, the language of being seen.

As they worked side by side, Georgina found herself listening for his breath between the rustle of parchment and the scratch of quill. It was something quieter. Steadier. A rhythm she'd been missing.

Once, when he rose to cross the room for more parchment, she looked up and found herself watching him, not as a partner in investigation, but as a man she had come to know without defenses. And when he looked back and smiled without question, the smallest part of herself relaxed.

When he read a pompous letter aloud in a ridiculous voice, she laughed, sharp and sudden and real. It lit something unnamed and unguarded inside her.

Alex watched her in profile as she bent over a ledger, sunlight catching the edge of her brow. The furrow between her eyes, the slight purse of her lips, he'd seen officers glare at maps the same way before battle. But she was no soldier. She was something rarer: someone who still believed that truth was worth chasing. And being beside her made it easier to believe in things he'd long since buried.

Georgina teased him when he nearly spilled ink across the margin of a delicate ledger. Alex retaliated by returning to the pompous letter from a shipping clerk, reading it aloud with such exaggerated inflection that Georgina's laughter rang out, bright and unexpected.

"You're a menace," she said, dabbing her eyes.

"But an entertaining one," he replied.

He poured more tea for them both, and when her fingers brushed his, she didn't retreat. Neither did he. The contact was brief, but the pause after it lingered.

Later, they moved into the library. He offered her a book, one of Rowland's, full of marginal notes and thoughtful commentary. She teased him for reading the end before the beginning, and he countered by reading a passage aloud with such dramatic flair that she laughed until she couldn't catch her breath.

They ended side by side on the carpet, surrounded by old maps and worn ledgers, cross-referencing port records. At some point, their fingers brushed again, and this time, they stayed. She didn't speak. Neither did he. The silence held.

Mrs. Hemsley had appeared, as if summoned by instinct, with a tray of tea and a tart Georgina vaguely remembered mentioning two weeks ago. It sat mostly untouched.

A few minutes later, Mrs. Bainbridge arrived with wind-blown curls and a wrapped parcel of receipts. "I'm only staying until Barrington agrees that I was right," she announced. "Then I'll collect my victory and leave him to his ledgers."

"You might be here a while," Georgina murmured.

"Nonsense. He thrives on defeat. Especially mine."

She swept toward the study with a flourish and a smile. Moments later, her voice could be heard declaring, "If he thinks dry biscuits will distract me from my accomplishment, he has severely underestimated my affection for lemon cake."

He had meant only to bring her a fresh folio.

But when he entered the library and saw her half-curled on the carpet, chin propped on her hand, ink smudged on her wrist, and a faint smile lingering from some silent thought, he forgot the reason entirely.

"You look far too serious," he said, drawing her gaze. "Are you decoding a secret treaty or counting how many times I nearly spilled the ink today?"

She grinned. "A bit of both."

He dropped down beside her with a soft groan. "My back may never forgive me for this floor."

"Shall I call for a cushion?"

"No," he said, stretching out his legs. "Your company is cushioning enough."

She laughed, unexpected and warm. And it hit him like sunlight after storm clouds.

He laughed too, shaking his head. "That sound… I've missed it more than I knew."

"Laughter?"

"Yours."

She faltered, not from uncertainty, but because it felt so tender. So real. There was a time she would've mocked such softness, called it fanciful or false. But not now.

"You have a gift, Georgina," he said softly. "You make hard things bearable. And somehow, you still make me laugh when I least expect it."

Her throat tightened. "It's easy with you."

He drew her closer, as if the space between them had become a thing to defy. "Then let it be easy. At least for now."

Their lips met, finally, fully, not from hesitation, but from clarity. A sealing of something long understood but never named.

When they parted, it wasn't from doubt, but from reverence, an unspoken promise neither was ready to voice, yet neither would let slip away.

He brushed his thumb gently along her jaw before standing, as if memorizing the feel of her smile.

They sat on the narrow garden bench just beyond the drawing room doors, the last amber light stretching across the lawn. The air was cool, but she didn't feel it, not with his arm around her shoulders, not with the echo of that kiss still stirring between them like a vow.

Crickets sang in the hedgerows. The wind carried the scent of roses and sea.

Neither spoke at first. Words were too small.

She leaned into him, her hand resting lightly against his chest, where his heartbeat kept time with her own.

He looked out at the soft colors of the sky, then down at her. "You once said you didn't believe that kind of love was real."

She nodded, her cheek brushing the fabric of his coat. "I thought that kind of love was just something we told ourselves to keep hoping. I didn't believe it was real."

"And now?"

She tilted her face toward his, her smile touched with wonder. "Now I know better."

He drew her in, and for a long, quiet moment, they watched the horizon fade together, two hearts no longer waiting.

He held her close, the warmth of her against his side grounding him in a way battlefields and brotherhood never had. This wasn't survival. It was gentler, something that asked for nothing but presence.

The ghost he carried fell silent here, as if even they paused to listen to her heartbeat.

And for the first time in years, he gave it freely.

Chapter Twenty-Four

THE GARDEN WAS still, the air holding the hush of early light. Dew glistened on the rose petals like pearls spilled across velvet, and the ivy along the stone walls drank in the morning warmth without complaint.

Georgina stepped through the open doorway and paused beneath the archway, her slippered feet quiet on the worn flagstones. The shawl around her shoulders, once wrapped tightly in habit, now hung loose and forgotten. She wasn't cold. She wasn't anything but… calm.

Her eyes drifted toward the yew hedge, and there he was.

Alex stood just beyond the curve of the walk, sleeves rolled to his forearms, collar undone, the breeze catching at a lock of hair he hadn't bothered to tame. One hand rested on the back of the old bench, with his fingers curled against the lichen-mottled wood. His gaze was distant, fixed on the horizon beyond the hedgerow, where the sea met sky in a blur of silver.

He didn't turn when she approached. But when the soft pad of her footfalls reached him, his posture shifted. Her shoulders relaxed, head tilted slightly, as if he'd been listening for that sound.

"You're up early," he said, still looking outward, his voice low and warm as the sun on stone.

"So are you," she replied.

Now he looked at her, and the corners of his mouth tugged upward. "Habit, I suppose."

She stepped closer, trailing her fingers along the hedge as she came to stand beside him. "Let me guess, you're surveying the land? Calculating sheep movements? Checking for criminally lazy gardeners?"

"That and making sure the bees haven't unionized."

She smiled, and he gestured toward the bench. She didn't hesitate.

The wood was cool beneath her skirt, but the sun reached them there, dappled through the branches overhead. He sat beside her, close but not crowded, his arm brushing hers just enough to make her aware of it.

They watched the light shift across the garden, neither speaking for a time.

"I never liked this corner of the grounds," she said eventually. "Too quiet. But today…"

She didn't finish the thought.

He turned his head slightly, not pushing, just listening.

Georgina traced the line of mortar between the stones with her gaze. "I used to come here when Rowland was away. I would sit on this bench and try to find order in the garden. Something to match the order I couldn't find in myself."

"And did it help?"

"No," she said, then smiled. "But the roses were loyal."

"Back then, the garden couldn't answer what I didn't yet know how to ask. But today…I don't need answers. Just this."

Alex leaned back slightly, elbows resting on the bench's edge, face tipped toward the sun. "This was where you once accused me of being insufferable."

She blinked, surprised. "When?"

"You were sixteen. I said your handwriting lacked discipline. You told me I lacked a soul."

"I was right."

He chuckled, the sound low and genuine. "You were furious. You stomped off and wouldn't speak to me for a week."

"I made a vow never to forgive you."

"And yet here we are."

She tilted her head. "I suppose even sixteen-year-old girls are allowed to change their minds."

He looked over at her then, not teasing, not amused. Just… seeing her. Not the widow, not the legend she'd become in town, not the woman who'd outwitted the Order. Just Georgina, with her shawl slipping from one shoulder and her fingers curled softly in her lap.

"You've changed," he said quietly.

"And so have you."

His gaze dropped to her hands. She turned one palm upward between them.

An invitation.

She turned her palm a fraction more, a yes without a sound.

His hand moved slowly, not tentative, not unsure, but as if the gesture mattered. As if it had meaning.

When his fingers slid into hers, the breath left her chest in a quiet sigh.

No urgency, only warmth, just the kind that settles rather than sparks. And the sense of something true.

They sat like that as the garden brightened around them, the morning unfolding not with fanfare, but with the grace of something longed for and finally found.

The morning passed the way honey slips from a spoon, slow and golden and without need of rush.

After breakfast, Georgina found herself in the library with the tall windows flung open to the sea breeze and the scent of rosemary rising from the pots below. She was curled into the corner of the settee, a book in her lap, but her eyes kept drifting to the empty armchair across from her.

Not empty for long.

Alex appeared in the doorway, his sleeves rolled again, and a half-smile was already forming. He carried two cups of tea, one slightly fuller than the other.

"I took a gamble," he said, setting the cup on the table beside her. "Mrs. Hemsley said you usually take it with lemon. I added honey."

"You remember that?"

"I've made worse guesses."

She lifted the cup, sipped, and nodded once. "It's perfect."

He took the chair opposite her, one leg stretched lazily before him, cup in hand, the picture of contentment. The silence between them now was lived-in, a comfort rather than a space to fill.

"What are you reading?" he asked.

She turned the book so he could see the spine. "A treatise on garden design in Florence."

He narrowed his eyes in mock suspicion. "Is that the one that recommends marble fountains in every corner?"

"Every second corner, if you please," she said, grinning. "And fig trees shaped into heraldic beasts."

"I look forward to seeing the griffin topiary you'll demand in the west field."

"You joke, but I think you'd secretly enjoy having a few statues bow to you on your morning walk."

He took a sip of tea and didn't deny it.

When she laughed, it wasn't guarded or polite. It was the kind of laugh that tipped her head back slightly, eyes shining with amusement she didn't try to suppress.

"You do that," he said, watching her.

"What?"

"Laugh like you mean it."

"I suppose I do."

She tucked her legs beneath her, more at home in her own skin than she could remember being in years. The book slid forgotten into her lap as the breeze ruffled a curl near her temple. Alex leaned forward and reached, carefully, to tuck it behind her ear. This time his fingers lingered at her shoulder, a soft touch that didn't press nor withdraw.

Her breath caught, but she didn't move away.

He withdrew his hand as if the contact had been a kind of promise, one he wasn't yet ready to press. But he didn't look away.

"I missed this," she said, the words spoken as much to herself as to him.

He didn't ask her to explain. "So did I," he said simply, as if it were the most ordinary truth in the world.

Instead, he stood and offered his hand. "Come walk with me."

She blinked. "Where?"

"It's nowhere in particular. But if you'll walk it with me, I'll not ask for better."

She took his hand, rising with the ease of someone who'd already decided. No question. No hesitation.

Just the feel of his fingers lacing with hers once more, and the sun spilling across the corridor as they stepped out together.

The sky outside had turned the color of washed copper by the time Georgina finished dressing. She stood in front of the mirror in her bedroom, fastening the last amethyst earring with steady fingers. The stone caught the low light of the autumn afternoon, glowing with quiet confidence. Her gown was simple, a deep sapphire wool that fell gracefully and did not demand attention. She hadn't chosen it to impress anyone.

And yet, as she glanced down to smooth the bodice, a smile played at her lips.

She crossed to her dresser and tucked the small velvet box of jewelry back into its corner, where her mother's cameo and Rowland's signet already lay. Then she picked up her shawl from the foot of the bed and made her way downstairs.

In the drawing room, Barrington stood by the hearth, swirling a glass of port as he spoke to Mrs. Bainbridge, who was examining the rows of books on the far wall. Alex leaned against the mantel, hands tucked into his trouser pockets, his posture relaxed but alert, the light from the fire painting his features in warm relief.

Three heads turned as she entered.

Only one pair of eyes made her breath catch. It was, absurdly, like a thread pulled taut between them.

Alex's gaze swept over her, not in possession or astonishment, but in silent appreciation. As though he saw not just the woman before him, but everything she had endured and chosen to become. He said nothing. He didn't need to.

"I see dinner is not merely an occasion for nourishment," Barrington said, raising his glass. "You've brought decorum to a table sorely lacking it."

Georgina inclined her head with mock solemnity. "You're welcome."

Mrs. Bainbridge sniffed. "You're the only one in this house with an ounce of sense. I told him not to wear that waistcoat."

"It's a perfectly respectable waistcoat," Barrington muttered.

"Only if one respects hay."

Georgina bit back a laugh and accepted the arm Alex offered. His hand rested lightly at her waist as he guided her to the table, and though the touch was brief, it was grounding. Familiar, in a way that made her stomach warm.

Dinner was unhurried and abundant, roast pheasant, stewed apples with cinnamon, fresh bread, and a Stilton Mrs. Hemsley had declared "still fit to serve." Conversation flowed easily, peppered with stories from London and subtle barbs traded between Barrington and Mrs. Bainbridge. Alex listened more than he spoke, but when he did speak, it was with that low, steady timbre that always made the room lean in.

Georgina, seated beside him, found herself watching his hands more than she intended to, taking in how they curled around a wineglass, how one fingertip caught a drop of gravy before it could fall. It was not longing she wanted, not exactly, more like belonging.

After the last spoonful of cobbler had been claimed and the fire had dimmed to glowing embers, the four of them drifted back toward the drawing room. The warmth of the meal lingered in the air and in their limbs.

"I'll have Cook set something aside for breakfast," Mrs. Bainbridge said, rising with a firm nod. "I doubt anyone here will want to rise early, but that's no excuse for going hungry."

Barrington helped her to the corridor, offering her his arm with gentlemanly precision.

Georgina and Alex remained behind, standing near the mantel. The quiet between them wasn't silence. It was rest.

She looked up at him, her expression soft in the firelight. "That was… a lovely evening."

"It was."

"They feel rare. Lovely evenings."

"They shouldn't."

She turned slightly toward him. "You said that like a promise."

He met her eyes, and something in his gaze changed. It didn't darken, not deepen. It focused, like a man making a decision in full light.

"I meant it as one."

His hand found hers, not as a question, but as an affirmation. And then, slowly, he lifted it to his lips and pressed a kiss to the back of her fingers. Her breath caught, but she didn't move.

He stepped closer.

She tilted her face up, no hesitation, no distance left between them.

When he kissed her, it was without preamble, without tension. Just warmth and certainty. His hand slid to her cheek, cradling it gently as her fingers curled into his coat.

It wasn't a beginning. It was an arrival.

When they parted, neither spoke for a long moment.

His thumb traced once, barely, along her cheek, a promise he chose to keep.

"I should…" she whispered, nodding toward the stairs, though she made no move.

His thumb brushed the side of her jaw. "I know."

She smiled then, the kind of smile that came only when a person felt safe enough to mean it.

"Goodnight, Alex."

"Goodnight, Georgina."

She turned and ascended the stairs, her hand grazing the banister, the echo of his kiss still warm on her lips.

The autumn sun filtered softly through the lace curtains in the breakfast room, painting delicate patterns across the tablecloth. The windows had been opened just enough to let in the scent of the garden with its damp leaves, a hint of woodsmoke, and the faint sweetness of drying lavender.

Georgina sat at the table in a pale day dress, the bodice modest and crisply pressed, her hair swept into a simple twist. A plate of toast rested untouched beside her, and a teacup cooled near her hand. She held a pen lightly between her fingers, a single sheet of parchment before her.

Dearest Eliza,

Forgive my delay. If you're willing, shall we meet today? The park behind the bookshop at half past eleven?

—G.

She blew gently on the ink to dry it, then folded the note in half and sealed it with a small wafer. By the time she looked up, Alex had entered the room.

He entered with his coat slung over one arm, his cravat neatly, if hastily, tucked into place. His hair was still damp from washing. His face was unusually unguarded.

"Mrs. Hemsley insisted I eat something before I saddle a horse. I didn't argue."

"Wise."

He crossed to the sideboard, poured himself a cup of coffee, and leaned against the edge of the table. He didn't sit by her, just near.

"You're riding out?"

"Sommer Chase," he said. "Carver sent word early. He wants to speak with me."

"Today?"

He nodded. "This morning, if possible."

"What does he want?"

Alex shrugged, but there was no tension in the gesture. "Didn't say. Likely something tedious. He said to come alone."

She tilted her head, studying him. "You're not troubled."

"Should I be?"

"No," she said after a pause. "Only… you've that look you get when you're thinking five moves ahead."

He smiled faintly. "Only five?"

She grinned, and for a moment, it was as if they'd never spent a day apart.

He reached for her cup and stole a sip. He set the cup down, then touched two fingers briefly to the spot he'd kissed last night, as if confirming the promise still held.

"I'll be back before supper," he said.

"I thought I'd go into town," she said, turning slightly toward him. "Eliza's probably ready to disown me."

Alex smiled, then stepped forward and kissed her forehead gently.

"I'll see you this evening," he said.

She looked up at him, her hand briefly resting against his chest. "Don't let Carver drag you into anything impossible."

"He wouldn't dare."

She let him go then, with a small smile, and watched from the breakfast room window as he crossed the courtyard and mounted his horse. Brutus trailed after him to the gate, tail wagging, the quiet guardian of a morning that already was a memory. The morning sun caught in the edge of his coat as he rode toward Barrington's home.

She pressed her palm to the cool glass, silly, sentimental, and let the warmth there stand in for his hand until evening. Behind her, the tea had grown cold.

Chapter Twenty-Five

I T WAS JUST past four o'clock when Mrs. Hemsley laid down her embroidery and realized something was wrong.

The fire in the drawing room had burned low. The house was steeped in a hush that had once been peaceful but now rang hollow. No footsteps in the corridor. No voices drifting from the stairwell. No Georgina.

She set her needle aside and rose from her chair with a slow, deliberate motion.

There was no message.

Georgina had written one that morning. Mrs. Hemsley had seen it handed off to the footman herself. A note to Miss Eliza, asking to meet behind the bookshop at half past eleven. A short outing. Familiar. Safe.

It was now past four, and Georgina had not returned.

Mrs. Hemsley moved through the lower rooms with practiced efficiency, no drama, no panic. But with each empty chair, each unruffled curtain, the disquiet in her chest deepened.

In the library, only dust motes kept her company.

The breakfast room had been cleared, the dishes long since washed.

Georgina's room was tidy. Unlived in since morning.

She called to one of the footmen who'd been polishing silver near the dining room.

"Has Lady Ravenstock returned?"

"No, ma'am. Not since she left this morning. She said she'd

only be a few hours."

"And the gentlemen?"

"Mr. Barrington rode out to Sommer Chase. Said he'd return in time for dinner."

She hesitated. "And Lord Weld?"

The footman shook his head. "No one's seen him since he left early. Not sure where to."

She pressed her lips together. Alex hadn't said where he was going, but that wasn't unusual. Still… both men gone. Georgina overdue.

"Has a note come from Miss Eliza?"

"Not to my knowledge."

Mrs. Hemsley turned sharply. She crossed the entry hall, opened the front door herself, and stood beneath the covered portico for a long moment, watching the drive.

Nothing.

The stables yielded no fresh word. The horses had been watered and fed. The grooms had seen no sign of Lady Ravenstock since she'd left, and no one had been dispatched to collect her.

She returned inside, the hem of her gown darkened with dust, and gave her instructions without raising her voice.

"Ready the carriage," she told Brandon. "I'm going to Sommer Chase."

"To speak with Lord Barrington, ma'am?"

"To speak with someone," she said.

And without spending time to change her gown or sending word ahead, she gathered her gloves and her resolve and prepared to find out exactly what in God's name had happened to her ladyship. She thought of the way Lady Ravenstock had begun to laugh again, freely at last. The sound of it still echoed faintly in the halls she was about to leave.

The sound of carriage wheels on the gravel cut through the stillness like a warning bell.

Mrs. Hemsley paused in the act of fastening her cloak, the heavy wool hanging from her shoulders in a half-knot. She turned as one of the footmen passed by the open front door, wiping his hands on his waistcoat.

"A carriage just arrived from town, ma'am."

She didn't wait for a name.

The knock came before the bell could ring.

Mrs. Hemsley reached and opened the door. Her expression was already set in expectation.

Eliza stormed in before a word could be spoken.

"Where is she?" She demanded, cheeks flushed from the wind, curls tumbling from beneath her hat. "Where is Georgina?"

The air snapped tight.

Mrs. Hemsley stepped aside to allow her in fully. "You tell me. She was to meet you at half eleven."

"She never came," Eliza said, her voice sharp, not from anger, but from something far more brittle. "I waited. I waited an hour, and then I walked the entire length of the park, thinking she'd been delayed. I even went to the bookshop to ask if she'd stopped in. She hadn't."

Mrs. Hemsley closed the door behind them and gestured toward the drawing room. "Sit down."

"I don't want tea."

"I didn't offer it."

Eliza stalked inside, pacing a short line near the hearth. "I thought she might have returned here without telling me. But when I saw the state of the drive, no carriage, no new tracks, then I knew."

Mrs. Hemsley folded her hands at her waist. "We haven't seen her since she left this morning. She said she was meeting you. No one else."

"Well, she didn't," Eliza snapped, then caught herself. She let out a shaky breath. "I'm sorry. I'm just—"

"Worried," Mrs. Hemsley said calmly. "As am I."

Not after she'd finally let herself believe she was safe again. That she could walk freely without fear. And now this.

They stared at one another for a moment. Two women of

very different natures, drawn together by the same fire.

"Has anyone been sent to look for her?" Eliza asked.

"I was preparing to ride to Sommer Chase," Mrs. Hemsley replied. "Mr. Barrington left for there earlier this morning. I thought he might have some word."

"And Alex?"

Mrs. Hemsley hesitated. "Left at dawn. No word since. No one seems to know where."

Eliza's brows rose. "She didn't say she was meeting him?"

"No. Only you."

Eliza folded her arms, wrapping them around her own rib-cage like a shield. "She wouldn't disappear. Not without telling someone. Not after everything."

"No, she wouldn't," Mrs. Hemsley said firmly.

She turned to the footman now standing in the corridor. "Send for Mr. Barrington's man, if he's returned. Then tell Brandon to bring the carriage to the front."

"Yes, ma'am."

Mrs. Hemsley looked back at Eliza. "You'll stay here. In case she returns."

"I'm coming with you."

"You're not. If she arrives and finds the house empty—"

Eliza exhaled through her nose, frustrated, but nodded. "Fine. But if she's not back in an hour—"

"Then we'll raise hell together," Mrs. Hemsley said.

And with that, she turned, cloak snapping behind her as she strode out toward the carriage.

The wheels of the Ravenstock carriage hadn't even stopped groaning when Mrs. Hemsley stepped down onto the gravel with the force of someone who had no intention of being received. Not received. Obeyed.

The wind tugged at her cloak, snapping the hem against her boots as she marched up the short stone steps to the door of Sommer Chase and rapped twice, sharply, without patience.

The door opened a moment later, and Kenworth, ever

poised, blinked only once.

"Mrs. Hemsley. We weren't expecting—"

"Clearly," she said, brushing past him. "Where is Mr. Barrington?"

He gestured, unruffled, toward the study. "With Lord Weld, ma'am."

Her eyes flicked to him, surprised. "Weld is here?"

"Yes, ma'am. They've been in conference nearly an hour."

"Good."

She swept down the corridor like a gust of judgment and flung open the door to the study without an announcement. Of course. He had come here straight from breakfast, just as he'd said. And yet, why hadn't he known?

Inside, Barrington stood near the hearth, a sheaf of papers in one hand and a decanter in the other. Alex sat in one of the leather armchairs, one booted foot resting on the opposite knee, his posture deceptively relaxed.

Both looked up at the intrusion.

"Mrs. Hemsley?" Barrington blinked. "Is something wrong?"

"You might say that," she replied, voice cool as pressed linen.

Alex stood. "What's happened?"

"I'd ask you that very question." She stepped inside, allowing the door to swing shut behind her. "Where is Lady Ravenstock?"

Alex's brow furrowed. "She's in town. She said she was visiting Miss Eliza."

"She never arrived."

Silence cracked across the room.

Alex's breath stilled. For one heartbeat, he saw her as she'd been that morning, her hand warm against his chest, her smile still lingering, and then it vanished.

"What do you mean?"

"She wrote a note this morning and asked that it be delivered to Miss Eliza, arranging to meet at half past eleven behind the bookshop." Her eyes locked on his. "It is now after four o'clock. Eliza arrived at Ravenstock in a fury, having waited an hour and searched half the town. Georgina was nowhere to be found."

Alex was already moving. He pushed the chair back with a thud, then crossed the room.

"I thought she'd be out of harm's way," he said, more to himself than to her. "I left before breakfast. She said she was meeting Eliza. There was no reason to question it."

Barrington set down the decanter. "She didn't go with you?"

"No."

Mrs. Hemsley's voice was flint. "Then where is she?"

Alex's mind was already running ahead. "Did anyone see her leave?"

"A footman said she departed as usual. On foot. With her shawl. No carriage was ordered."

"That was hours ago."

He turned sharply to Barrington. "Summon your man. Tell him to check every path between Ravenstock and the town square. Speak with the bookseller, the grocer, the postmaster, anyone who might have seen her."

Barrington didn't argue. He left the room at once.

Mrs. Hemsley crossed her arms. "I should have gone with her."

"No," Alex said, reaching for his coat. "I should have stayed."

He strapped on his gloves in silence, jaw tight, his eyes already narrowed with purpose.

"I'll find her."

"You'll take someone with you."

Alex didn't answer. He simply opened the door and disappeared into the corridor, his footsteps already pounding toward the courtyard.

By the time the lamps were lit in the drawing room, the warmth of the day had fled, leaving the windows streaked with breath and the fire sputtering in the grate.

Mrs. Hemsley sat stiff-backed in her usual chair, a shawl draped over her shoulders and a cup of untouched tea cooling beside her. She'd returned from Sommer Chase nearly an hour earlier, with no answers and a heaviness that wouldn't lift.

Eliza stood near the window, arms folded tightly, watching the empty drive as if willing Georgina to appear by force of will alone.

Mrs. Bainbridge had come down from her room without being asked, summoned by instinct or some other sharp intuition, and now occupied the settee, a blanket over her knees but no comfort in her posture.

The door opened quietly.

Alex stepped in, the wind still in his coat. His face was unreadable, drawn in hard lines.

"No sign of her," he said.

Barrington followed behind him, removing his gloves with uncharacteristic distraction. "We checked every path into town. Not a trace of her passing. No purchases, no shopkeepers, no footsteps remembered. Not one person recalled her at all."

"She was meant to meet me," Eliza said again, voice thin. "She never came."

Alex leaned one hand against the mantel, the knuckles white. "Then we assume she never reached town."

Mrs. Hemsley rose to her feet. "I'll check the study."

"For what?" Barrington asked.

"For anything she might have left behind."

They all remained where they were as she swept from the room, her footsteps clipped and echoing in the stillness.

It wasn't more than five minutes before she returned, her expression unreadable, a crumpled piece of paper clutched in her hand.

She passed it to Barrington without a word.

He unfolded it carefully.

Two words. That was all.

Greyline Holdings.

"We've seen that name before," Alex said, in a low, clipped tone. "It was in Rowland's ledger. Where did you find that?"

"In the wastebasket by the desk."

"That's Rowland's old study," Barrington murmured.

"It's the only thing in there that wasn't in order," Mrs. Hemsley said.

Alex took the paper, turned it over once in his hand. "She went to Greyline."

Eliza's voice broke. "Then why didn't she come back?"

No one answered.

Outside, the wind picked up, scattering the last of the fallen leaves across the gravel. Inside, the silence grew thick with names unspoken and one thought no one dared to voice aloud. Wherever she was, she no longer walked alone.

Chapter Twenty-Six

THE MORNING HAD opened gently, the mist rising off the fields, the leaves clinging to dew, and the quiet rustle of a house not yet fully awake. Georgina stood in Rowland's study, one hand resting on the worn back of his old chair, the other holding the edge of a file box she'd left untouched for weeks.

She had not planned to come here today. But the hush and the sense of something unfinished had drawn her. Alex had already gone, and the absence of his presence was like the lingering warmth of a fire after the flame had died. She hadn't asked where he was headed. She trusted him. Trust, she knew, asked as much as it offered. He had learned to let her choose her battles. This one, she chose alone.

And now, here she was, surrounded by shadows that no longer hurt as they once had.

The crate on the floor still bore Rowland's handwriting: *W.R. – Ledgers West Accounts.* She knelt beside it, brushing a film of dust from the lid. One of the hinges had started to rust.

Inside were neat stacks of papers, tied with ribbon or twine. Some were labeled. Others not. She sorted them gently, careful not to disturb the order, though she suspected it mattered little now. Most were dry, investment summaries, modest dividends, and rent rolls.

Until she reached the bottom layer.

One unmarked file contained several receipts and a torn memorandum, with the top half missing. The remaining fragment was dated from nearly six months before Rowland's death and bore the name:

Greyline Holdings – Schedule B: Disbursements

She frowned.

She'd seen the name Greyline before, passing on shipping manifests or property transfer documents. But never in connection to Rowland. Never linked to anything significant.

Beneath the slip was a note in Rowland's hand. The ink was smeared in one corner, as if he'd dashed it off and never returned to it.

Hold for follow-up. Ask Barrington re: Everly's investment arm. Check if tied to 'GH.'

Her stomach clenched. The letters blurred for a heartbeat, not from fear but from the echo of Alex's warning that danger never travels alone.

Everly. That meant the Order.

Georgina stood slowly, the page still between her fingers.

She could wait. Let Barrington sort it. Let Alex shield her again. But every instinct in her body rebelled at the thought of standing still while others decided her fate. And some part of her, the sharp, stubborn, and tired of being protected part, refused to do that. Not this time.

She crossed to the writing desk, selected a fresh sheet of paper, and began to write.

Eliza—

I hope you're well. Would you mind delaying our walk slightly? I'll meet you at half past eleven, in the park as planned.
Yours,
G.

She sanded the ink, folded the page, and called for a footman to have it delivered to Miss Eliza.

Then, without rushing, but with the same focused calm she'd used to handle barristers, bankers, and whispered threats in drawing rooms, she changed her gown, selected her gloves, and pinned her hat precisely. She passed the staff in the corridor with a polite nod and slipped out the front door without explanation. For a fleeting moment, she imagined Alex standing at the gate, half-smile in place, telling her to be careful. She answered him in silence. *I will.*

The air was crisp with the scent of chimney smoke and fallen leaves. She walked with purpose, the hem of her cloak brushing against the gravel as she followed the lane down to the village.

There was always a carriage for hire at the White Bell Inn. No questions asked. A small errand, no longer than an hour. Eliza wouldn't mind the delay.

She would be back in plenty of time.

The Greyline Holdings offices were located in a narrow brick building near the edge of town, where the streets grew quieter and the scent of salt and coal mingled in the air. It bore no sign of wealth or power. There was no polished brass plate, no livery at the door, just a modest knocker and a name discreetly painted on the window above.

Georgina stepped down from the hired carriage and paused to gather herself. Her gloves were buttoned. Her reticule hung neatly at her wrist. She looked every inch the composed young widow she had learned to be.

Inside, the office was dim and spare, the front room dominated by a counter and two tall stools. A clerk looked up from behind a pile of ledgers, startled to see her.

"Good morning," she said smoothly. "I'm Lady Ravenstock. I believe you have some holdings previously managed by my late husband."

The clerk rose at once, bowing quickly. "Of course, my lady. Do you, did Lord Ravenstock have a scheduled appointment?"

"No," she said, not unkindly. "But I'm sure someone can

spare ten minutes."

He hesitated, clearly unused to titled women arriving without notice, especially not ones with eyes this direct.

"I'll see if Mr. Hargraves is in," he murmured, then disappeared through the rear door.

She stood in silence, glancing over the neat but weathered appointments, the chipped paint near the wainscoting, the faded registry log on the counter. Everything clean, quiet, respectable.

The clerk returned. "He'll see you in the back room, my lady."

"Thank you."

Hargraves was a broad man with thinning hair and the uneasy air of someone who didn't like surprises. He rose when she entered, but didn't offer a chair until she had already claimed it.

"Lady Ravenstock," he said with an approximation of warmth. "What can we help you with today?"

She placed her gloves on the desk and offered him a calm smile.

"I came across a reference in my husband's estate papers. Greyline Holdings – Schedule B: Disbursements. Dated some months before his passing. It wasn't filed with his other investments."

Hargraves lifted his brows but kept his expression unreadable. "Greyline maintains many partnerships, my lady. Not all are public."

"I'm aware. I'm simply hoping to understand whether my husband was an active investor or something more passive. I'm trying to get a sense of... obligations he may have left behind."

"Obligations?"

"Quiet ones," she said lightly. "The sort that don't make it into probate but have a way of returning if ignored."

He glanced at a ledger on his desk, fingers drumming once. "Your husband was listed among our limited partners, but only for a brief period. He divested before the summer."

She inclined her head. "Why?"

"I couldn't say."

"Of course you could. But I understand you won't."

He offered a small, practiced smile. "I believe Lord Ravenstock handled those matters privately," Hargraves said, his hand resting lightly atop a closed ledger. "We were not always invited to inquire."

"Yes," she said softly. "He did."

There was a pause.

"I appreciate your time," she said, rising smoothly. "Please don't trouble yourself with sending word if anything changes. I prefer to ask my own questions."

She turned, gloves in hand, and walked with quiet precision from the room.

The air outside was cooler than it had been an hour ago. A breeze stirred the edge of Georgina's cloak as she stepped back onto the street, the autumn sun caught in the angles of the brick buildings around her. Somewhere, a bell chimed the half hour.

She drew her gloves on one finger at a time, then descended the short stone steps of Greyline's office. Her breath came steady, though her thoughts did not.

She drew her gloves on one finger at a time, her breath steady, though her thoughts were not.

A gentleman stood just beyond the gate.

He leaned with casual ease against the iron post, his hat tipped slightly forward, his gloved hands resting lightly on a walking stick he didn't seem to need. His coat was impeccable. His expression was serene.

The breeze shifted. It carried something unfamiliar, clove, maybe. Or cedar oil. Not unpleasant. But out of place.

As she passed, he stepped away from the post and bent slightly, not blocking her, but close enough to be noticed.

"You dropped this," he said, holding out a handkerchief.

It was finely embroidered. Pale cream linen. Her initials, GR, stitched in soft gold.

Her fingers hesitated, too long, perhaps, and the air between them tightened. Then, because to refuse would be to reveal the tremor in her pulse, she reached for it.

Chapter Twenty-Seven

THE PARK BEHIND the bookshop was nearly empty at that hour, the sort of place one chose for quiet company rather than solitude. It was the kind of morning that was too quiet, too expectant, as if the world itself waited for someone who never came. The leaves had fallen in drifts along the garden paths, too damp to stir. A row of hedges stood trimmed in polite attention, and the wrought-iron bench beneath the sycamore still bore the imprint of an early frost.

Eliza stood beside it, her arms folded. Her boot tapped once, then not again. A small, quiet rhythm she refused to let become anxious.

Georgina was late.

Not dreadfully so. Only ten minutes. Eleven, at most.

She pulled the note from her reticule, smoothing the fold with the back of her glove.

Half past eleven. The park behind the bookshop.
Would you mind delaying our walk slightly…

It had come that morning, written in Georgina's steady hand, precise as ever, the letters looped but never frivolous. Eliza had smiled when it arrived. Of course, she didn't mind. Who could refuse a request from a friend so fastidious?

She checked the square again. There was no sign of her.

There were others in the park, a governess with two children trailing hoops through the gravel, a pair of older gentlemen discussing something in serious tones, one of them gesturing with a pipe, but none of them were Georgina.

Eliza began a slow walk along the hedgerow, her steps deliberate, unhurried. It wasn't like Georgina to forget. But perhaps she'd become delayed at home. Or gone to the market on a whim. Or found something in Rowland's papers that needed sorting.

Or—

No. There was no or. Georgina was the sort who arrived five minutes early and stood pretending not to notice the time until one struck the half.

She looped back to the bench.

It was nearly noon.

Eliza stared up at the bare branches above her, the brittle sky beyond. The kind of day that held no promise of change, just cold truth in clean air. She disliked it intensely.

She waited seven more minutes. Then she walked away, not in haste, but in rising silence.

The sound of her own footsteps followed her crisp and even, but too loud for comfort through the narrow side street leading back into town. Eliza hated walking alone when she was meant to be walking with someone else. It wasn't fear that quickened her pace. It was the memory of Georgina's steadiness, the way her friend's presence always balanced the air around her. Without it, the world tilted. It always made her feel like she'd missed something. A message. A signal. An entire conversation that never had the chance to begin.

Georgina wouldn't have forgotten. That wasn't her way. If something had come up, she would have sent a note, likely with a brief apology and a promise to reschedule. But she hadn't.

Still, there were reasons. There were always reasons.

Eliza reached the far end of the market square and turned in at Madame Pembroke's, the bell over the door chiming like a peal of laughter.

The shop smelled faintly of starch and violets. Lace in every shade of ivory hung like clouds above the counter. A girl in pale blue came out from the back and brightened when she saw her.

"Eliza! Miss Pembroke isn't in just now, but I'm happy to assist—"

"I'm actually looking for Georgina," Eliza said with a smile, stepping forward. "Or perhaps Mrs. Bainbridge. I wondered if they'd come in for a fitting?"

The girl blinked. "Not today, miss. Mrs. Bainbridge was here earlier in the week to view a few samples, but nothing was booked for today."

"No?" Eliza forced a breezy tone. "She mentioned she was thinking about narrowing down fabric for the wedding."

"She said she'd send word when ready." The girl tilted her head. "Did you want to see what she chose?"

"No, no," Eliza said quickly. "That's not necessary. Thank you."

Back outside, the sun had shifted westward, softening the glare on the cobblestones. The air still smelled of salt and coal and something sharp, perhaps roasted chestnuts. She crossed the square and made for the bookshop. The same one Georgina had mentioned in her note.

The bell rang. Familiar comfort.

The bookseller behind the counter gave her a pleasant nod. "Looking for anything particular today?"

"Not today," she said. "I was meant to meet a friend near the park and thought she might have come in first."

He tilted his head, thinking. "Lady Ravenstock, you mean?"

Eliza smiled. "Yes."

"Haven't seen her today, miss. Though a few days ago she asked after that pamphlet on maritime trade."

"Of course she did." Eliza laughed once, softly. "Thank you."

She wandered for a moment longer than she needed to, tracing her gloved fingers along a row of volumes she didn't read.

Outside again, the clouds had begun to gather near the horizon.

The tearoom was on the next corner. A pale pink door and rose-shaped windowpanes. She ducked her head in.

Empty, save two matrons and a scowling child with jam on his collar.

"Have you seen Lady Ravenstock this morning?" She asked the server near the window.

The girl shook her head. "Not since last week. She ordered lemon."

Eliza offered a polite thank-you and stepped back into the wind.

She hadn't realized until now how many places she expected Georgina to be. The tearoom. The bookshop. Even the apothecary was her final stop. Perhaps a headache had kept her from their walk. Or perhaps she needed tincture for something else. It would explain the note. The delay.

But the shopkeeper only blinked at her through a pair of thick spectacles and said, "Lady Ravenstock hasn't been in. Not for some days."

By the time Eliza left the shop, it was nearing one o'clock.

She had to meet Everly.

Still no Georgina.

The bell above the clock tower struck one as Eliza turned onto High Street.

She had not meant to hurry, but her feet had carried her briskly all the same. Her gloves were warm from her hands, and her cheeks stung faintly from the wind. A part of her still hoped, foolishly perhaps, that Georgina would appear at the last moment, pulling her cloak tighter, apologizing for the delay with that soft, even voice that never rose in fluster.

But there was no one waiting.

Everly was already there.

He stood just outside the jeweler's, his back to the shop window, one foot crossed casually over the other. His cane rested against his leg. His hat was in place. He might have been a drawing.

He smiled when he saw her. Not broadly. Not greedily. Just enough. Something about that smile was measured, almost rehearsed, like a phrase he'd practiced until it no longer sounded like words.

"Eliza."

She returned the smile, more from habit than ease. "You're early."

"I am rarely late," he said, offering his arm. "You look well."

She took it without hesitation.

As they turned toward the south end of the square, she glanced over her shoulder, as though expecting to see someone trailing behind. Georgina, perhaps. But the street was ordinary people walking, wheels clattering, a pair of children chasing a hoop past the bakery.

"I thought I might be bringing someone," she said lightly.

"Ah." He didn't ask who.

"She was meant to meet me in the park but didn't arrive. I checked a few places, nothing urgent, I'm sure. Just... not like her."

Everly turned his head slightly, the gesture almost too restrained to be called interested. "Do you think she's unwell?"

"No," Eliza said quickly. "No. Georgina isn't the type to fall ill without informing every person she's seen in the last forty-eight hours. No, if I had to guess, she's buried under a heap of ledgers and forgot to come up for air."

"Ah. A very modern ailment." He chuckled softly. "She's fortunate to have you watching over her."

The words settled on her shoulders, warmer than they ought to have been. She adjusted her grip on his arm.

"You mentioned you wanted to speak privately," she said, redirecting the conversation.

He smiled faintly. "Did I? I suppose I only meant to enjoy your company without the distraction of half the town listening in."

Eliza shook her head, amused despite herself. "You do make

it sound so mysterious."

"And you do make it so easy to pretend," he said.

They walked on in silence for a few moments, the town falling behind them.

"Shall we?" he said, tipping his head toward the lane that led toward Ravenstock. "I imagine your friends may be there already."

She'd insisted on doing things her own way. And now no one knew where to look for her.

"They might," Eliza replied. "Or Georgina might have slipped in without telling anyone. It's still rather unlike her."

He didn't press. He simply adjusted his stride to match hers and offered, with quiet concern, "If there's anything I can do to help…"

The Ravenstock carriage had not been brought around, which Eliza took as a sign that no one had gone out in it. Good. That meant someone would be home.

She and Everly approached on foot, the last turn in the drive crunching softly beneath their boots. A low wind had stirred the leaves into half-hearted motion, but the manor itself looked perfectly still. Too still. Even the curtains hung motionless, as if the house itself were holding its breath.

At the door, she didn't wait for a servant. She opened it as if she lived there.

"Lady Eliza," came Mrs. Hemsley's voice from the entry hall. She appeared from the corridor, wiping her hands on a towel, her brows rising. "We weren't expecting—"

"No one's seen her," Eliza said, stepping in quickly. "She never met me at the park. I went looking. I've been to Pembroke's, the bookshop, and the tearoom. No one's seen her today. Not since this morning."

Mrs. Hemsley's face didn't change, but something inside her posture did. She folded the towel over one hand with quiet precision.

"I see," she said.

"This is Mr. Everly," Eliza added, gesturing behind her. "A friend. He was kind enough to accompany me back."

Everly inclined his head. "Your servant, ma'am."

Mrs. Hemsley nodded once, calm but polite. "We've not seen Lady Ravenstock since she left the house. She said she would be meeting you."

"She was meant to," Eliza said, voice rising just a note. "And she never arrived."

"Perhaps she returned without saying—"

"I checked her room. I checked the study. The staff says she hasn't come back," Mrs. Hemsley cut in, not harshly, but with that clipped tone that came when she was already five steps ahead in her thoughts.

They stood in a triangle of silence near the drawing room door.

Everly's voice broke the silence first. "Would it be forward of me to offer assistance? I know the town and its people rather well. If you'd like someone to make quiet inquiries, I'd be glad to help."

Mrs. Hemsley glanced at him. "Your concern is appreciated."

"She may simply have lost track of the time," Eliza offered, though her tone betrayed that even she no longer believed it. "She had a note to send this morning. Perhaps she's gone to speak with someone about Rowland's estate."

"Perhaps," Mrs. Hemsley agreed softly. "Or perhaps something else entirely."

A footman appeared at the end of the corridor. "Shall I inform Lord Barrington and Lord Weld, ma'am?"

Mrs. Hemsley nodded. "At once."

Eliza turned toward the front window. The sun was beginning its downward arc.

"I can't explain it," she said. "But it's not like her."

"No," Mrs. Hemsley agreed again. "It isn't."

The drawing room had gone still. Eliza stood by the window, one gloved hand pressed lightly to the drape, watching the shadows lengthen across the drive.

"I should have remained there longer," she murmured.

"You waited long enough," Mrs. Hemsley replied. "If she meant to meet you, she would have been there. She's not careless."

Everly was seated near the hearth, perfectly at ease. He had offered to take another look in town, but Mrs. Hemsley had waved him off with quiet authority. "There's no use hunting shadows," she'd said. "Not until we know where to look."

Eliza turned from the window. "You don't think she's simply… decided to take a detour?"

"I think she's been gone too long without explanation."

That was when Mrs. Hemsley moved, quietly, deliberately, toward the corridor that led to the study.

"She spent time in there this morning," she said over her shoulder. "Didn't say what, but if she left a trace, it will be in that room."

Eliza followed her with her eyes but didn't speak.

Ten minutes passed. The wind stirred again outside. Somewhere upstairs, a floorboard creaked. It was an ordinary house sound that was now too loud.

Then Mrs. Hemsley returned, a scrap of crumpled paper in hand.

"I found this in the wastebasket," she said, holding it out.

Eliza stepped forward.

Only two words. Written cleanly in Georgina's unmistakable hand.

Greyline Holdings.

"She found something," Mrs. Hemsley said. "And didn't tell anyone."

"She meant to," Eliza whispered. "She was going to tell me everything."

But the paper said otherwise. The silence between them now was sharper than absence.

It was intentional.

A knock rattled the door.

A footman stepped in, breath slightly short. "Lord Barrington and Lord Weld have just returned from Sommer Chase, ma'am. Shall I show them in?"

Mrs. Hemsley didn't answer immediately. She looked down at the scrap of paper in her hand.

"Yes," she said at last, the words measured, certain. "Bring them in." She looked down once more at Georgina's handwriting. "Whatever we thought we knew, this changes everything."

Chapter Twenty-Eight

BY EARLY EVENING, Ravenstock had fallen into the quiet of a house holding its breath.

The corridors, once bustling with the rhythm of daily tasks, were hushed. Lamps burned lower than usual. Doors stood ajar, ready for someone to return and push them fully open. The air held the scent of rain that had not yet fallen and of something else, something absent.

Alex stood in the front hall, boots planted wide, his voice low but firm as he gave instructions to Peter Simms, one of Barrington's men. Simms was an investigator by trade, methodical, sharp-eyed, and discreet. His gloves were already on, the leather creased at the knuckles.

"Take the north road. All the way to the river. If you see a coach, any coach, stopped or changing horses, you question the driver. Don't let him ride off until you've seen what's inside."

Simms nodded once and vanished out the front door, swift and silent.

He was already halfway through fastening his riding cloak when Barrington appeared at the top of the stairs, shrugging into his coat.

"You're still assuming something's wrong," Barrington said. "She may simply have followed another trail. She's done it before."

Alex didn't look up. "She hasn't done this before."

"There's no reason to think she's in danger."

"Except she missed an appointment. Except she left no word. Except she hasn't come home."

Barrington frowned, but his voice stayed calm. "She's methodical. She'll come back when she's finished."

Alex adjusted the strap on his saddlebag. He didn't argue further. The facts sat poorly in his gut. Georgina was independent, curious, and determined, but not careless. Not when others were depending on her.

Mrs. Hemsley appeared quietly from the corridor, holding out a flask. "You'll take this. And you'll be back by full dark."

Alex paused, took the flask. Their eyes met.

"Unless I find her," he said softly. He hadn't meant the words to sound like a vow, but they settled in the room as one.

He turned and walked out into the dusk.

Barrington stood before the mantel in the study, the fire crackling low. A map lay open across the table, dotted with carriage routes, trade roads, and footpaths. Candlelight caught the fine edge of his profile, throwing sharp shadows across the pages.

Eliza hovered at the edge of the room with her arms crossed tightly over her chest. She had not changed out of her walking dress. The hem of her skirt was still faintly damp from the park path, though she hadn't noticed it until just now. Her gloves were clenched in one hand. Her other arm was wound tightly across her waist, as if to hold her own center still.

"We know she went to Greyline Holdings," Barrington said, his voice quiet but clipped. "We know she changed her meeting time with you to give herself more time beforehand. And we know she never arrived."

His finger tapped once on the map. Then stopped.

Eliza stepped closer, her voice low. "But why would she go alone? She's not reckless."

"No," Barrington agreed. "But she is deliberate. If she thought she could gain information without drawing attention, she would have done it herself."

"She would have told someone."

"Not if she didn't think it was dangerous."

Eliza studied the edge of the map. There was a small ink blot near the word Alnmouth. It looked like a tiny, perfect bruise.

"Are you worried?" she asked.

Barrington hesitated. "Not yet." He didn't look up. "She's resourceful. If she needed time to follow something privately, she'd take it."

"Without telling anyone?" Eliza said. "Without sending a note?"

He glanced at her then, but only briefly. "She may have meant to."

The wind stirred against the windows, rattling one of the shutters in a soft, restless rhythm.

Eliza turned from the table and paced once toward the hearth, then back again. "And if she found something? Something she didn't expect?"

Barrington didn't answer right away. The fire popped. Somewhere in the hallway beyond, footsteps passed. They didn't pause.

"She's strong," he said at last.

"I know," Eliza said, her throat tight. "But even strong women disappear." The words slipped out before she could stop them, the sound of fear pretending to be reason.

Barrington's eyes finally lifted to meet hers. "Then we'll find her."

Outside, the wind scraped the windows again. But inside, the study remained silent.

Eliza and Everly stood near the hearth in the drawing room, just beyond the reach of the fire's warmth. Shadows clung to the corners of the room, the flicker of the flames not quite brave enough to chase them all away.

Everly held an untouched glass in one hand. His other rested lightly against the back of a chair, as though he had simply wandered in for polite conversation. He looked entirely at ease, and perhaps that was what unsettled Eliza most. When the rest of the house was fraying at the edges, he remained composed. Calm. Almost reassuring.

"If there's anything I can do," he said, voice low and unhurried, "please say so. I know the harbor well. There are men there who keep their ears open more than their mouths. Quiet men. Loyal ones."

Eliza managed to smile. It was small and brief, like a candle struggling against the wind. "That's generous of you. Thank you."

Everly studied her, but not too intently. Just enough. His expression, a faint crease of concern between his brows, but nothing too dramatic, was perfectly schooled. Nothing that might look like performance.

"Someone like Lady Ravenstock doesn't simply vanish," he said. His tone was mild, but something in it made her skin prickle, calm and too smooth to be kind.

"No," Eliza murmured. "Not her."

"She's far too clever. Far too cautious. If she's gone quiet, there's a reason."

The words were meant to comfort. And they did. They soothed her, just enough to stop the trembling that had reached her fingers.

He paused. "I'll speak to a man I trust," he added. "He's kept quiet about worse. If she passed through the harbor alone or with someone, he'll know."

Eliza hesitated. "Are you sure? I wouldn't want to put you in a difficult position."

"It's no difficulty." Everly offered a faint smile, one almost too well-measured. "Let's just say it's long overdue."

She let out a breath. "You've been very kind."

He tipped his head, brushing the brim of his hat as he offered her the ghost of a bow. "I'll return once I've learned something."

His coat collar lifted against the wind, and footsteps quiet on the stone, he was gone.

Eliza stood for a long while after the door had closed, her eyes fixed on the empty space where he'd stood. She wasn't waiting for him to return.

She was waiting for Georgina.

But Georgina didn't come.

A knock at the service door came just after sunset, followed by the quick shuffling of boots and a muttered explanation from a kitchen maid. A village boy had brought word: someone had seen a woman matching Lady Ravenstock's description near the old toll road. Cloaked, walking alone, boarding a small, dark carriage.

It was vague. It was secondhand. But it was something.

Alex was out the door before the maid had finished the tale. Barrington went with him, coat only half-buttoned, sword strapped hastily over his shoulder.

Back at Ravenstock, Eliza remained in the drawing room, the ticking of the mantel clock growing louder with every passing moment. She paced in measured loops, crossing and re-crossing the same narrow patch of carpet. Her boots clicked faintly on the floor. Mrs. Hemsley sat in her chair by the hearth, her knitting untouched in her lap. The fire gave off little warmth.

Outside, the wind had picked up, whistling through the chimney like a voice trying to speak but never quite finding the words.

The minutes stretched. Then slowed. Then snapped.

Hoofbeats. Distant at first, then louder, sharper.

Eliza stopped mid-stride.

The door opened, spilling cold air into the hall. Alex stepped inside, his coat still damp from the road, his face pale beneath the grime.

"It wasn't her," he said. His voice scraped low, dull with fury, and that frightened her more than anything. "A washerwoman. Wrong age. Wrong height. Wrong everything."

He'd let hope take root. That was the worst of it. He'd built his hope out of her name, out of the memory of her voice, and now the sound of it splintered in his chest. Let it bloom in the space between hoofbeats. Now it was rotting.

Barrington followed behind him, slower. "She had the same cloak," he offered, as if that justified their hope.

Mrs. Hemsley rose without a word and left the room.

Eliza didn't speak. She looked at Alex, then at the space behind him as though she might still catch the flutter of a familiar cloak, the glint of golden hair, a voice raised in apology.

But the space behind him remained still. Outside, the wind swept the leaves along the path.

⇶⇷

LATER THAT NIGHT, long past the hour when most had gone to bed, Eliza sat curled on the edge of Georgina's chaise in the window alcove, wrapped in a shawl that smelled faintly of rose water and salt.

She hadn't meant to come in here. Her fingers had turned the handle before her heart could catch up.

It was as Georgina had left it. The inkstand was covered. The chair pushed in. A shawl, half-folded, lay across the end of the bed. One of her books, Darwin, of all things, was open to a marked page, the ribbon slightly askew. A hairbrush rested on the vanity, its silver back catching the moonlight, a single strand of blonde hair still caught in its bristles.

The scent in the room was familiar. Lavender from her soap. Dust warmed by the sun. A whisper of ink and wax.

Eliza drew her knees up to her chest and rested her chin on them. The shawl slipped from one shoulder. She didn't bother to fix it.

She had gone over it, the park, the note, the shops, the walk back to Ravenstock, again and again. Nothing out of place. Nothing she could undo. The silence between them had not been troubling. Georgina had smiled the last time they spoke.

She should have waited longer. Followed. Asked one more

question. Something. Anything.

The fire in the grate had burned low, casting long fingers of gold against the far wall, pulsing gently as if trying to fill the space with warmth that no longer held.

A breeze stirred the curtain. Outside, the wind moved through the trees with a sound like breath drawn in but never released.

Eliza stared into the dark.

"Where did you go?" she whispered. The question hung between the walls like the echo of a breath, waiting for someone who would not answer.

The room did not answer.

Chapter Twenty-Nine

THE MORNING SUN fell across the long table in the breakfast room, soft and golden, too warm for the mood it illuminated. The light touched silver and porcelain, glinted off the rim of the butter dish, but none of it reached the hearts of the people seated at the table. The tea had gone cold. The toast sat untouched. Ravenstock was not a house at rest. It was a house holding its breath, waiting for its walls to whisper something useful.

Eliza sat beside an empty place, her hands clasped tightly in her lap, knuckles white against her gloves. Her cup of tea had cooled, untouched, the rim stained faintly with the mark of her first sip. She did not remember taking it. Her shoulders were set, spine straight, but her eyes had the dazed softness of someone trying to remember what normal used to feel like. The tick of the longcase clock in the hall was louder than usual. Somewhere upstairs, a door creaked, then fell silent again. Even the fire burned softly, as if afraid to intrude.

Across from her, Barrington stood near the fireplace, unreadable, the fingers of one hand curled loosely around a folded letter. He read it, then read it again, as if willing the words to change. They did not. His other hand was closed, his knuckles pale, as if he'd forgotten he was still holding something.

Alex sat with his back half-turned from the table, one arm braced against the chair beside him. He had poured a cup of coffee and forgotten it. The dark surface had gone still, reflecting his hollowed features. His riding boots were still dusted with the road. He had not slept. Not really. His gaze drifted, unfocused, toward the window, although he wasn't watching the wind. He was listening for a footfall that never came.

The quiet was not companionable. It was cavernous.

Then came footsteps. Light, well-measured.

Everly arrived late. Apologetic. Breezy.

"Forgive me," he said, brushing imagined dust from his coat. "I stopped at the harbor this morning to speak with a contact. No word yet, but I'm hopeful."

Hopeful. The word struck like glass against stone.

He took the empty chair beside Eliza with practiced grace. She offered him a tired smile because it would have been rude not to. She had spent the morning fighting back the tremor in her hands. His voice, so calm, so easy, was almost a relief. Until it wasn't.

The room tried to resume the rhythm of polite conversation. Barrington asked about the weather, and someone remarked on the wind picking up, but every word fell like a feather into water, vanishing without a ripple or a reply. No one spoke of Georgina. No one dared.

A footman entered with a fresh pot of tea. His heel caught on the rug, and he stumbled, not badly, but enough to jostle the tray.

A splash of tea landed across Eliza's sleeve.

She gasped, dabbing at the fabric with her napkin, but Everly rose at once. "Allow me."

He reached into his coat pocket and withdrew a square of pale linen.

He handed it to her, unthinking.

Eliza took it, grateful, then froze.

Her eyes dropped to the corner. Fine stitching. Cream silk thread. Two letters: G. R.

For a beat, the world slowed.

"I meant to return it," Everly said easily. "She dropped it at the bookshop last week. By the time I reached the door, she was already gone."

Eliza looked up at him, searching his face.

He gave her a small smile. Calm. Undisturbed.

"I'm glad it found its way home."

She forced a nod, murmured her thanks, and turned back to her tea.

Her fingers trembled against the porcelain. She didn't drink. Couldn't.

It wasn't until after breakfast, when the others had drifted away, that Eliza found herself in the hallway just outside the drawing room. Alex was there, standing near the window, arms folded tight across his chest. Mrs. Hemsley moved quietly between rooms with a folded sheet of correspondence in one hand. There was a stillness in the air, not calm, but held.

"I need to show you something," Eliza said softly.

Alex turned. His expression was tired, wary. "What is it?"

She reached into her pocket and unfolded the square of linen.

Mrs. Hemsley paused in the doorway and stepped closer.

"He gave this to me at breakfast," Eliza said. Her voice was flat. "He said Georgina dropped it at the bookshop last week."

Mrs. Hemsley didn't even need to look closely. "That's hers," she said at once. "She made only one like that. Took it with her yesterday."

Alex took it gently, turning it over in his hand. The monogram gleamed. He traced the edge with his thumb. The linen was still smooth, as if freshly pressed. It hadn't spent a week tucked in a coat pocket.

Something cold settled in his chest, not shock, not anger, something older. Recognition.

"He lied," Eliza whispered. Her voice cracked. "He lied to my face."

She defended him. She believed his civility meant safety. And now Georgina was missing. The words clung in the air, fragile and irreversible, the way truth always sounded when spoken too late.

There was a long silence. Not hesitation, but grief. The kind that comes when certainty replaces hope.

Alex looked toward the hallway where Everly had gone. Then to Barrington, who had just entered behind them.

Barrington's voice was low, steady. "Let him go."

"Close enough. We will follow." Alex glanced once toward Eliza, not pity, not comfort, just the shared knowledge that this had become personal.

Mrs. Hemsley turned away first, her hand closing slowly around the corner of the wall as if bracing herself. Eliza didn't move. Alex nodded once.

The storm had shifted.

Peter Simms returned mid-morning. His coat was dusted with road dirt, his expression unreadable.

"I asked again at the White Bell," he said. "Yesterday, we asked if Lady Ravenstock hired a carriage. The answer was no. Today, I asked if anyone else hired one."

Barrington straightened. Alex turned sharply.

Simms nodded. "A man matching Everly's description hired a coach near noon. Paid in cash. No name given. He left with a woman. She was blonde, cloaked, and polite. They were seen heading southwest."

He paused. "They never arrived at the park."

Barrington's gaze flicked toward Alex. "There's not much that way," he said softly. "Not unless you mean the mine."

Eliza pressed her hand to her mouth. Her eyes had gone glassy, but no tears came. Not yet.

Alex closed his eyes. His voice, when it came, was flat. "He's gone?"

Barrington didn't look away. "He won't outrun us."

He turned slightly toward the hallway and gave a short, almost imperceptible nod. Then, quieter, to Alex, he said, "For now, let's keep that to ourselves. We don't confirm a damn thing until we're certain."

Simms disappeared down the corridor like smoke. No footsteps. No sound. Just the wind closing the door behind him.

Mrs. Hemsley lowered herself into a chair as if her knees had given out. Eliza didn't move. Alex gripped the mantel so tightly that the tendons in his hand showed white.

The air was alive with fire. It wasn't fear, it was a reckoning. One that was long overdue.

They weren't searching for Georgina anymore. They were hunting the man who thought he could take her and vanish. And none of them would rest until he learned what that mistake would cost.

Chapter Thirty

THE ROAD SOUTHWEST of Sommer-by-the-Sea narrowed quickly.

By the time they'd passed the last of the hedgerows and scattered farmsteads, there were no more milestones. No more foot traffic. Just coarse gravel, thick brambles, and the occasional half-toppled stone wall overgrown with moss. The autumn wind funneled through the hollows like a whisper passed too many times between people. The hooves of their horses thudded dully against the rutted track, muffled by damp leaves and packed soil. Even the birds were silent.

Alex kept to the ridgeline, reins loose in his gloved hands, eyes never leaving the track below. Simms rode half a length behind, silent as ever, his coat collar turned up and his gaze alert.

A single crow passed overhead, its cry stark against the hush. Alex didn't flinch, but he noted it. His senses were strung tight as wire.

They had watched Everly calmly leave Ravenstock. No rush. No secrecy. The same polished indifference he always wore like a well-cut coat. Now, more than an hour later, his carriage was little more than a black smudge on the road ahead.

"He's headed toward the old quarry," Simms said quietly. "Near the woods just past the second rise."

Alex nodded. He knew the place. Most locals did. The mine had long since shut down. It was too shallow and too unstable. There had been a cave-in twenty years earlier. Two men had died. The company had boarded it up, posted a warning, and moved on.

But men like Everly didn't need stability. They needed privacy. And if they needed secrecy... they didn't plan to leave witnesses.

They crested a hill, and Alex pulled his horse to a halt, raising one hand. Below, half-obscured by the rise and a copse of wind-stunted oaks, sat a low stone building with a slate roof gone uneven. The chimney smoked faintly. There was no sign of livestock. No cart. No activity. The surrounding land was bare, too bare as if anything that could bear witness had already been swept away.

Everly's carriage pulled into view. It turned off the main road and disappeared behind the slope.

Alex dismounted. So did Simms.

They moved to the edge of the rise and knelt behind the heather, watching.

Ten minutes passed. Then twenty.

Finally, the door opened. Everly stepped out and spoke briefly to a man in a heavy coat. The man nodded once and disappeared back inside. Everly remained a moment longer, looking out at the landscape as if admiring the bleakness. Then he turned and followed the man inside.

Simms murmured, "One entrance. One man on guard. Maybe more inside."

Alex didn't answer. His eyes were fixed on the closed door. Locked. No sound. No movement.

But she was in there. He felt it. Every instinct, every muscle in his body knew it like he knew his own heartbeat. It wasn't logic that told him. It was the quiet pull that had bound them from the beginning, the knowing that neither of them ever needed words to find the other.

"You go back," he said at last, his voice low and firm. "Tell Barrington. Bring them back quickly." He didn't look away from the door. "I'll be here when it opens."

Simms hesitated, then nodded. "I'll be back with Barrington as soon as I can."

Simms turned and slipped away into the trees.

Alex stayed where he was, unmoving, watching. Waiting. The wind stirred the heather. The chimney smoked. But the door remained closed.

SIMMS MET BARRINGTON in the Ravenstock study, a map already unfurled across the table. Candlelight glinted off brass compasses and a row of sealed envelopes. The windows were shut against the wind, the curtains drawn. Outside, dusk had fallen fast.

Simms gave the report. Direct. Efficient. A single entry point. No visible movement apart from Everly and a presumed guard. Chimney smoke confirmed recent habitation. There was no reason for anyone to be there unless they were hiding something.

Barrington's brow furrowed. "It could be a decoy. Or a trap." He rubbed a thumb across the edge of the map, as if he could smooth out every path that might end badly.

Simms looked at him. "You think he staged the whole thing?"

"I think he knows we're close," Barrington said. "Too close. We've been knocking over stones for weeks. They're running out of places to hide. If Everly was sent to clean up the mess, he might want us watching him while the rest of the Order disappears."

"They could be holding Lady Georgina to force a trade," Simms stated, his voice matter-of-fact.

Barrington nodded grimly. "That's my concern. They know what's at stake. You, Alex, and I know how long Rowland had been working to expose them. What Georgina found might be the last piece. And if they lose that—"

"They fall," Simms finished.

Barrington tapped the map. "Which is exactly why we tread

carefully. They've cloaked their desperation in bravado. But if they feel the ground give way—"

"They'll drag her down with them," Simms said.

Barrington met his eyes. "Exactly. That place should have been empty."

"That's the quarry site," Barrington said, tapping the map. "The mine entrances run along the back wall, here, and here. Only one is stable. The others collapsed years ago, or so we thought."

"Any word from Tresham?" Simms asked without looking up.

"Still buried in ledgers at Cambridge," Barrington replied. "If there's a pattern we missed, he'll find it."

Barrington looked up at Simms. "You think she's in the quarry."

"I do, and so does his lordship."

Barrington considered the layout, then pointed. "Simms, east ridge. Eyes on the rear." He tapped the map again. "Alex and I go through the front."

"We're wasting time," Simms said. "Every minute we wait—"

"We cannot afford to make any mistakes. None," Barrington said firmly. "We go in blind, we lose her. Or they make certain we never find her again."

The words hung in the air like smoke.

By nightfall, Ravenstock had changed.

No more pacing the halls. No more guessing at shadows. The uncertainty had become action. Even the staff moved differently, quieter, more watchful. A footman extinguished one of the front hall lamps early, and Mrs. Bainbridge kept to her rooms with the door shut. The manor itself seemed to understand something unspoken was about to unfold.

In the barn, Simms laid out the equipment: rope, lanterns, two pistols, and extra powder wrapped in oilcloth. He inspected each piece in silence, testing the flints, adjusting the harness straps.

Barrington stood nearby, sleeves rolled, reading through a worn notebook filled with hand-drawn layouts of the quarry. "There's an access hatch above the main entrance," he said, almost to himself. "If it's still there, it could give us a second angle."

Eliza entered with a basket. Bread. Apples. A flask of broth. Her face was drawn but steady. She placed the basket near the door, then turned to Barrington.

"I know you'll bring her back," she said. She didn't ask. She declared it. The steadiness in her voice wasn't belief in chance. It was the belief in them, in the men who loved Georgina enough to cross the dark for her.

Barrington only nodded. Words wouldn't have served. Not when the air between them held everything neither could name. What if he failed? It wouldn't only be Georgina he lost. It would be all of them.

Mrs. Hemsley came next, a folded cloth in her hands. "She'll need this," she said. "It's her favorite shawl. The green one."

He should have paid more attention to Georgina. But now wasn't the time for regret, only results. Barrington accepted it without speaking, tucking it carefully into his pack.

Outside, the wind was rising. It moaned against the shutters and stirred the trees like a warning. The scent of rain hung in the air, sharp and cold, but the sky was moonless, starless, waiting. And inside, the house held its breath.

Barrington looked at Simms. "Midnight. We ride quiet. Douse the torches half a mile out. We go in as shadows." He paused. "We come out with her. That's the only thing that matters."

Simms met his gaze. "Agreed."

The last bell of the night tolled just as they crossed the outer gate. The sound followed them down the road, a warning, a promise, a reckoning yet to come.

Chapter Thirty-One

ALEX WAITED IN silence.

The rain had come and gone twice. The wind had quieted. Still no movement. No light behind the shutters. No sound beyond the distant rustle of trees.

He would have seen them if they'd left. He was sure of it.

Just after midnight, the faint crunch of hoofbeats reached his ears. He rose from the heather as two riders emerged along the lane.

"No change," he said. "No one's come or gone."

"Then let's go in quietly." Barrington gave a single nod. They dismounted in silence, weapons ready, and moved as one through the mist-wet underbrush.

Half-hidden at the end of a narrow lane, the two-story structure looked untouched by time or by guilt. The shutters were drawn. The chimney was cold. The garden gate hung straight. There was nothing in its quiet face to suggest it had once held a prisoner.

But Alex knew she was inside it. So did Barrington. Simms said nothing, but he moved like a man who already knew what they would find.

They entered just after one in the morning. Lanterns low. Pistols drawn.

The house was empty.

No dust, no broken furniture. Nothing abandoned in haste. Just absence. Just silence. The parlor had been wiped clean, though the scent of coal still lingered. Upstairs, the beds were made. Drawers closed.

But it wasn't right.

In the kitchen hearth, a small mound of ash still held the faintest trace of warmth. Not hours old. Minutes.

Barrington ran a hand over the mantel. "They were here. Not long ago."

Alex crossed to the rear of the kitchen. There shouldn't have been another exit. But the bolt slid back easily, and the door opened without resistance. He stepped outside, just outside the kitchen door. His fingers brushed through the damp soil, pausing on a pair of fresh indentations.

"Two horses," he murmured. "One carriage."

Simms appeared beside him. "Headed south."

Alex looked up sharply.

Barrington exhaled. "The mine."

No one questioned it. No one argued.

They turned back toward the door. But Alex paused, then stepped into the hall. He moved with purpose now, past the kitchen, past the empty drawing room, to the narrow stairs that led to the upstairs chamber.

The bedroom was still. Cold.

He knelt near the dresser and swept his hand along the floorboards.

A shape, soft, familiar.

A glove. Cream leather, finely stitched. At the thumb, the tiny mark where she'd once pricked herself threading a needle. Alex turned it in his hand. For a moment, he simply held it, the shape of her hand pressed into the leather like memory refusing to fade.

Inside he found a folded page.

He opened it slowly, reverently. Ink. Curling script. A torn edge from a ledger.

Barrington stopped short, his tone caught between relief and dread. "That's Rowland's."

Alex didn't answer.

He read the page. Then read it again.

Greyline Holdings. Schedule B. Disbursements. Everly.

He looked up. "She left this for us."
Barrington nodded. "She's not waiting to be saved."
They left the house with new fire in their step.
The mine awaited.
The ride was swift and dark. Fog clung low across the fields, as if trying to slow them down. The path narrowed near the ridge, then fell away into a dry cut of land where even the weeds grew crooked.
The quarry rose like a scar.
They left the horses in the trees.
Simms took the east ridge as planned. Barrington and Alex moved low across the brush, toward the mine entrance. It was a rough-hewn arch framed in stone, half-obscured by creeping brambles. An old iron door stood ajar, its hinges streaked with rust, its edges blackened by age and soot.
There was no sound. There were no guards.
Barrington drew his pistol. Alex tested the latch. Together, they went inside.
The air grew colder immediately, damp and sharp with the scent of earth and coal. Lantern light pressed against the walls, damp stone, timber braces, and old rails sunk into the floor. The mine sloped gently down, splitting into a narrow corridor that ran straight, then turned, then branched again.
They followed the main passage, lanterns low, the silence shifting from hollow to taut. Then a voice echoed from the shadows ahead.
"That's far enough."
Everly stepped into view, flanked by two men. Georgina stood behind him, her hands bound, her expression calm but wary.
Alex didn't move. Didn't breathe.

Everly smiled. "Let's talk about what she's worth to you." He straightened and brushed dust from his sleeve. "I was beginning to wonder if you'd come."

Georgina stood just behind Everly, her wrists bound. Her chin was lifted, but her eyes flicked to Alex, steady and sure.

Alex stepped forward. Barrington stood just behind, his pistol raised but steady.

"You have something to say. Say it." Alex glared at him.

"I do." Everly tucked his gloves into his coat pocket, unhurried. "You've been digging. So have I. And we both know where this ends if you push further." He withdrew a folded paper from his coat. "This is what I'm willing to offer. Georgina's release. Her safe return. And no more interference."

Alex didn't blink. "You don't get to decide what 'safe' means."

Everly's smile thinned. "In exchange, I want Rowland's records. All of them. And your silence. No inquiries. No tribunals. No leaks to Whitehall."

"You think we'll walk away," Barrington said.

"I think you know what happens if you don't." His tone sharpened. "The Order isn't dying. It's shifting. It always has."

Georgina's voice cut through. "And it always leaves blood in its wake."

Everly turned. "You—"

"I know exactly what I'm saying." Her wrists were bound, but her fingers moved deftly, drawing a folded page from her sleeve. "This shows your payments to collapse the supports at Ashdown Hill. The deaths. And here—" she turned the page "—more payments, same plan, different mine. You weren't just after Rowland. You meant to bury Carver next."

Everly drew his pistol and raised it, aiming squarely at Alex.

A shot rang out from the shadows, sharp and final.

Everly jerked backward with a grunt, one hand clutching his side. His pistol clattered to the ground.

Carver stepped into the light, smoke curling from the barrel of his gun.

"That was for my family. And for every man you buried to keep your secrets."

"You think this ends with me?" Everly swayed, eyes wild. Blood soaked his coat, his breath shallow with rage. "You have no idea what's coming."

He grabbed for Georgina as he tried to rise.

Alex pulled her away.

Everly stumbled. His shoulder slammed into the support beam. There was a sickening crack.

The wood groaned, and dust poured from above as the post shifted under Everly's weight. A brittle snap echoed down the tunnel, then another, and another.

Barrington's eyes widened. "Move!"

The ground shuddered. Somewhere behind them, the wood fractured with a deafening roar.

They ran. Smoke swirled in the tunnel now, mixing with falling debris and choking heat. The air itself seemed to rebel.

Another shudder rolled through the tunnel, this one stronger. Cracks raced along the ceiling. A lantern shattered on the floor, flames licking the walls before vanishing in the haze. A beam splintered above them with a shriek and crashed to the floor just behind Alex's heels. He didn't slow. Georgina stumbled. Barrington caught her by the elbow and kept her moving. Georgina kept pace, her breath shallow but steady.

Behind them, Everly groaned.

Alex skidded to a halt and turned back.

"No," Barrington barked.

"He's wounded," Alex snapped. "He'll die."

"And you'll die with him."

Georgina turned and met Alex's eyes. "Go. He made his choice."

But Alex was already moving. He found Everly crawling toward the wall, half-conscious, blood all over him.

"You want to live?" Alex growled, crouching. "Then move

faster."

He grabbed Everly by the arm and hauled him up. Together, they staggered forward.

Barrington had cleared the mine entrance. Simms appeared outside, shouting for them to get out. The last beam groaned like something that was alive. Then the world dropped. The floor pitched sideways. More timber gave way behind them in a thunderous roar, and for a moment, it was as if the entire mine exhaled its last breath.

The earth lifted under Alex's boots.

Georgina screamed his name.

The mine groaned once more, then fell still. Dust choked the air. No one moved.

The hours blurred. Shouting, digging, prayers whispered to broken stone.

Then came the scramble: boots and tools, urgent voices cutting through the dust.

The rest was sound and silence. Orders barked. Steel on stone. Someone crying. Someone praying. And all around them, the burden of waiting.

And when the sun finally crested the ridge, Georgina stood just beyond the edge of the trees, wrapped in her green shawl, her arms folded tightly against her chest. Her face was streaked with dust and sweat, her knuckles scraped, but her spine was straight.

She had nearly unraveled, but she'd held fast. Like a thread drawn tight. Like the truth itself.

The mine entrance was gone, having collapsed in on itself, now sealed with rubble and ash.

Then a sound. A shout.

Simms and Barrington tore through the wreckage. A hand emerged. Then a shoulder. And then Alex. He staggered into the light, covered in grit and blood, limping but whole.

Georgina ran to him.

She didn't speak. Just wrapped her arms around him and held on. The world might have been burning around them, and she would still have known that feel, the warmth and quiet strength of him, the proof that hoping had never been in vain. The strength in her grip wasn't relief. It was determination. He had come back to her. She would not lose him again.

He murmured her name like a vow, and her breath hitched as tears traced paths through the dust on her cheeks.

He bent to kiss her, not possessively, not even gently, but with the aching relief of a man who thought he might never feel this again.

She pulled back just enough to look into his eyes, and in that gaze was everything. Fear, fury, and forgiveness. She didn't let go. She wouldn't. Not now. Not ever.

He leaned his forehead against hers and let out a faint, battered breath. "That's twice now," he rasped. "You're going to make a habit of this."

Her laughter turned to tears, brief but unshakable.

Behind them, Simms helped drag Everly from the wreckage. His coat was torn. His expression was blank. His hands were shackled.

Barrington approached, his jaw set. "He'll talk now. If not to us, then to Parliament. This ends the Shadow Order."

Alex didn't take his eyes off Georgina. "No. This ends their hiding."

Carver stood nearby, covered in grit, his sleeves torn, his hands raw from the dig. He hadn't rested. He hadn't stopped.

Alex faced him. "You saved more than one life today."

Carver gave a nod, nothing more.

The wind stirred through the trees. Dust still hung in the air.

They survived. They had him. And in the fragile hush that followed, with dawn breaking over the ridge, it was, just for that breath of time, as if light had finally chosen their side.

Chapter Thirty-Two

THE SUN HAD fully risen by the time the coach rumbled up the drive. Alex's horse, reins looped and trailing, was tied to the back of the coach. He'd chosen to ride beside her, not ahead.

Ravenstock Manor stood quiet, dignified, and unaware of the night's violence. But the stillness didn't last. As the wheels crunched to a halt, the front door burst open.

Mrs. Hemsley descended the steps at a near run.

"Thank the Lord," she breathed, eyes fixed on Georgina. "I told them you'd come home."

Georgina stepped down with care, one hand still linked with Alex's. Her face was pale, drawn with fatigue and smoke, but her gaze remained steady.

"I'm all right," she said softly. "We're all alright."

Behind her, Simms and Barrington dismounted. Everly, bound and bloodied, was hauled from the second conveyance and immediately flanked by two of Barrington's men. He didn't speak. He didn't look up. His coat was torn, his expression unreadable.

Eliza appeared at the door with a blanket wrapped around her shoulders. She stared at Georgina as if trying to reconcile the woman before her with the image she had feared.

One of the Brigade stood aside, and she saw him. Everly.

Her face changed.

Georgina caught her breath. "Eliza—"

But Eliza stepped back without a word and vanished into the

house.

Barrington nodded to Simms. "Put him in the cellar. And don't take your eyes off him."

Simms led Everly away. The manor door closed slowly behind them.

Alex reached for Georgina's hand again. "Come inside."

She didn't hesitate.

⫸⫷

THE DOOR TO the cellar creaked on its hinges as Eliza descended, the hem of her morning gown trailing lightly behind her. The lantern she carried lit only a small cone of stone and dust, but the figure in the corner was unmistakable.

Everly sat on a wooden chair, one wrist chained to the wall. His coat was gone. His shirt was stained. And yet, when he looked up, he tried for a smile, but it faltered.

"Eliza," he said softly. "You came."

She didn't move closer. She placed the lantern on a narrow table and folded her hands before her. "You should stop saying my name like it still belongs to you."

He tilted his head. "You're angry. I understand."

"You have no idea what I am."

He gave a small, rehearsed sigh. "I didn't want you to be involved. I told you that from the beginning. If you'd listened—"

"Don't," she said sharply. "Don't you dare pretend this is something you protected me from."

Then Everly said, quieter, "I never lied about how I felt."

Eliza's chin lifted. Her voice, when it came, was calm. Too calm. "And I will never forgive myself for believing you."

He flinched slightly.

She stepped closer, not afraid. Not anymore.

"I've been thinking," she said, her tone thoughtful, almost musing. "Another woman might have slapped you. Or screamed.

She'd waste her energy on you, thinking it might matter." She paused, just long enough. "But I'm not her. I wouldn't waste the gesture." She tilted her head, voice unwavering. "That would make this about anger. And you don't deserve that from me."

His mouth tightened, jaw flexing.

She leaned closer, close enough for him to see there was no anger left, only truth. "You don't deserve to be hated. Or hunted. You deserve to vanish, to be forgotten. To become nothing. You won't matter. Not even to history."

Then she turned, retrieved the lantern, and walked out without looking back, her head high.

The door shut behind her with a quiet finality.

Barrington stood in the library, sleeves rolled to his elbows, a map of the northern coast spread out across the long table. A half-written letter sat beside it, weighted down by a pocket watch. The seal of the Home Office had already been pressed into the envelope beneath it. His brother would receive it within the day.

"Your mother sends her love." Mrs. Bainbridge sat in a nearby chair, a cup of tea forgotten in her hand. "She was quite helpful. I was with Edward yesterday," she said, voice still clipped from travel. "I joined his entourage and sailed to Alnwick with them. I told him about the wedding. He was most generous."

Barrington gave her a sidelong glance. "And did he offer you anything else?"

She reached into her reticule and pulled out a folded page. "This."

He took it, scanned the contents, and nodded. "It will do."

Alex entered without knocking.

"She's resting," he said simply.

Mrs. Bainbridge stood, composed as ever. "Then I'll leave you both."

Barrington didn't look up. "Good." He made another mark on the map, drawing a faint line along a series of port towns. "There are still two men we haven't accounted for. Everly's closest allies. I expect they'll go to ground. Or worse."

"They'll run," Alex said.

Barrington nodded. "And that's fine. Let them run. It gives us time to force the rest of the Order into the light."

He picked up the letter, then let it fall back to the desk. "Edward will push for inquiry. Disbandment. Names named."

"Will it be enough?"

Barrington met his eyes then, serious and tired. "It will be loud. And sometimes that's all you need to rattle what's left standing."

Alex crossed to the window. Outside, the gardens lay in gentle quiet, touched by the gold of early afternoon. "I keep thinking about that mine," he said. "How fast it all turned. If she hadn't fired—"

"She did," Barrington said.

"She did," Alex agreed, quieter. "But I don't think this is finished."

"It's not."

They stood in silence for a moment longer.

Then Barrington added, almost as an afterthought, "There was a message this morning. From Carver."

Alex turned. "And?"

"He's in Devon. But he's been warned that something's wrong. He's heading back north."

Alex's jaw set. "They'll go after him."

Barrington nodded once. "We'll be ready."

GEORGINA WAS IN the morning room, a cup of tea cooling between her hands. The lace curtains stirred gently with the sea breeze, and the light that spilled across the floor was soft, almost forgiving. Somewhere beyond the cliffs, the tide turned, steady, certain, a rhythm that had outlasted fear and fire alike. But her posture was stiff, like she hadn't yet remembered how to relax.

Alex paused in the doorway.

She didn't look up. "You came anyway."

"I always will."

That brought her eyes to his. The smallest wry, reluctant smile touched her lips. "You're not supposed to say things like that."

"Too late."

He crossed to the chair opposite hers and sat without permission. She studied him and his bruised knuckles, the tear in his coat, the weariness in his eyes.

"You didn't have to go back for him," she said quietly.

"No," Alex agreed. "But I did."

"You nearly died."

"But I didn't." He looked at her, then added, more gently, "You saved my life."

It still felt like a memory borrowed from someone braver. She looked down into her teacup. "I fired a pistol. I didn't—"

"You did," he said, his voice low. "You didn't wait for rescue. You didn't flinch. You fought."

Georgina took a breath, held it, then let it go slowly. "And now?"

He didn't answer right away. Instead, he reached across the small table and took her hand. Her fingers curled against his. He brushed a smear of coal-dust from her knuckle with his thumb, an idle, tender motion that steadied her more than any words could.

"Now," he said, "we wait for them to make their next mistake. And we finish this."

She reached up and brushed her thumb along the small cut near his temple, a touch light enough to seem accidental but steady enough to make him still. For a heartbeat, the war outside the room ceased to exist.

The first time they'd stood together in conspiracy, she had feared what it might cost. Now, sitting across from him in the quiet morning light, she feared nothing at all.

She didn't speak. But she didn't let go either. For a moment, the house seemed to exhale with them, and in that shared stillness, she let herself picture mornings like this, small, ordinary, and utterly theirs.

Chapter Thirty-Three

SIMMS RETURNED JUST past midmorning, his coat damp from mist and travel, his boots stained with red earth.

Barrington and Alex met him in the front hall. Georgina stood halfway down the stairs, one hand resting on the banister.

"I found it," Simms said, breath tight. "A farmhouse west of the ridge. Locked from the outside. No sign of recent occupation."

"Anyone there?" Barrington asked.

"No. But someone wanted us to find it." Simms handed over a small leather pouch. "Letters. Ledgers. Payment records. All organized. All very… neat."

Alex opened the pouch and skimmed the top sheet. "It's too clean."

Georgina descended another step. "Clean?"

"Nothing here condemns anyone above Everly," Alex said. "In fact, it paints him as the architect of the whole operation."

Barrington's jaw tightened. "They're sealing the breach. Feeding us a narrative."

"They want the story to end here," Georgina said softly.

Simms gave a short nod. "There's more. A second set of prints made by heavy boots. But no carriage tracks. They walked in. And out."

"Someone watching?" Barrington asked.

"Not that I could see."

Georgina crossed the hall, took the pouch from Alex's hands, and studied the papers inside. Her eyes scanned the entries, one after another.

"They left just enough truth to satisfy Edward," she murmured. "And just enough fiction to protect the one who gave the orders."

She looked up at them. "This isn't a conclusion. It's a warning. They're telling us to stop."

Alex met her gaze. "And if we don't?"

Her fingers curled around the pouch. "Then we begin a war."

Georgina, Barrington, Alex, and Mrs. Bainbridge gathered in the study an hour later. The documents were spread across the long walnut table, sorted by Simms with practiced efficiency.

Names. Dates. Codes. And silence.

"This looks exhaustive," Mrs. Bainbridge said. "But it isn't."

"It's smoke," Barrington said. "Everything pointing inward toward Everly, toward those we've already taken down."

Alex leaned over the table. "And none of it explains how they survived for so long, how they stayed funded. How did they remain hidden?"

Georgina traced a name on the edge of a ledger with her fingertip. "Because the source is still hidden. Still powerful."

Barrington nodded. "And likely watching."

"There are no more offices," Simms added from the corner. "We've been tracking activity for months. This was the last known physical location outside of London."

"They've collapsed inward," Georgina said. "What's left of the Order isn't spread across counties anymore. It's embedded. Quiet. And close to the seat of power."

Alex looked to Barrington. "Do you know who it is?"

Barrington was silent for a long moment. Then: "I have a theory. But it won't stand without proof. And what do we have here? This is curated. This was meant to close a door, not open one."

Mrs. Bainbridge folded her hands. "Then what do we do?"

Georgina answered first. "We hold. We gather. We plan. And we don't stop until the real story comes to light."

Mrs. Bainbridge reached into her bag. "There is one more thing. You asked me to keep this. She set a small, lacquered puzzle box on the table.

Georgina blinked. "I did. You had mentioned that one of your students might be able to solve it. I hadn't thought of that box in weeks."

"She did solve it," Mrs. Bainbridge said gently. "Yesterday. I thought you'd want it back."

Georgina lifted the lid.

Inside, folded carefully between two layers of linen, was a single sheet of paper. Her breath caught as she opened it.

Alex stepped closer, reading over her shoulder.

"It's Rowland's handwriting." She turned the paper over. "Just a few lines." She read it aloud.

"I followed the money. It ended with the crown. But it passed through the raven's nest first."

The silence that followed was immediate.

Barrington exhaled slowly. "Then we know where to look."

Edward, from the doorway, spoke for the first time. "And we know how high this truly goes."

No one said more. The reckoning had only just begun.

BARRINGTON STOOD BY the fireplace in the drawing room, flipping through a stack of letters Edward had sent from Alnwick. The final page, penned in a careful hand, bore the Royal seal.

"Your mother sends her blessing," Mrs. Bainbridge said as she entered, shedding her cloak with a graceful twist. "And a guest list that rivals a coronation."

Barrington chuckled. "Of course she does."

"She'll host the wedding in London. Early spring, at Clarendon House."

He set the letter aside and crossed to her. "And what do you want?"

Mrs. Bainbridge tilted her head. "The same thing I've wanted for years. You."

He kissed her then, not cautiously, but with all the intent they had once tucked away behind duty and distance. When they broke apart, she rested her forehead against his and smiled.

"You're sure about this?" he asked softly.

She nodded. "I've never been more sure of anything."

A knock interrupted them. Kenworth stepped into the room with a slight bow.

"My lord. Your brother has arrived."

Edward entered briskly, dressed in travel clothes, his expression sober.

"I came as soon as I read the report. You were right," he said, nodding to his brother. "There's one more. I have a theory, but nothing that would hold in court, and he's not going to fall easily."

Barrington exhaled. "Then we make ready."

Edward glanced between the two of them. "You've done well here. But the fight isn't over."

"No," Barrington said. He looked at his fiancée, then at the fire. "But for now… we let them rest."

Edward raised an eyebrow. "And after that?"

Barrington's gaze didn't waver. "Then we finish what we started. And we start where Rowland left off."

Mrs. Bainbridge glanced toward the hallway. "Eliza said to send her regards. She's gone to Madam Pembroke to see the new fabrics that have recently arrived. For now, she said her part here is done."

Barrington nodded slowly. "Tell her she did more than she knows."

THE WIND OFF the sea was cool, but not cold. Evening light filtered through the lace curtains in Georgina's sitting room, softening the sharp edges of the day. The faint scent of salt lingered on the breeze, a reminder that the sea kept its own promises, relentless, enduring, and free.

Alex knocked once before stepping inside. She was at the window, arms folded across her chest, eyes on the water beyond the trees.

"You're supposed to be resting," he said.

"I will," she replied. "In time."

He crossed to her, slow but certain. "You were right, you know. About everything."

She turned toward him. "It doesn't feel like victory."

"It isn't. Not yet."

She studied him for a long moment. "Will it ever be?"

"I don't know." He paused. "But I know what I want when it's over. And what I want now."

Georgina's throat worked. Her hands gripped her arms more tightly. "Say it."

"I want you," he said. "Without hiding. Without waiting for the world to stop spinning."

She crossed the room and took his face in her hands. "Then take me because I want you, too. No more hesitating."

"Then we begin here," he said. "And build something they can't tear down."

He kissed her firmly and full, and with certainty. The taste of salt and smoke still clung between them, a reminder of everything they'd survived to reach this quiet moment. But she didn't draw back. Instead, she leaned into him, her hands slipping from his face to his shoulders, then around his back, holding him as if to make sure he wouldn't vanish.

He responded in kind, his arms wrapping around her, pulling her against him until there was no space left between them. The kiss deepened. It wasn't urgent, but sure, reverent, like the closing of a wound. Her breath caught when he shifted, when his hand slid up her back to cradle the nape of her neck. She pressed her forehead to his and laughed, just a little.

"This isn't decorous," she whispered.

"No," he murmured, his lips grazing hers again. "But it's real."

He lowered his mouth to hers again, slower now, less fire and more promise. She melted into it, her fingers fisting in his coat. When they parted, barely, she looked into his eyes. The air between them pulsed, thick with everything unsaid.

"Stay," she said. "Don't go back to your room. Not tonight."

He didn't smile. He didn't speak. He just kissed her again, softer still, and led her gently away from the window toward the warmth and the firelight, where the door closed behind them with a quiet click, and in the hush that followed, nothing else mattered.

She kissed him once more, not in surrender, but in certainty. Whatever storms remained, they would meet them together, not in silence, but in defiance.

Their reckoning was no longer something to survive. What had begun as duty had become devotion, quiet, fierce, and unbreakable, the kind that could weather more than storms. It was something they had chosen. Together.

The End

About the Author

There was never a time when *USA Today* Bestseller, RUTH A. CASIE hasn't had a story in her head. When she was little, she and her older sister would dress up and act out the ones Ruth creative. Today, Ruth writes exciting and beautifully told legendary historical romances that are both rich and engaging. Her stories feature strong women and the men who deserve them, endearing flaws and all. Her stories are full of, 'edge of your seat' suspense, mind-boggling drama, and a forever-after romance.

She lives in New Jersey with her hero, three empty bedrooms and a growing number of incomplete counted cross-stitch projects. Before she found her voice, she was a speech therapist (pun intended), client liaison for a corrugated manufacturer, and vice president at an international bank where she was a product/marketing manager, but her favorite job is the one she's doing now—writing romance. Ruth hopes her stories become your favorite adventure.

Fun facts about Ruth:

1. She filled her passport up in one year.
2. She has three series. The Druid Knight is a time travel romance. The Stelton Legacy is a historical fantasy about the seven sons of a seventh son. Havenport Romances are contemporary romantic suspense stories. She also writes for the Pirates of Britannia connected world.
3. She did a rap with her son to "How Many Trucks Can a Tow Truck Tow If a Tow Truck Could Tow Trucks."

4. When she cooks she dances around the kitchen.

5. Her sudoku books is in the bathroom and that's all she'll say about that!

Social Media Links:

Website:
ruthacasie.com

Instagram:
instagram.com/ruthacasie

Facebook private reader's page, Casie Café:
facebook.com/groups/963711677128537

Facebook Author Page:
facebook.com/RuthACasie

Twitter:
twitter.com/RuthACasie

BookBub:
bookbub.com/authors/ruth-a-casie

Amazon:
amazon.com/author/ruthacasie

Goodreads:
goodreads.com/author/show/4792909.Ruth_A_Casie

YouTube:
bit.ly/3hI5eQr

www.ingramcontent.com/pod-product-compliance
Lightning Source LLC
Chambersburg PA
CBHW060356310726
48976CB00003B/837